"All Right,"

he said, chuckling. "You know, Madelyn, you really need to loosen up a bit. Not everything about life is a fight."

She drew herself into a slender, rigid, and aloof posture, and Taylor had the uncomfortable sensation of having let something valuable slip away.

"Live in my shoes awhile, Mr. Champion," she said distantly. "Then we'll talk about fighting."

LINDA SHAW

is the mother of three children and enjoys her life in Keene, Texas, which she shares with her husband. When Linda isn't writing romantic novels, she's practicing or teaching the piano, violin or viola.

Dear Reader:

Romance readers have been enthusiastic about Silhouette Special Editions for years. And that's not by accident: Special Editions were the first of their kind and continue to feature realistic stories with heightened romantic tension.

The longer stories, sophisticated style, greater sensual detail and variety that made Special Editions popular are the same elements that will make you want to read book after book.

We hope that you enjoy this Special Edition today, and will enjoy many more.

The Editors at Silhouette Books

LINDA SHAW
One Pale, Fawn Glove

Silhouette Special Edition
Published by Silhouette Books New York
America's Publisher of Contemporary Romance

SILHOUETTE BOOKS
300 E. 42nd St., New York, N.Y. 10017

Copyright © 1985 by Linda Shaw

Distributed by Pocket Books

ISBN: 0-373-09224-5

First Silhouette Books printing March, 1985

10 9 8 7 6 5 4 3 2 1

Map by Ray Lundgren

Silhouette, Silhouette Special Edition and
colophon are registered trademarks of the publisher.

America's Publisher of Contemporary Romance

Printed in the U.S.A.

Books by Linda Shaw

Silhouette Special Edition

December's Wine #19
All She Ever Wanted #43
After the Rain #67
Way of the Willow #97
A Thistle in the Spring #121
A Love Song and You #151
One Pale, Fawn Glove #224

Silhouette Intimate Moments

The Sweet Rush of April #78

One Pale,
Fawn Glove

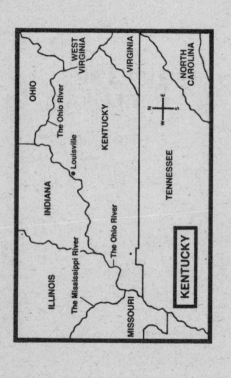

Chapter One

The taxi pulled into the entrance of the long, winding drive and sat, purring, like a cunning yellow cat.

Over seventy-five vehicles, most of them vintage, surrounded the old Victorian mansion like lesser jewels around the Hope diamond. The house was more splendid now than when it had been built, thirty years before Kentucky joined the Confederacy. Somehow it had survived the Civil War. Today it was a showplace, a tax assessor's bonanza of painted brick surfaces, lavish lawns and arrogant, thrusting chimneys.

Madelyn immediately regretted coming. She leaned forward, gazed out the window, and rehearsed reasons for the driver to take her back.

Beyond the drive, sprouting out of the grounds like cheerful summer flowers amid a forest of dark morning suits, were the most beautiful and politically powerful people in the state. A public address system was booming

9

out, "Testing, testing," and caterers darted around like moths, trying to keep out of everyone's way while they prepared an elaborate buffet. A television crew, stringing cables and setting up lights for a filming, shouted directions over the hubbub. Everywhere were red, white, and blue placards hammered to stakes: "Put a Prince in the Presidency. Vote for Owen Prince."

What was the old saying? "Fools' names and fools' faces always appear in public places"? She imagined her own name sprayed in garish grafitto across the glossy white brick of the governor's mansion: MADELYN GREY WAS HERE.

After today someone could probably paint her caricature beneath the lettering—a serious, twenty-two-year-old face framed by seal brown hair that was sleeked severely back to drop in a shank to her waist. Her brown eyes would be disconcertingly alert, her nose narrow and discreet; it had learned a long time ago to keep out of people's business. The mouth would be smiling, always, because nothing hid feelings like a smile, and along her curved upper lip would be painted the predictable prankster's mustache with playful handlebar swirls at the ends. Perhaps even a Vandyke beard on her chin as the final irony.

"Don't drive all the way up," she said to the driver. "Let me out here."

The cabby didn't often get out and open a door. Today he did. Climbing out, Madelyn reached into a handbag that draped over her shoulder and removed a twenty-dollar bill. She considered it a moment and steeled herself to place it into his hand—a back-breaking fare to come from the opposite side of Old Louisville to here.

"Wait for me." She resisted the temptation to tell him that she needed the money a lot worse than he did.

The driver placed the bill into a fat roll with his others. She was a pretty and appealing girl, but he wasn't inclined to worry about anyone's financial status who could walk out of a houseboat anchored on the Ohio River and say, "Would you take me to the governor's mansion, please?" He hadn't been in this business twenty years for nothing.

He eyed the inappropriateness of her pleated gabardine slacks and wine-colored blouse. "You one of the television people?"

"No." She sighed. "I just picked the wrong day to come."

"It was in both the papers. Didn't you see it? And in a few weeks the big fancy money-raisin' to-do? Lots of people flyin' into the state then. There's an airstrip out back of the mansion, y'know. Showed it in the paper. A hundred dollars a plate they say it'll cost to come to the la-de-dah dinner. Myself, I can't see any food worth a hundred dollars."

She tried to appear properly enthusiastic. "That's a lot, all right."

"Guess it takes a lot of money to get elected president of the United States."

"I'm sure it does."

The cabby appraised her with what Madelyn supposed was disappointment and gave her a dour sniff. "It was in both the papers."

When would she have read the Louisville papers? Between rising at dawn to frantically finish the portrait and her trip to the hospital before she called the cab? Madelyn settled her bag resolutely upon her shoulder.

The driver leaned forward to search for her change of heart. "Want me to take you back?"

Paying this fare once meant that she would eat less for a while. If she paid it twice, she wouldn't eat at all. "I'll be back in a few minutes," she said grimly.

The cabby watched her walk with slender and striking grace across the Kentucky blue grass toward the beautiful people. He lit himself a cigarette and leaned his hips back against the fender to wait. Gals her age usually came in two classes: trivial, giggling ones and the hard, four-letter-word ones. She was different—no artificial tricks about her, no sir. Serious and alive, like some highly charged energy was buried inside just waiting to go off. A man would turn his head twice at a young woman like her.

Madelyn was so absorbed in her reason for being there that she didn't see the man fall into step beside her. "You must be a member of the campaign staff," he said.

Glancing up, she got the impression of an athletic body clad in a reassuringly rumpled tweed jacket on the top, faded jeans on the bottom, and a tie that had "garage sale" written all over it. His alert twentyish eyes twinkled at her in an irresistibly disarming way, and she could imagine him cursing his curly red hair every morning.

"Hi." He managed a Kentucky drawl in one syllable. "I'm Randy Morrison. I haven't seen you around before."

The badge pinned to the lapel of his sport jacket designated him as a member of the press. "That's because I've never been around before, Randy Morrison. I'm not part of the campaign."

"Is that a fact? Miss . . . Mrs. . . . ." Her self-effacing smile was the most refreshingly delightful thing he'd seen in a long time, he thought.

"For six terrible months it was Mrs." she said. "Now it's Miss again. And thanks for the offer, but I won't be here very long."

"Short and sweet?"

"Short anyway."

"Oh?"

He followed her up the polished marble steps that mounted the portico. People were shoulder to shoulder at the bar set up on one end—elite, combat-trained politicians whose glitzy repartee slammed like tennis balls from court to court.

Madelyn grew more uncomfortably aware of how her clothes were sticking out amid all the fabulous georgettes and silks and Dior designs. She wouldn't even pass as a peon member of the press.

"You know who I thought you were?" Randy asked, wondering if she would go out with him.

Over her shoulder, Madelyn countered, "Mel Gibson?"

He laughed. "That English actress with the hyphenated name. She was in that television series, you know the one with the butler. Real pretty."

"Lesley-Ann Down."

"Oh, heck. You've heard it before."

Yes, she'd heard it before, but it was still nice. "I'm thinking of going into the movies."

The cork of a champagne bottle popped from somewhere out on the lawn. Gaiety floated up with the bubbles. "To Owen Prince. Long live the prince!"

Madelyn thought of trying to shoulder her way through to the door but decided that that would only call more attention to her alien status. She forced herself to walk slowly along with everyone else in the crowd.

On both sides of the glassed entry were positioned men with two-way radios bulging like .38s beneath their suit jackets: Owen Prince's security. The time was past when governors moved among the populace without bodyguards and security.

"Are you going in?" she said to Randy.

He grinned. "All the press members are supposed to meet on the lawn in a last-ditch powwow before the speech."

"Then you're going the wrong way."

"I've got a few minutes. You wanna fall in love?"

Laughing, she indicated the *Daily Times* identification on his badge. "You're a reporter."

"Since I started college. I'm not famous. I'm not even good. I just work dog cheap."

He was sweet, and Madelyn didn't want to hurt his feelings. "I know the feeling."

"Which? Going to college or working cheap?"

"Working cheap." College wasn't something she dreamed about anymore.

"And where do you perform this cheap but honest labor? You don't mind if I throw the honest in there, do you?"

"McMillan Studios," she said, laughing.

"Ah." Randy's sandy brows shot up in a fresh respect. "A photographer."

"Not quite. Sometimes a client wants a portrait done in oils." Her work wasn't something she generally talked about. She inched along with the crowd. "I do that."

"Must be satisfying."

"I'm not feeding the hungry of the world, Mr. Morrison."

"Neither am I." He laughed. "But I don't worry about it."

"Well, I do."

Her tone was so patently grave that Randy gave her a second glance. He didn't know if he'd ever heard anyone say that, but he didn't doubt her for an instant. They had reached the door by now, and one of the security men withdrew a clipboard from beneath his arm. On it was a long list of names.

"Madelyn Grey," she said politely, smiling and tossing a sidelong glance at Randy.

The man looked at her blouse for a badge. Finding none, he ran an efficient fingernail up and down the list. On the opposite side, Madelyn's right, the second man scrutinized her height, giving attention to her well-fitting but quite ordinary slacks, especially the front pockets that clung softly to her flat stomach and narrow waist. He moved down her legs to her worn leather loafers. On the way up he noted her long ringless fingers, her natural-tone makeup, her severe hairstyle, her lack of jewelry. His eyes came to rest upon the enormous floppy bag slung over her shoulder.

Riffraff, she could hear him thinking. She guessed there would be trouble now.

"You with the television people?" asked the guard.

She shook her head. She had hoped this would be easier.

"I'm sorry, Miss Grey." The first man sounded as if he suspected an automatic weapon was in her bag. "I don't seem to find your name on our list."

"That's because it isn't there. I'm here to see the governor."

"If you're not attending the speech—"

"It's quite important."

"That may be so, but—"

"Couldn't you just—"

"Hey, lady, if you're lookin' for trouble, you've come to the right place to find it!"

Madelyn recoiled, lifted trembling fingers to her lips. Had she been insane to think that Owen Prince would give credence to an ill woman's words? A mentally ill woman's words?

"Tell your father where we are," Abigail had said as she lay upon a plain bed in the state hospital for the mentally deranged.

Madelyn had lifted her mother's hand without undue surprise. She couldn't remember how many fathers Abigail had told her about in the last eighteen years. All different, all nonexistent.

"What father, Mama?" she'd said with an unspoken plea for patience to the staff physician standing on the opposite side of the bed. "What's his name?"

Abigail pushed herself higher up on the pillows. "Now, don't look at me like that, Madelyn. I'm not making this up."

Abigail wasn't used to having medical doctors and psychiatrists come to sudden attention regarding her case. In the past she'd been lucky to confer with an underpaid counselor once a month. "I'm sorry," she went on. "I know I shouldn't have waited until now to tell you. I haven't wanted to tell anyone."

Madelyn pondered the brown eyes of her mother—large, sensitive eyes that had reflected much anguish during the last years but always with a common denominator: the mother's love for the daughter. Now they sparked with a strangely convincing mixture of sanity and maternal regret.

Tenderly kissing her mother's cheek, she said, "Tell me again, Mama."

"How do I? I swore I never would. Owen Prince is his name."

The shock virtually obliterated Madelyn's voice. Numbly, inaudibly, she shaped her mouth about the name. "Owen Prince?"

"He will have worried, darling. Not about me but about you. Tell Owen I'm sorry for everything, clear back to the beginning, the fight over the money, everything. Tell him he shouldn't hold what I did against you. If I could do it all over again . . ."

Madelyn didn't know who was the most flabbergasted at Abigail's convincing display of lucidity, she or the doctor who was writing furiously upon his chart. "Mama, do you know what you're saying?"

"That I cheated you of more than you can know."

No, Madelyn thought, her mind splintering crazily in a dozen directions at once. Not more than she could know; more than Abigail could know. Owen Prince was the governor of the state of Kentucky. He was currently campaigning to be the next president of the United States of America!

Any person who had lived very long around Louisville necessarily knew something of the Prince story. The nationwide search for Owen's first wife had made—and still did make—money-making newspaper copy. During that period of Prince history the family had resided in Richmond. After his first marriage, Owen had amassed a fortune with race horses. Even now, the fleetest horseflesh in the state was stabled in the elaborate buildings behind the governor's mansion.

Eight and a half months after Owen took Virginia to be his wife she presented him with a set of twins. The twins were such a spectacular surprise in themselves that few took note of their slightly early arrival. Virginia Prince was a fiercely pretty young socialite in those days, popular with everyone and the daughter of millionaire Gerald Youngblood who had served for many years as president of the Tennessee Horse Breeders' Association.

Virginia always joked that if she didn't become a jockey, she would marry one. (Some, those few who knew of the twins' "premature" appearance, said she probably should have.) She could hardly wait to recuperate from the twins to resume her riding. Before they were a year old she undertook the rigorous training of Owen's prize thoroughbred stallion, Bounty Fair.

The Morgan breeding that Virginia was accustomed to in horses traditionally produced a quiet, even-tempered animal. Bounty Fair had the skittish high spirit of his Darley Arabian ancestors flowing in his veins. Yet Virginia worked hard and did well. Bounty Fair took the blue ribbon his first time on the track. Everyone, even Owen, congratulated her on a job well done.

Then it happened, the day Virginia laughingly placed her three-year-old daughter, Waverly, in front of her saddle as she and Bounty Fair posed for photographers. The accident injured Virginia's brain, the doctors diagnosed. Sometime later, in a haze of mental confusion, Virginia took the twin girl, all records of her birth, and disappeared from the face of the earth.

How many publicized searches had there been? Madelyn

wondered now. Five? Six? And until a week ago none of them had touched her life. She had been familiar with Kentucky's first family the way a teenager knows Hollywood second-handedly from *The Inquirer*.

Abigail's spurt of lucidity had not lasted after her shocking news. It was catatonia now, staring at the walls, refusing to eat, to sleep, to move. Abigail needed much more than she was getting and there was nothing that she, Madelyn, could do. In desperation—for only out of desperation would she have followed through with this—she was standing at the door of the most prominent house in the state of Kentucky.

Madelyn looked up at Owen Prince's security. She had raised her own self on pennies, educated herself, taken care of Abigail, and had made that stupid, stupid mistake with Darrell White. To have a stranger throw her into a collective pool without considering what everything had cost or even asking why, was an injustice almost too great to bear.

"Look," she said with a rashness that was not her habit to display, "will you tell the governor that his daughter wants to see him?"

It was one of those noticeable silences. Randy Morrison jerked about as a senator's head turned. And that of Louisville's attorney general.

"What did that young woman say?" hissed the assistant to the comptroller as he pulled down his glasses to peer incredulously over their tops.

The owner of a food franchise who was good for a quarter million in campaign donations exchanged a stunned look with his wife. "Well, I'll be damned, Mother. It's little Waverly Prince."

A member of the press reached for his pen and, with a bored, blasé skepticism, stated in a nasal monotone: "She'll have a hard time proving it if she is."

This wasn't going at all like she planned. Madelyn could hardly believe that she'd said it. Randy Morrison, however, suddenly smelled the trail of the once-in-a-career story that every small-town reporter dreams of. He protectively grabbed Madelyn's wrist.

"Look, guy," he growled to the guard, "the lady is with me. Come on, Madelyn, let's you and I take a stroll about the old home place. You can talk to me and I'll talk to you. Maybe we'll both talk to the governor, who knows? Eh, guy? Maybe we'll just come back and—what do they call it?—interface? Yeah, we'll interface. Come on, Madelyn."

Voices began whispering behind hands, and the security man consulted mutely with his companion. Their shoulders passed messages of uncertainty; it was highly unlikely, but still . . .

"Just a minute, you."

The official call rang out to include them both. Thinking that he would live to regret this in a mighty way, the security man said, "All right, all right. I'll let you talk to Mr. Champion. If he wants to let you see the governor, that's up to him."

He stepped to a telephone and murmured a few words into it, covering the receiver with an impatient palm as he waited. The young punks this generation spawned!

Madelyn's confusion was a blank glance at Randy.

"Taylor Champion," Randy answered her query. "My editor-in-chief at the *Daily Times*."

"Champion? What does he have to do with anything?"

Randy pulled a face. "Aside from the fact that his paper is endorsing the governor for the next president, a lot. The Champ is Owen Prince's son. Adopted, but sharing the inheritance with Wallace Prince. He and the governor?" He crossed his fingers. "They're like that. Why do you call yourself Madelyn, Madelyn?"

Still quaking from her audacity to do this thing (and the

Prince inheritance had never once occurred to her), Madelyn lifted her hands. "Because Madelyn Grey is my name. At least, it's the only one I remember. Look, I'm sorry, Randy. This is crazy. I shouldn't have said what I did about being Waverly Prince."

"But if you are—"

"That's just it, I don't know if I am or not. All I know is what my mother told me."

"Then what's the problem? Good grief, if anyone would know, she would. Why hasn't she come forward before now? She must be nearly fifty. Where is she? Do you know what a story like this could mean to me?"

Bystanders were going to incredible lengths to pretend they weren't hanging onto every syllable. Madelyn supposed that had she been one of them, she would've eavesdropped too: the Case of the Missing Daughter.

"My mother can't come forward," she whispered from behind her hand.

Randy's freckles seemed to pale. "Is she dead?"

"She's in a hospital." Madelyn met Randy's query with the reluctance she always felt when she talked about Abigail's illness. "A mental hospital."

Randy Morrison crossed his arms over his chest in a quaint, old-fashioned stance and tapped his jaw, uncertain of what to do. "Of course she would be, what with her injury. You know, Madelyn, you might as well have marched in here and said you were the missing bride of Howard Hughes. The Prince fortune will be split three ways if you can prove this. One third, even after taxes, sure ain't chicken feed."

Madelyn tried not to flinch and turned her head with pretended languor. "The money doesn't interest me."

His hilarity bounced off the walls. "You'll be the only one, then. Listen, I'm serious. If anything comes of all this . . ."

"It won't. I won't even make it to the governor."

"Talking to Champion's just as good. Prince doesn't brush his teeth without asking the Champ first. But when you talk to 'im . . ."

Madelyn fixed the reporter with a frown. "What's the catch?"

"Hang on, hang on. Champion's a good newspaperman, maybe even a great one. But he can be a tough cookie. He doesn't take any lip from anyone, and well . . . you're a woman."

Well, she couldn't help that!

"The feeling is"—Randy lowered his voice—"and I say this with a certain amount of authority, that the Champ's not overly fond of women."

"I see." She wasn't particularly wild about men, either; not after Darrell.

"Oh, there's nothing weird about him. He was married once. His wife was killed in a car wreck."

"I'm sorry."

"She was with her lover. They were both killed."

If Madelyn hadn't thought things were hopeless before, she did now. She was about to say so when the security man returned from the telephone with brows that distinctly said: *There is no way you can win, so don't get ideas.*

"Mr. Champion is already out at the platform with the governor," he told her. "I'm going to let you wait in the library, Miss Grey. But if there should be any problem, I mean *any* problem, this man and I will be here."

"In other words," Randy mumbled from the side of his mouth, "you can't rip off any of the artifacts, Madelyn. Don't throw dynamite in the fireplaces, or put poison in the bourbon decanter."

"That," snapped the testy guard, "is not funny, Mr. Morrison."

Randy winked at him. "It wasn't meant to be." He

assumed a karate stance and held his hands readied to chop, chop. "All right, Madelyn, give 'em what-for. And remember, I get dibs on the story."

"Randy, I think Mr. Champion should look out for his job," she called over her shoulder as she left. "He just might look up one day and find your sign on his door."

"I love the way you talk," Randy called back, laughing.

"This way, please." The guard was moving sullenly down the corridor, and he played his irritation to the hilt. "How do you spell your name?"

"Grey," Madelyn replied, feeling the intimidation of this zaniest of odds, yet tiptoeing to peer over the guard's shoulder at the chart as he wrote. "G-r-e-y."

He smiled because he was going to have the last word. "Before I can let you go in, Miss Grey, I'm going to have to search you."

The room was certainly extravagant enough for a president, Madelyn thought as her artist's discriminating eye swiftly evaluated it. She couldn't identify the carpet beneath her feet, but the tapestry on the wall was undoubtedly an Aubusson, the chandelier a Settecento. It seemed a bit obscene to sit on a damask-covered Chippendale in slacks that cost nineteen dollars, so she retucked her blouse, checked her nails, smoothed back her hair, and stared anxiously out the window toward the speaker's platform.

Madelyn had been in the seventh grade when she learned that she had an IQ of one hundred seventy. Her teachers had suddenly rushed to their class roles to see who she was and had appropriately beamed: "Why, how very blessed you are, Madelyn. We expect great things of you."

Blessed? Her particular brand of brilliance wasn't the cocky arrogance of computer wizards or mathematical acrobats; it was an artist's excruciating and deeply private sensitivity. Which she probably could have learned to compensate for had she been given the chance, but there was Abigail. While her lesser-endowed friends were going on the pill and getting high, Madelyn had to keep house and pick Abigail up at the truckstop every midnight. Madelyn viewed the 'good life'' from a distance and tried to devise some way, *any way,* to rise above what she was.

All Madelyn knew of sophistication she learned by imitation. Since she couldn't learn it from Abigail, she learned it where she could. Television lent her a sense of fashion. Magazines taught her to sew. She learned interior decorating and rudimentary carpentry from books, and also how to cook. But she learned other things—opera and music from public television, and great literature, art from Louisville's countless galleries. She was insatiable. For fifteen dollars she bought an outdated set of Encyclopaedia Britannica and read it all in one summer, the volumes propped against the milk carton at breakfast before she went to work.

Early on, long before the blessed event of the IQ tests, Madelyn had discovered the secret of how she could fit into society. She could draw better than anyone else. For a number of years she was the amusement of her classmates and the astonishment of her teachers. It didn't last, of course; life didn't hold back for a wallflower genius who lived in a book and who never went on dates or to parties or class proms.

When she was fifteen Madelyn thoughtfully pondered a ''Draw Me'' advertisement for an art course in a magazine. She sketched it in a couple of minutes and sent it off. Back came a form letter that informed her she couldn't possibly afford the course. But it served to ignite a spark in her. Her only hope, she knew now, was study. Study and more study.

When Madelyn finally confided in a high school art teacher, his interest went as far as public school limits and a thankless job would allow. Her work won amateur prizes and attracted the attention of several private citizens of a Louisville art funding agency. The teacher sent her to an eccentric and long-time friend of the arts, David Hirschfield. Hirschfield, a great bear of a man with an art sense that was unequalled anywhere, became, in an irregular sort of way, Madelyn's mentor.

For Madelyn, college wasn't an automatic next step after high school. By then Abigail's deterioration was complete. David Hirschfield arranged a small scholarship, encouraging Madelyn to do enough pieces that he could show to a colleague in the hope of getting some permanent financial aid.

She did show, at the respectable Chancellor Gallery. To Hirschfield's fury and Madelyn's misfortune, she was made a sacrifice to newspaper critic Ellwyn Muse's bloody pen.

Ellwyn Muse had been, and still was, one of Louisville's most eligible and talked about bachelors. He used his position with *The Register,* Louisville's competition for the *Daily Times,* to keep his profile high and his glamor formidable. Being introduced to Louisville's art culture by Muse was tantamount to an actor's winning an Oscar. Madelyn hadn't turned twenty when she grandly found herself among the nominees.

Madelyn's one commendable strength, she believed, was that she suffered no illusions about herself; she looked at her life and her talent with an honest and practical eye, and the little head games that professionals played with each other had never been part of it.

After receiving a full dose of the Musian flattery ("If you will put yourself in my hands, my dear, I will mold you into one of the greats. I will give you this city and the world upon a platter.") and still failing to see Muse as anything except a man who held some rather second-hand opinions about art, she discovered one of the ugly realities of life.

Muse expected her to bend her knee. If not from respect for his position, at least in token acknowledgement of the politics of the game.

Madelyn's superlative sense of honor wouldn't allow her to play the hypocrite. Muse was dumbfounded; people begged for his affections and went to unbelievable lengths for one generous flick of his pen. Immediately she became his conquest, and he lavishly doubled his efforts to win from her a proper awe. His flattery was outrageous. Didn't she know who he was?

Her greatest mistake, Madelyn decided later, was that she hadn't realized that honesty had no more place in the arts than it had anywhere else. Muse's public crucifixion had come in three days and before the eyes of three hundred and fifty thousand people.

"We find Miss Grey's work," he wrote in the Sunday section, *"to be strangely boring. Her choice of subject matter somehow gets derailed and her attempts to be sexy come across as a dirty elementary school prank. It is labored and tests our patience. Frankly, we found her whole moral tone to be contemptible and tiresome in the extreme."*

Because Madelyn worked from the deepest, most internal center of herself, Muse's critique wounded her beyond Hirschfield's ability to patch her up. For months she went around in a haze of pain so keen that she was like an animal grieving itself to death. Work at the easel was unthinkable. She got a job waiting tables in a pizza house in order to take care of Abigail, and she tried, with all the strength left in her, to stop feeling anything.

Finally, alone and desperate, she took a job at McMillan Studios and worked on the fringes of her talent. Slowly, like someone venturing into the water after nearly drowning —one inch at a time—she began to study again: the angst-imbued art coming out of Germany and Italy:

Koberling and Middendorf, the sexual flare of Caravaggio and the wildness of Enzo Cucchi. She began experimenting —aggressive pieces, highly charged works that reflected her struggle to survive—and ventured off on drastic tangents from anything she'd done up to then.

It was Abigail's deterioration that drove Madelyn to marry Darrell White. Hirschfield was beside himself; something monumentally unique was buried inside Madelyn Grey, something more than he would ever know for himself, but he had no idea in the world of how to go about unearthing it. Cursing Ellwyn Muse for a Nazi butcher, he pleaded with Madelyn not to marry.

Madelyn never deceived herself that she loved Darrell White. But Darrell wasn't a bad young man, and for a few months she thought the miracle would happen; she would fall in love with him and at least she wouldn't be alone with her pain and her responsibility for Abigail. And then Darrell's creditors caught up with him.

To an introverted, already damaged girl of twenty, the harassment of money lenders was unbearable. It was a stormy, disillusioning time, and the only thing good about it was that the end came quickly. Madelyn was far too humiliated ever to go back to Hirschfield again.

And now, listening to Owen Prince's silver oratory coming over the loudspeakers, Madelyn wondered anew whose genes besides Abigail's had made her what she was. She couldn't remember ever having been near Owen Prince. Except for Darrell, no man had really been in her life. And she couldn't remember the mansion, either. Who was Abigail? And who was she? Where was she meant to go?

Owen's big voice boomed out over the estate: "And you, Floyd Griffen, didn't I hear you say the same thing just the other day?"

"That you did, Governor!" Floyd glanced proudly around at his friends as if to say, "See how he cares about

us? He knows us all by name. What a great man, Owen
Prince!''

The applause was deafening.

Prince, a beefy six feet six with a drawling manner
reminiscent of Lyndon Johnson in the early days, loved to
use gigantic terms like Responsibility and The Future and
Our Great Country. Even so, Madelyn had heard talk—
everyone had—about things that weren't so good.

Madelyn caught sight of the security man who had been
weaving his way steadily through the people. He motioned
to a man who stood slightly apart from the crowd. Taylor
Champion, she guessed, and unconsciously flinched as his
dark head bent to listen.

Taylor Champion was slightly shy of six feet, but because
he was slender and his body as disciplined as his wits, he
gave the impression of hard, harnessed power. He wasn't a
particularly handsome man, not in the way of movie idol
beauty. Yet in a room of good-looking men a woman's eye
would invariably find him first. He wore his dark suit with a
rebellious gypsy grace, and his black hair was cut in a
rakish, above-the-ears style that few men would find
becoming. His nose was hawkish, but it was narrow and
long, well suited to his rugged cheekbones and the rather
full sensuality of his lower lip.

Though Madelyn couldn't see the color of his eyes, she
glimpsed about thirty-five years' worth of cynicism knitted
into their edges. His right hand had been in a trouser pocket
when the security man walked up. As he listened he
removed it and, turning, squinted at the very window where
Madelyn stood.

He could see her!

A shocking awareness rippled along Madelyn's nerves.
What was she, insane to think she could parley with a man
like Taylor Champion? He would make Ellwyn Muse seem
like an altar boy!

She was suddenly much too warm, and she stepped

fearfully back into the swirl of brocade drapes, pressing a hand to her runaway heart and trying to catch her breath. "I've really done it this time," she whispered.

She glanced around the room like a mouse horrified of the arrival of the cat. If she moved quickly and calmly, it would be a relatively simple matter to walk out the front door, cross the lawn, get into her waiting cab and leave, all without being seen. Couldn't she do that? Yes.

Grabbing up her bag, she hurried to the door. Opening it, she stepped through and looked first one way and then the other.

All through its various restorations, the corridor of the Prince mansion had retained its integrity. From the foyer, it divided the house in two and ended at the back where it split into a T. There, three huge windows, ceiling high, were draped with gauzily patterned sheers, and on each side corridors led to the flanking Tuscan towers which were private homes in themselves. Before the windows stood a gorgeous eighteenth-century table and a vase of hothouse flowers.

The corridor was deserted now. Everyone was out listening to the speech.

Madelyn's shoes tapped lightly as she hurried toward the foyer. She resisted the urge to break into a run—*calmly, calmly*—but as she neared the portico she couldn't help it. Her hands were clammy when the security man stepped from behind the shrubs and began climbing the marble steps.

"Oh, murder!" An impression flashed onto the screen of Madelyn's mind: herself suffering through a dreadful Gestapo ordeal with the security guard, and Taylor Champion standing by writing everything down. She saw herself in headlines the next day.

Spinning hard about, she began half walking, half running back in the direction of the wings. The front door opened and shut behind her.

"Miss Grey?" The guard's demand echoed down the empty corridor. "Miss Grey!"

She didn't dare answer but continued to hurry until the sound of other footsteps came to meet her—deliberate, masterful steps that clicked smoothly along the east wing. And other footsteps with them, less pronounced.

Madelyn stopped walking. She knew, deep in her most desperate and reliable instincts, who belonged to at least one pair of those steps.

He had removed the coat to his suit, and as he and Randy Morrison came into view, it was draped across his arm in a length of navy blue. Randy was a good four inches taller than his editor, but Champion still gave the impression of being larger. He had been making some remark, and when he saw Madelyn he stopped where he was—silhouetted against the sun streaming through the windows, sun-bronzed and compelling, a monument.

Madelyn saw now that Champion's eyes were blue and about as nonsensical as a machine gun. A thin scar angled down the edge of his jaw and became lost in his promised shadow of beard. If there had ever been a boy beneath all his urbane exterior, he had disappeared long before now. Capable was the only word that could possibly apply to Taylor Champion, and he emanated one of the most staggering sexual auras she had ever felt in her life.

He assessed her skeptically, and Madelyn's heart jerked. "You wanted a word with me, I believe?"

Flushing like a child about to be punished, she said lamely, "I changed my mind. I was just leaving."

"I see. Then you're a bit confused, Miss Grey. That"— he gestured to the foyer—"is the door."

"I know where the door is!"

"Really?" His brows rose in an insult. "Yes, well, that's some progress at least. I suppose since you're here, we might as well talk. I can hardly wait to hear your story."

How callously he said it, the wretch! She pictured him

behind an editor's desk—the crease between his brows intrepid as his two index fingers pounded a smoking typewriter to write things most people would never have the courage to think, let alone print.

Behind her, the front door opened and shut. She drooped; the security man had just deserted her. Sighing, she said: "It isn't a story."

He moved nearer with a tread that made no mistakes, and his scrutiny pierced to her bones. She felt stripped of everything: words, facades, the right to appeal.

"Too bad." He smiled an ice-sweet smile. "Stories are my favorite thing."

Well, she'd known better, hadn't she? Madelyn motioned to the place where the guard had been, then to Randy who was watching his editor from a reverent distance. "I explained to both these men that I . . . well, the fact is, Mr. Champion, I came here thinking I would at least be allowed to speak with—"

"Your father?"

"No!"

Champion's mouth drew skeptically downward.

"Yes," she corrected herself instantly. Then she shrugged. "How do I know if he's my father?"

" 'Will you tell the governor that his daughter wants to see him?' Isn't that what you said?" Champion gave his head a sardonic jerk toward his reporter. "Have I misquoted her, Randy? You know how I hate to misquote someone."

Sheepish, for the grilling was uncustomarily tough, even for Champion, Randy lifted his shoulders in a feeble apology to Madelyn.

"But the security man wasn't going to let me in the house," she insisted.

"Then the governor isn't your father."

"You're twisting my words, Mr. Champion."

"Then he *is* your father?"

"I didn't mean . . . I'm not saying—"

"*Exactly what are you saying, Miss Grey?*"

He had stepped so near that her face tipped audaciously up to his, and now she prayed he couldn't hear her heart pounding. "What I'm saying is that I don't know if Owen Prince is my father. Why d'you think I came here?"

He towered over her like a warlord bent on justice, and Madelyn refused to flinch, though she was seized with an appalling need to grab hold of something to keep from falling.

"I think you came," he said with low, damning intensity, "to find out how much money it was worth."

Madelyn had learned the hard way that a person didn't stand up to a man like Champion unless she didn't mind being served up as a sacrifice. But her instincts of personal dignity and honor, though temporarily buried, were by no means dead. Her forehead was that of a duchess.

"Even the thief on the cross got his day in court, Mr. Champion," she said in a tight, gritty voice. "You can stop with the hammering now."

When Taylor had walked back into the house after listening to Eliot's report that a con artist was on the premises, he expected to find a number of things. Someone older, he'd thought; not older, but certainly more hardened than Madelyn Grey. She wasn't a bad-looking girl. As a matter of fact, she was quite lovely: fine classical bones that composed a face which changed constantly with emotions he found difficult to label. She wore her cheap clothes with a surprisingly regal elegance. Some rare women were like that, their chic coming from somewhere inside, its very effortlessness being its charm. Why was she trying to pull off something this obvious?

He felt a twinge of embarrassment for having provoked her and took several steps that placed him even with her. "I'm being rude," he said with silky cordiality as he extended his hand. "Allow me to introduce myself proper-ly. I'm Taylor Champion."

Nonplussed, Madelyn blinked down at his hand as if it were that of Benedict Arnold and took a step backward. It wasn't only because she didn't trust him; her hands were those of an artist, and no matter how much she pampered them they were rough from turpentine and pigment. She was suddenly, and for a reason that escaped her, mortified by them.

"I know who you are," she said huskily and folded her hands within themselves.

"And you've already met Randy."

Not turning around, she threw the younger man a guarded look over her shoulder.

"I'm happy to make your acquaintance, ah . . ." Tay-lor's glance found her ring finger, and his smile couldn't have been more charming. "Miss Grey. Or should I call you Ms. Grey?"

"You don't have to call me anything." Madelyn, slowly, and with conspicuous reluctance, accepted his hand.

His hand was dry and serious, Madelyn discovered, and enormously strong. If it had been the movies, the audience would have been in stitches as he gradually tightened his grip and broadened his smile. She stared at him in horror, then back down at his hand about to break the bones of her own.

Dear God! Her eyes flared wide, and her breath made a tiny choking sound in her throat. *He's going to bring me to my knees here in the corridor!*

The battle was swift, the victory total. He wasn't even a good sport about it. Chuckling, he released her hand and stepped back.

"Actually, Madelyn," he said with soft irony as he kept an eye upon the indicative pulse in her throat, a lovely throat, it occurred to him, "I have to tell you that I've seen better scams. Yours isn't all that bad, but it lacks a certain originality. Others have tried this, you know. No one has ever pulled it off.''

Madelyn trembled with an overpowering desire to slap his face. When he leaned forward, Taylor thought that she actually might, but she arched away, her head thrown splendidly back, her eyes huge and nearly black with fury.

''Uh, uh, uh,'' he chided, waving his forefinger like a ticking metronome. ''A soft anger turneth away wrath, Miss Grey. You, as an authority of the thief on the cross, should know that. Don't say something you'll regret.''

In the distance the governor was finishing his speech. Applause was ringing out. The high school band that had been bused in for publicity was striking up ''Hail to the Chief.''

''My regret, Mr. Champion,'' she whispered with reckless abandon, ''is that I've had the bad luck to ever know of your existence.''

Before Taylor realized that she would dare, she whirled nimbly away. His suit coat slithered to the floor, and he grabbed at the back of her blouse as she slipped millimeters beyond his reach. It had been a long time since someone had caught him that much off guard. He was chagrined at the thought of explaining it to Eliot.

''Damn!'' he muttered under his breath and started after her.

Madelyn had no conscious hopes of escaping as she stole away; she was just running. Guests had begun streaming up the steps now, and they pressed through the door and into the foyer in a colorful wave: the tide rolling in to the shore. If she could, by some miracle of justice, make it to the lawn, perhaps he would let her go.

She almost did make it. Shielding her face, she pressed her shoulder against the oncoming wave of bodies and ran headlong into the governor of Kentucky.

"John Brown!" he boomed and caught her with thick, meaty hands that nearly knocked her off her feet. "That's all we need today—a hit and run."

Madelyn's jaw dropped. Nervous laughter twittered from those who saw. In a completely calm part of her brain she saw how clumsy this all looked from a distance, and she made one reflexive half-turn to prevent herself from being buried in the grave of the governor's flesh. The fate she suffered was even worse; she stumbled, pell-mell, into Taylor Champion.

It was, as it turned out, a kaleidoscope of slow-motion tableaus, none of which was extraordinary in itself but which seemed to Madelyn to be earth-shattering: Taylor's pelvis making forceful and vivid contact with hers, his hand clapping down upon the side of her buttock to balance himself and his knee plunging intimately against the inside of one thigh. She was trapped there, the threads of her hair snagging on his buttons, her breath mingling with his and her hand resting upon his hip as if she were inviting his embrace.

It wouldn't have been so bad if everything had proceeded with a natural reversal. But nothing pulled away or undid itself. She and Taylor stared at each other in a consciousness so acute that it didn't allow for a smile. In that fragment of warped time, deeply hidden away, Madelyn saw the isolation in him. She could understand why Randy thought Champion was hard. Even now he was divided; part of him was touching her while part of him was recoiling. He had lived a lot in his lifetime, she guessed. Perhaps too much.

Then the seconds overbalanced. She and Taylor Champion both knew they had betrayed themselves by waiting too long. With a jerk they came apart.

Oblivious to the tiny drama enacted beneath his nose, Owen Prince was lustily staging one of his own. He forced the incoming wave of people to hold.

"What's a little lady like you doing in the path of moving

machinery?'' he shouted and removed an imaginary hat to sweep it before Madelyn's path, Errol Flynn style, complete with plumes and swagger.

Madelyn's reply was unintelligible. Even after she detached herself from Taylor's body, she was so unnerved that she was incapable of tearing her eyes from his face. The part of him which had touched her, a very male part, was frowningly divesting her of every thread she was wearing.

"Taylor!'' the governor called out. "Just the man I'm looking for.''

"Ahh, Governor . . .'' Disrupted from his absorption, Taylor compelled his gaze to shift from Madelyn, and he awkwardly cleared his throat. "If you'd wait just a minute, Governor . . .''

Owen Prince's crafty politician's mind caught Taylor's concern. Instantly every word took on the complexity of a double meaning. "Taylor?''

"Another claimant to be a Prince-ess.''

The announcement was made under Taylor's breath and with only half his attention. What was there about this girl? He'd been prepared to chew her up in little pieces, and here he was wondering what secrets she had hidden behind those wide, very old eyes.

The governor gazed at Madelyn in astonishment. "I'll be damned. So innocent.''

"I, umm . . . I wouldn't jump to conclusions,'' Taylor grimly intoned.

There was a stunning moment when no one knew what to do. Madelyn sensed the energy of the two men wanting things to maintain an outward normality. Taylor swiftly catalogued the reactions around him and decided that the most that could be done was to keep the lid on.

"If you have any ideas of creating a scene, Miss Grey''—he bent forward to whisper in the vicinity of her hair—"I suggest that you forget them.''

Madelyn's nerves tightened about her bones. "If it's a

scene you don't want, Mr. Champion, I suggest you let me out of here.''

"Shut up and smile," he said and did so himself.

"What?"

A strobelight flashed. Then another.

Blinding dots swam through Madelyn's head, and Taylor moved nearer her side, smiling as if their little chase and parry were only an illusion, as if they were, and always had been, on congenial terms. He placed a hand solicitously beneath her elbow and closed his fingers about its bones.

Through his own urbane grin he said for the benefit of the photographers, "Smile for the camera, Miss Grey. Hello, Kurt. Good to see you.''

The governor turned aside and murmured something into his wife's ear. Edwina Prince, a small porcelain figurine with a sense of protocol second to none, obediently began to move as security cleared a path for her. Madelyn found herself neatly sandwiched between the governor and Taylor Champion as her direction was reversed without any effort on her part and the three of them backtracked along the long corridor.

When a privacy of some fifty feet separated them from guests the governor's expression changed from smiles to thunder. He positioned himself before Madelyn, feet flagrantly astride, and flicked open the buttons of the suit coat, hooking his thumbs in the pockets of his vest and drumming his fingers like a parent confronting a naughty child.

"Now," he demanded sternly, "suppose you tell me what the hell you're doing, young lady.''

Taylor stepped back, leaving Madelyn a victim to the official Prince temper. "She came here in a cab," he explained. "She walked in with one of my reporters and told Eliot that she was your daughter.''

"One of your reporters?''

"Morrison.''

"He had nothing to do with this," Madelyn vehemently protested, but she doubted that the governor heard her.

Prince jabbed his thumb at her. "Is she with the paper?"

Taylor had to keep from grinding his teeth. Sometimes Owen had the sense of a duck. "No, Governor."

Cheeks glowing with anger, Owen leaned forward and said, "Would you mind if I had a look in that handbag, Miss Grey?"

Madelyn crossed both arms over her bosom. "I most certainly would mind!" She gestured in the direction of the security men at the foyer. "Your shock squad already searched me." She tossed back her head with what she hoped looked like outrage. "Unless you two are planning to strip me down here in the hall."

The gubernatorial brows lifted disapprovingly. "There's no call to be abusive, Miss Grey."

For the life of her, Madelyn couldn't think of a reply adequate to the irony of that.

"Well," the governor said emphatically, "her timing couldn't be worse, Taylor."

"Possibly."

"Extremely clever."

"Has potential, at any rate."

Owen Prince was as sensitive to ripples of public opinion as a delicate piece of electronics. To say his election would be a close one was an understatement. He had planned this campaign for the last four years, though he gave the impression of having reluctantly accepted it at the insistence of a loving and zealous constituency.

His strongest asset, to his thinking, was that he understood and cared about the struggling poor of the nation. Unfortunately, the struggling poor couldn't provide him with the financial backing he needed to run for the presidency. Not since the Carter administration had a man come from the South with a deck so stacked against him.

So his purpose was to swing some of the conservative votes in the state his way. Conservatives were funny people; they liked things predictable and cool, very cool. The slightest breath of scandal—like the appearance of another glory seeker to be his daughter—would be looked upon with an extremely jaundiced eye, as grandstanding among other things.

Owen fixed his gaze upon Madelyn with the ruthless ambition that had gotten him this far.

"Get rid of her," he said to Taylor and started walking away.

Chapter Two

There were still times when Taylor Champion could close his eyes and see the stretch of his life on the rough streets along the Ohio River. Home was a dingy flat five flights up with an alcoholic uncle who took a diseased sort of pleasure in hitting him.

After his jaw had been laid open and his mouth wired together, he had learned to live on the streets—a fourteen-year-old who watched the aftermath of John Kennedy and Camelot close up: big-city riots and flesh sold on the streets, the coinage of words like "establishment" and "pigs" and "grass." He learned quickly, surviving by sheer wit, stealing and not getting caught, working with the men who supplied the drugs and not becoming contaminated—a miserable and hopeless life, the only one he had.

He was on his second juvenile probation when he stole from the wrong man. Owen Prince thrashed Taylor within an inch of his life for breaking into his house. As revenge, Taylor hot-headedly broke in again, robbed it of every piece of jewelry Edwina owned, then dumped it all in Owen's center desk drawer as a sort of off-key triumph.

Owen saw something in the young street thug with the flashing rebellious eyes—a bitter fighting pride. Though he didn't know exactly why, he took Taylor into his own home. The first year was a battlefield. Virginia Prince had been gone a year, and Edwina, Owen's genteel little bride nervously coping with a four-year-old Wallace who was also not her own, finally threw up her well-bred hands and declared to Owen that it was Taylor or her.

Whether or not it was revenge, Edwina never knew; Owen made Taylor his adopted son. Edwina stayed, primarily because of Wallace, who was shrinking farther and farther into his shell. In time she took both boys to her generous heart. As Taylor emerged from his teens—no one knew how much of the credit went to Edwina's diligent mothering—he grew more stable. Gradually he transformed into a taciturn, long-haired young thinker with an admirable brand of sophistication all his own.

Then came Owen's heart attack. Taylor Champion, at twenty, became Owen's arms and legs. Owen owned the *Daily Times;* Taylor rolled up his sleeves and began to learn the trade. Louisville grew used to the razor-witted jeans-clad reporter whose face seemed to turn up anywhere things were happening—from high society charities to drunken brawls and knife fights along the waterfront.

The student began to teach the teacher until Taylor outgrew Owen Prince. He cut his hair and stood back to look at what was happening in the world as the United States pulled out of Vietnam. He hassled the banks and investors until he was able to buy the *Daily Times*. He wrote about everything: inflation, pollution, crime, the war, the stock market, the generation gap, immorality, riots, cyclamates, traffic, racism, and skyjacking. And Taylor became his own private man, seeing things about his wheeling-dealing master-politician father that he didn't agree with. A dozen times he tried to leave Owen's shadow.

It wasn't that Taylor minded picking up Owen's pieces now and then; his debt was unpayable and the interest high. So when responsible people began coming privately to him in the hope of reaching the governor's ear, Taylor thought he saw a way. He tactfully began appealing to Owen, dropping a few words here, a bit of advice there, coming up with answers when there seemed to be absolutely nothing but a brick wall, and steering him into directions that proved over and over to be the right ones. Owen's successes became a matter of record. His dream of the presidency evolved into more than a wistful thing he mused about from his office window.

Taylor was glad to keep behind the scenes—a frosty iceberg with nine-tenths below the surface—but there were times when he grew weary. Like now, when he must keep Owen from making yet another mistake.

Throwing a woman off the premises went against the public grain at any time. But this one? A girl with a misty passion in her eyes that unsettled even his own crusty cynicism? A girl who made him remember, in a way he didn't have a name for, a hungry ache that he used to feel in his innocence?

"Governor?" he called, his concern unconsciously sending his fingers to the scar on his jaw.

Turning, Owen Prince pondered momentarily, then swiped his arm at one of the errand boys on his payroll. "Lew!"

"Yessir?"

"Get my checkbook," Owen said with a ponderous sigh and cracked his knuckles. "And be quick about it."

Circumstances shifted without warning beneath Madelyn's feet as she watched Owen Prince's aide disappear into a room. A checkbook? Because of her? Without even listening to her story about Abigail? She turned stunned and uncomprehending eyes to Taylor.

"Well," Owen defended himself to Taylor, "do you know any other way? It's cheap, believe me." Owen impatiently waved Lew forward with the checkbook. "Come on, come on."

Astonishment quivered in the pit of Madelyn's stomach. What was happening here?

The governor spread open the checkbook on the table before the windows. He held his pen poised like a dagger about to let blood. "Well," he demanded of Madelyn, "how much, young lady?"

Then, of course, it all became quite hideous and nasty. Madelyn was struck speechless. Owen Prince scribbled something down and ripped out the check, and the sound seemed to echo grotesquely to the foyer and back: *fraud, fraud, fraud*.

Unconsciously she stepped toward Taylor, needing his understanding in a way she would never have dreamed possible. "It would only take a minute to explain," she whispered and stumbled into the troubled blue pools of his eyes. "This isn't what you think, Mr. Champion."

Taylor's disturbance mounted as he experienced a strange and unwelcome urge to take Madelyn into his arms and protect her. *From whom?* he wondered vaguely. Owen Prince or himself?

"What I think doesn't matter here," he said tightly.

Owen Prince thrust the check into Madelyn's hand, and she got the impression of several zeros. She thought of Abigail sitting in her chair, of the years before that when Abigail had waited tables and borne the pawing of lewd men before she would apply for welfare.

No. She would be her mother's pride. Madelyn placed a fold in the check. Then another. As if it were nitroglycerin, she placed it meticulously upon the antique table and, without looking back, began the desolate journey to the door—past the security men, past Randy Morrison, past the open space where she'd collided with the governor, and out into the brilliant sunlight and the six marble steps where, beyond her, two hundred guests wandered about the grounds.

But guests only, for the press, having been disappointed by the trite clichés of the governor's speech, were waiting in a pack. Glimpsing a chance to sate their hunger, they closed about Madelyn like wolves about a fresh carcass.

Microphones were thrust, cameras were aimed, and questions were shouted rapid-fire. Madelyn was hardly able to keep on her feet amid the jostling. She raised both arms to protect her head and struggled, after one final glance at Taylor, to plow through them.

"We've just heard that you claim to be the missing daughter of Governor Prince," one man yelled. "Would you comment on this?"

"How long have you known you were Waverly Prince, Miss Grey?" shouted another.

A woman with a tape machine strapped to her shoulder accidently struck Madelyn in the face with a microphone. "Why haven't you come forward before now?"

"Do you have documented evidence of your claim, Miss Grey?"

Someone grabbed her arm. "How much money are you asking? Are you willing to take a settlement?"

Madelyn cried out, fought the man's hands off her. "Leave me alone! Please!"

"Madelyn, Madelyn! Over here!"

Madelyn strained to see through the press of bodies. "Randy!" she cried.

Randy grabbed at her over a man's shoulder but got elbowed in the stomach for his trouble. "Watch it, buddy!" he screamed.

"Up yours, kid. Miss Grey, would you be willing to take a polygraph test?"

"I have nothing to say!" Madelyn shouted. *Lord, if you'll keep me from getting trampled to death, I'll never do this again, not even for Abigail.*

"What were you and the governor talking about? What did he say to you?"

"Nothing, nothing." At last Madelyn saw her cab, a flash of yellow, a compass in a wild and killing storm. "Let me through. Please!"

"Is this part of a campaign tactic, Miss Grey?"

"No comment."

"I'll call you, Madelyn," Randy shouted from the lawn.

From somewhere behind her, Madelyn heard the governor's voice amplified. She guessed that Taylor Champion was smiling at all this. She wanted to weep. Ducking her head, she crawled inside the taxi, hollow-eyed and avoiding the driver's I-figured-something-like-this-would-happen look.

"Take me back to the river," she said with a groan.

"Sure thing, ma'am." He slipped the car into gear. "Gotta warn you, though. The meter was really pickin' 'em up and puttin' 'em down for a little while. It's gonna cost you."

"I don't care, I don't care."

"Then we're in business."

All eyes fastened upon the yellow cab as it crept, rumbling, along the oak-lined drive. Taylor watched it along with the rest. His personal sense of loss was deeply troubling, and he knitted his brows together and telegraphed a message to the governor: *This is leaving a very bad taste in my mouth.*

"What about it, Governor?" someone was yelling as the reporters along the fringes deserted Madelyn and retraced their steps to try and extract information from the governor. "What did she say?"

"Now, you all know me," Owen lavishly bluffed. "I'm

always open to questions. Come up to my office first thing tomorrow and we—''

"How many years has it been since the disappearance of Virginia Prince, Governor?''

"Eighteen,'' another supplied. "There was one search back in '73. Then again in '79.''

"Just think, Governor,'' someone had the gaucheness to call out, "if this girl turns out to be Waverly Prince, she will have come from nowhere to be daughter of the president of the United States. Not something to be taken lightly.''

Taylor, knowing that a 'press conference' out of control had ruined better men than Owen, strode quickly to Eliot and muttered, "Get these guests away from the press before this thing explodes.''

"What d'you want me to use?'' Eliot countered. "Tear gas?''

Taylor's jaw bunched in a commanding knot. "If I have to do it myself, you won't like it. Announce that lunch is being served, that money's being given away, anything. I'll keep the press here.''

Eliot grimaced. "Yessir.''

Turning, transferring the grilling to himself with a technique so casual no one noticed, Taylor called out loud enough for those nearest to hear. "We don't take it at all lightly, Donald.''

Donald swiveled around. Taylor Champion was someone the working man could depend on for getting things done. "Are you going to make another investigation of Virginia Prince, Mr. Champion?''

There was an exchange of glances between Owen Prince and the newspaperman. Ever so discreetly Taylor's smile said: *You've very little choice now.*

"Of course!'' Owen Prince threw out his arms in grand magnanimity. "Haven't I always listened when this state speaks?''

"What'll happen if this young woman is Waverly?"

Taylor raised his hands and shook his head. "George, please . . ."

Behind the governer's silver brows was a quick-fire process of deciding between two evils. He could try to lie his way out of this with as few adverse ripples as possible, or he could take Taylor's advice and give the girl a hearing. And if things just happened to make him look a little better in the process . . . well, then, there was certainly nothing wrong with that. That was the name of the game, wasn't it? Capitalizing on what lay at hand? What was with that girl, anyway? He didn't trust someone who turned down money.

"I'll make up something to tell these people, dammit," he muttered to Taylor. "Go get her."

Taylor sprinted across the lawn in the smooth, self-contained run of a man comfortable with action. He reached the end of the lengthy drive before the cab did and veered deftly out into its path to wave it down.

The driver leaned out his window as he put on the brakes. "Lookin' to get run over, buddy?"

Ignoring the question, Taylor dragged his hand along the front fender in a warning that he would take any efforts to leave as a personal insult. Stopping at Madelyn's window, he stooped until his head was level with hers. He leaned inside the car.

Madelyn's eyes, Taylor noticed in a momentary flicker of distraction, weren't completely brown as he had thought at first. Tiny black lines radiated out from their pupils—lyrical ebony fronds painted with darkest India ink. Her lashes were so long and so thick that they looked glued on by an expensive beautician, and they formed a sooty fringe that he crazily wondered whether or not would tangle with his own.

He grinned. "All right, beautiful. You win this round. Get out."

Taylor's face hovered so near that Madelyn glimpsed

bridgework inside his scarred jaw. What was with this impossible man? First he mocked her, then he seemed attracted to her. Then he threw her to the wolves as if he couldn't care less. Now he was . . . coming on to her?

"Go to hell, Mr. Champion," she whispered daringly. She'd never said such words out loud to another human being, but now seemed a very good time. "With all possible haste."

Taylor's laughter rumbled richly up from his chest. He reached inside for the handle to her door, but she leaned across the seat to the driver and tapped his shoulder.

"Go!" she ordered and dodged Taylor's striking hand. "Go now!"

Knocked nearly off his feet, feeling like an idiot, Taylor's oath ripped with a proficiency that didn't do much for the driver's state of mind. He trotted alongside the car muttering obscenities and groping in his hip pocket for his wallet. Without looking to see what it was, he thrust a fifty-dollar bill in front of the driver's face.

"Will you stop this damned thing?" he yelled.

The brakes screeched, the asphalt took a bite of tire rubber, and Madelyn was thrown against the front seat like a crumpling manikin. Her bag went scuttling to the floor as the driver gripped the wheel in a swift reassessment of the free enterprise system. Scrambling to regain her balance, she sat panting and picking strands of hair out of her mouth.

The cabby spoke to her in the reflection of the mirror. "Sorry, lady." He lifted apologetic shoulders. "You know how it is."

Yes, she knew exactly how it was! Madelyn cringed as Taylor Champion swung open her door.

"Miss Grey?" His gaze slashed across hers. "You said you wanted to talk to the governor. Well, he wants to talk to you. Now, are you going to get out of the blasted car, or am I going to take you by that rope of hair and drag you out?"

The driver twisted around to gape, but Taylor's look sent

him ducking his head and wisely staring out the windshield again.

Madelyn was beyond any facsimile of prudence. She glared at Taylor's strident posture, which she considered horrendously unmannerly. "I nearly got trampled to death back there."

"That's going to seem like a teddy bear's picnic if you don't get out of the car." One side of Taylor's mouth curled wickedly. "I never exaggerate when it comes to violence, Miss Grey."

Considering the hungry press milling around at the edge of the lawn and Taylor Champion's stormy blue eyes, Madelyn made her choice quickly. She tumbled out of the car, whipped around, and slammed the door with a majestic rattle and started off across the lawn. A minicam was aimed directly at her.

Instantly defeated, she turned back and whispered to Taylor, "They'll devour me."

There was something so honestly needful in her that Taylor found himself acting oddly out of character. He drew her into the circle of his arm until they were more one body than two. "Stay close, then. I'll sacrifice myself, though I doubt they'll find me as tasty as a juicy bite of you."

He moved with such authoritative ease that Madelyn obeyed him without question. With her shoulder tucked neatly into the juncture of his and the side of her breast pressing firmly against his ribs, they walked through the crowd, which parted like the Red Sea.

"I think I've got it all figured out now," he said, bending his head to hers, chuckling. "You're an author and your publisher wouldn't get you on a talk show. This is all a publicity stunt. Right?"

The look Madelyn threw up at him didn't do her repulsion justice. "That's a disgusting thing to say."

He laughed. "Well, what did you expect?"

"Some human decency would be nice."

"Decency doesn't pay the rent."

Now he was teasing her, and Madelyn wasn't sure what he was thinking. Or if he was even as tough as his reputation or her prejudices had led her to believe.

"Well," she said grudgingly, letting herself be drawn a bit closer into the strong hollow of his body, "if decency's out, I guess we have nothing else to talk about, have we?"

"It would appear so."

"I'm not going to make excuses to you."

"That's your prerogative."

"You'll just have to think I'm a criminal."

"You've got nice legs, though."

Madelyn had never mastered the brilliant rapier retort, and she had never wished for it more than now. "All right, Mr. Champion," she said on a sigh as she leaned her weight against him, "you win. But I really think you should tell me what you think before I go up there and lay my head on the block."

Taylor stopped where he was, conscious of people watching, waiting for the next installment of the drama. "Do you want me to be honest with you?"

Her shrug of accession was small against his side.

"My instincts are that you're either the most clever little con artist I've seen in a long time, or someone who's so out of touch they don't even belong in this century."

One of Madleyn's hands was wedged against Taylor's chest. Shoving at him, she placed a reproachful distance between them. She had almost liked him for a moment, *almost*.

"Well, put your mind to rest, Mr. Champion," she said curtly. "I'm about as out of touch as they come."

Stepping as far away as she dared, she wrapped herself in a quivering silence.

Taylor's irritation lost its clarity as he watched Madelyn's resilient young stance. He'd thought a lot more than he'd said; she might have made a stupid move today, but for whatever reason she was fiercely, magnificently proud, and she had a bone-deep sense of fair play. She would always believe that if she fought hard enough or lasted long enough, she would find justice right around the corner of life. It would always defeat her. He wanted to grab her again, to shake some sense into her lovely unrealistic head.

Then it hit him hard in his belly. What if she was who she said she was? What if she was Waverly Prince and he had been taking what would have been hers all these years? He hadn't asked for any of it; Owen had given only what he'd wanted to give. But still . . .

He moved closer and violated every instinct of common sense he possessed by slipping his hand back around her waist. "Look, Madelyn—"

"My name is Miss Grey!" she choked, her head down and her composure utterly disintegrating.

Taylor wavered between anger and sympathy. "All right *Miss* Grey. But let me tell you something before we get up there. I'm not your enemy. Do you understand that? Whether you meant to or not, you stirred up a hornet's nest here. Now, I can help you if you'll let me. I can see that the governor doesn't prefer charges, or I can step back and let it all come down on your pretty little head."

Madelyn pondered the hand resting upon her side: a hard, capable hand that took fantastic liberties. Would such a hand ever be tender? She imagined it touching her different-ly, like a man would touch a woman he was in love with. A nerve shattered somewhere along her spine.

Jolted, she stepped away. "Why would you intercede with the governor for me?"

"Oh, hell." Taylor clapped his hand to the back of his neck, looked away, then back. He couldn't remember spending this much time on someone even when he'd had the time to spend. He heaved a sigh. "How old are you, Madelyn?"

She bridled. "What does that have to do with anything?"

"Will you just answer the question?"

"I'm twenty-two, if it's any of your business. Which it is not."

"That's why." Pausing, as if he were taking a new perspective of her, Taylor cocked his head and the edges of his mouth threatened to smile. "Are you really only twenty-two?"

"Do you think I go around lying?"

It was a disastrous thing to say. Taylor comically rolled his eyes to the sky as if he were praying for mercy, and Madelyn, dropping her forehead to her fingertips in a rueful admission of the irony, relented.

"All right," he said, chuckling. "You know, Madelyn, you really need to loosen up a bit. Not everything about life is a fight."

She drew herself into a slender, rigid remoteness, and Taylor had the uncomfortable sensation of having let something valuable slip away.

"Live in my shoes awhile, Mr. Champion," she said distantly. "Then we'll talk about fighting."

He didn't risk asking why but pointed to the place where the governor was waiting. "There's one more thing I'm curious about before we get there."

She gave him a noncommittal shrug.

"Why didn't you accept the check the governor gave you?"

This question surprised her. At first she thought he was mocking her, but he wasn't. His brows showed honest concern. Newspaperman or not, Taylor Champion was a sensitive man; she was a connoisseur of sensitivity.

"I didn't intend to turn it down," she admitted. "When my mother said that Owen Prince was my father, I came here with every intention of getting help for her."

"Help?"

"She's in the state hospital for the mentally ill." Madelyn knew she might as well say it now; with one telephone call he could verify everything. "I don't need a father, Mr. Champion. I don't even want one, but my mother . . ." She looked out at the trees, the grand, gracious lawns with their flower beds and borders that kept someone employed full time. "She could use, if not a friend, someone."

Taylor found himself having to clear his throat. "Do you have a picture of your mother?"

Madelyn drew her bag off her arm. Her hands were shaking, and she didn't know if it was because Taylor's breath was falling so intimately and warm upon the side of her face or because he had asked about Abigail without that look people always got when they heard the words 'mentally ill.'

He studied the snapshot a moment. "Could I keep this?"

Self-conscious now, for when Taylor Champion wasn't hostile he was enormously attractive, she hastily closed her bag. "Of course."

He flicked open the button of his suitcoat and slipped the snapshot into an inner breast pocket. His shirt had worked out of his trousers at the back and she glimpsed a waist that was a band of tight, elastic muscles. Bodies were things that she studied—every muscle, every position, every nerve. Taylor didn't carry an ounce of extra weight on his body. His buttocks were lean and trimly curved, his ribs spare.

He shoved the shirt back down beneath his belt, and she looked quickly away.

"Taylor Champion, ladies and gentlemen," the governor shouted as they walked up. He gripped his girth with both hands as if he must prevent it from escaping. "If I ever do reach the White House, it'll be Taylor's blood that paved the way, drop by bloody drop."

Taylor accepted the unwanted applause with a thin smile.

"We were just talking this thing over," Owen Prince explained to Taylor as his constituency clung to every word. "Now, tell me, Taylor, in all the years you've known me, have I ever turned one person away who came to me for help?''

Taylor smiled again, a political smile.

''Have I failed to listen to each and every case?'' Owen went on. ''What I've decided to do, Taylor, is run a thorough check on Miss Grey. You handle it through the paper. Leave no stone unturned to help her. I say that's a pretty fair offer, don't you, Miss Grey? And goodness knows, if it all works out, I could do with a daughter around this place. Right, Lew?''

Lew colored. ''Right, Mr. Prince.''

''I want every person in this state to know he has a friend in this office, day or night. Right?''

''Right, Mr. Prince!'' they all said.

''All *right!*'' Enthusiasm caught like fire in a dry corn field. The governor was inspired. ''Miss Grey will have her day in court. Her place at the campaign dinner right here at the mansion.''

Madelyn and Taylor's looks collided. This was getting out of hand, Madelyn thought in panic.

''You tell it, governor,'' cried an enthusiastic voice.

''Maybe even a weekend holiday at the lake house.'' The governor played out his theme. ''What could be better?''

Wild applause.

Owen lifted his hands to calm the masses. He wanted this over and done with. ''Well, Lew, now that that's settled, why don't you and Floyd come with me? Taylor, when you get a chance, I want to see you. Now boys, back to business.''

Feet were suddenly departing across the Kentucky blue grass. The guests were moving on to more urgent and pressing matters. The governor had the reins of state well in hand, and all was well with the world. The members of the press, not convinced, still circled nearby—waiting, watching, drooling.

Madelyn and Taylor found themselves standing alone beside the steps and staring at each other like two boxers who have struck upon a fragile peace only to discover that they are slated for a championship bout in Madison Square Garden.

"There's no way I'm going to do that," Madelyn declared and hugged herself. "A weekend holiday at his lake house? Who does he think I am? Someone who can just pick up and go when she feels like it?"

"Do you have a choice?"

Her thoughts were somewhere else, on Abigail. "He doesn't believe I'm his daughter. Neither do you, for that matter. I came here for my mother, and I won't be a grandstand play for him to win a few extra votes, Mr. Champion."

"You might as well start calling me Taylor. We're going to be hand in glove for a while." He ventured an olive-branch grin. "Figuratively speaking, of course."

"Didn't you hear what I said?"

"Sure I heard." Taylor shrugged idly, glanced out at lines forming for the grand buffet. "The trouble is, you didn't say that to the governor."

"He's your boss."

"No he isn't."

"Oh, yes, I forgot. You're the heir. Well, Mr. Champion, I can't possibly hope to match the Prince money. Try to look at it patriotically, then. I'm saving you and the taxpayers a considerable amount by declining the offer."

As she started walking away Madelyn felt the now-familiar demand of Taylor's fingers banding her wrist. He turned her with an ease that made her jaw slacken.

"Look, Madelyn," he defended himself with a thumb jammed at his own chest, "first of all, I'm a newspaperman. Getting at the truth is my job. And it's also my job to see that nothing upsets the flow of this political campaign. Now, if Owen Prince wants an investigation of you, he'll get one. You will attend the campaign dinner. You will . . .'' His finger became less adamant and actually dared to touch the top button of her blouse. "You will be a good girl.''

Be a good girl? This was the moment when a liberated woman would have drawn back a hand and slapped the man's jaw. But he was taking a smiling inspection of her that Madelyn found both unnerving and dangerously flattering. It was a good thing he couldn't see inside her at this moment. If he knew how empty her life really was, how battered, how easily she could respect a man who had the courage to make decent rules and live by them—no, something infinitely more than respect, something terribly, terribly stupid—he would guess that it wouldn't take much to break her heart.

"I'm not going to fight you," she said, which was only half a lie. "But I don't like losing, Mr. Champion. And I don't like you." And that, she knew with a pang of conscience, *was* a lie.

Taylor drew his tongue across his lips and was tempted to blow, ever so gently, into her frilly curtain of lashes. "Well, I like you, Miss Grey," he drawled softly. "I like you a whole lot."

"I'm going home." She turned away in defeat.

"I'll take you."

He started toward the four-car garage that was connected to the mansion by a winding brick walkway. He had gone some paces when he turned back to see that she wasn't following.

"Are you coming?" He watched the wind capriciously tug a strand of her hair loose and toss it across her eyes. She was such a prickly, valiant little thing. "Or shall I leave you to them?"

He jabbed a thumb to the television camera staring with its unblinking eye.

Madelyn considered the unpredictability of a fate that

would place a stranger in a person's life and allow him such power. She had no doubts about surviving life; it had pulled its rug out from under her feet before. It was Taylor Champion. Who would protect her against him?

She pulled back the wisp of hair. "I'm coming," she said.

Chapter Three

By the time Taylor had walked alongside Madelyn to the governor's four-car garage, he knew he was in trouble.

Never had he considered himself to be a frivolous man. Not since he'd bent over Helen's grave with his promises made had he indulged in man-woman games. To him the approach was quite simple; women made the overtures if the overtures got made at all, and he lost track of how long it had been that way—a clean and uncomplicated lifestyle, no risks, no regrets.

Now, at thirty-five, this small-boned female idealist had appeared in his life. Every look from her was a suspicion that rankled him to the core. She was the most dangerous kind of female there was, that rare combination of girl-woman who has been the dream of men for time on end, a giver, an innocent. She was a babe in arms, for God's sake!

Yet if he were honest, there was something mysterious about Madelyn Grey that outdistanced him where it really counted, and that didn't rankle him, it fascinated him. So why hadn't he gotten Lew to drive her home?

She moved past him into the garage and stood cataloguing the chauffeur's domain, rotating like a graceful prima donna, her shank of hair floating along the slender concave of her waist.

After the frenzy of the lawn, the Prince garage was another world, a quiet, peaceful length of enclosed concrete that was nicer, even in its starkness, than a lot of people's houses. Here the governor's new Seville reigned king beside Edwina's sassy red 280ZX. Wallace's Lamborghini —his bonus for bringing Serina and their small son to live in one of the Tuscan towers—virtually shouted its monstrous price tag. Beyond them was parked Taylor's own restrained Mitsubishi, not a permanent resident anymore but always having a space.

A workbench, Madelyn saw, lined one entire wall. It was stocked with shiny cans of cleaning solvents and wax, lubricants and fresheners, everything to keep the national status symbol in the best possible condition. Laid out on a shop towel was a carburetor in the process of repair.

"Which car is yours?" she asked, bending over the carburetor in a jittery attempt to appear casual.

He chuckled. "You need a capitalistic symbol for your judgment?"

Her glance snapped over her shoulder. "I'm not judging you."

"Like hell you're not."

Taylor was leaning back against the Seville, hands thrust into pockets, hips settled back, and his legs immodestly spread. His brows winged toward the hook of his nose as he tried to figure her out. Madelyn wished him luck; she couldn't do it herself, and what she'd actually been doing was comparing all this wealth to her shabby three-speed bicycle chained to the dock at home.

"The Lamborghini," she said, brushing her unwelcome envy aside. "It matches your eyes."

He came away from the car in a lunge. "Sorry, I'm not color coordinated. Now what're you going to disapprove of, Mary Mary?"

"Is that what you thought I was doing? Disapproving?"

"Don't ever take up acting, Madelyn." He was surprised at the freedom of his quick laughter. "You'd starve to death."

She jiggled the butterfly valve of the carburetor. Nothing got past this man, did it?

"Well, you're wrong. Actually, I admire what you are." In the fringed edge of her vision she glimpsed an aggressive length of thigh move up behind her, a hem brush across the top of a flawless shoe.

"Admire is a pretty big word, Madelyn Grey." As if he, too, were suddenly enthralled by the carburetor, Taylor reached around her and poked about in one of the chambers. "Are you sure you wouldn't rather use another?"

"Do!" Madelyn jerkily amended. "I meant I admire what you do." In her awkwardness, she'd accidentally smeared grease on her fingers, and she glanced mindlessly about for something to wipe her hands on.

"I see. Running interference for the governor."

"No, I meant . . ."

Stilling, Madelyn realized that she didn't know what she meant, and she was coming off sounding like a lame brain. *"How* you do it, I suppose," she added, wanting dreadfully to end this line of questioning. "It's important, I think, not being for sale. I mean, being your own person and not a victim."

Chuckling, Taylor leaned against the workbench so he could see her better. Her skin was lovely and white, highly susceptible to changes of color, an enchanting barometer to her moods.

"Yeah," he said lazily. "I expect the Nobel Prize any day now. Madelyn, what are you doing?"

Having failed to find a grease rag, Madelyn had been, as covertly as possible, scraping her fingers off on the edge of the workbench. It hadn't helped at all, serving only to take one large streak of grease and turn it into a number of small messy ones.

How did this man succeed in keeping her on such a sharp edge? She sighed. "You could've been nice and pretended not to notice."

"Not notice you?" His laugh was short and to the point. "A man would have to be blind, Madelyn. Or an idiot."

The moment sparked momentarily between them: an exposed wire—live and capable of giving a nasty burn. "Of which you are neither, Mr. Champion?" she said warily without looking up.

"Exactly."

Much as a parent would extract a child's hand from the jelly jar, Taylor lifted up hers by his finger and thumb and fished in his hip pocket for a handkerchief. Flicking it open, he proceeded to wipe off her fingers one by one. So transfixed was Madelyn by the grace of his hands that she forgot to be self-conscious about her own. A tiny red TC was monogrammed in one corner of his handkerchief, and she stared at it as if he were a master hypnotist and it was a jewel sweeping back and forth on a chain.

"And neither am I nice," he warned as he brought the tip of his thumb to his mouth and, capturing her wide, astonished eyes, wet it with his tongue.

The stain on her wrist disappeared. Stunned, Madelyn made a fatal hesitation and knew that he felt it. His was the most unsmiling face she had ever seen. *What is happening here? What is taking two strangers and bizarrely making them feel everything?*

"Thank you," she whispered. She tried to pull away. "I-I'll try to be more careful from now on. Thank you."

Taylor turned up the satiny, vulnerable underside of her wrist. With a frown, he laid it against his scarred jaw.

It was nothing, she told herself. Nothing! Except that aura he gave off. Yet she felt as drained of strength as if he'd swept her up in his arms or touched her breast. She attempted a smile but failed. Some unseen winch had them in its grip: winding them together, infinitesimally, irresistibly.

As if someone had clipped him brightly across the shoulderblades, Taylor suddenly straightened. He bent his forehead to rest against the heel of his hand and raked his fingers through his hair.

He said, roughly aloof: "You'd better do that, Madelyn Grey. You'd better be more careful than you've ever been in your life."

"But you—"

"Don't ask me." The rugged angularity of his profile was what Madelyn saw. "I'm no chemist."

Chemistry? That was what they called it, wasn't it?

The winch snapped and sent Madelyn spinning out of control to earth. Chemistry was the most unreliable thing in the world—the mirage of fools, a short-term commodity that popped up from nowhere and disappeared just as capriciously. Everything in her life had been short-term: her mother, Darrell, her work, her happiness. No, not chemistry.

"Your handkerchief is ruined," she said with dull finality and thrust out her hand for it. "I'll get you another."

He faced her swiftly, offended. "Don't pretend, damn it!"

At this moment her pretense was her survival. But how could a man like him possibly know what that was like? "At least let me wash it."

Taylor wanted to shake her senseless. For one insane scrap of time he thought he'd touched a nerve in her and had wondered if he couldn't . . . what? Dream again? God, when was the last time he'd dreamed? Yet even now a dozen fantasies were blurring in his mind: the two of them, naked, clinging, her small hands upon him as they learned, he inside her as he learned, her heat, her tightness, the secrets of her mind. . . .

He looked away again. What was he thinking? "Offers to do the laundry usually come a bit later in the relationship, Madelyn."

He walked to the Mitsubishi, fit a key into the door, and swung it open. "Since we've discussed what I do for the world," he said with a stiff and formal courtesy, "you can tell me what you do for it while I drive you home."

Madelyn didn't want him seeing the nunnish way she lived. She didn't want him passing judgment on her profession with an Ellwyn-Musian viciousness, nor comparing her lifestyle with the sophisticated women he must know. She wanted this to be over!

She glanced about herself. Another twenty-dollar bill for a taxi would be better than this. "Do you mind if I use that telephone over there?"

His brows snapped. "Yes, I do mind."

"Why?" she flung back.

"Why do you want to use it?"

"It's none of your business, Mr. Champion!"

His mouth turned sensually down at the corners. "Get in the car, Madelyn."

When she refused with the proud determination that intrigued Taylor in spite of himself, he calmly proceeded to take off his jacket. He folded it meticulously with the lining to the outside, and placed it upon the fender of the car. Leaning back, he began systematically unbuttoning his cuffs and folding them back. He loosened the top button of his shirt, then his tie, stripping it loose and leaving it draped around his neck.

Was this what a man felt like when a woman did a

striptease? Madelyn wondered. It had been an utterly virile ritual, and her breath was shallow by the time he was finished.

"What next?" Her voice was deliberately abrasive; she wanted in some vengeful way to hurt him back. "Your belt? Why don't you just drag out a few chains, Mr. Champion? A whip? We might as well do the whole scene if we're going to do it at all."

"Oh, we're going to play a game," he drawled mockingly. His eyes were dangerous slits of cobalt blue as one of his legs swung up and planted itself against the wall: a human guard rail between her and the telephone, an ultimatum. "I do love games. They bring out the best in me. It's your move, Miss Grey."

She could, Madelyn supposed with diminishing rashness, make a dash for it and engage in a lot of silly scuffling around. But he would probably enjoy that. She stared down at his leg and traced it with an absent artist's perception from ankle to knee to the top of his leg and, before she could stop herself, the uneven masculine tautness there. Immediately she jerked her gaze away but not before his shift of weight warned her that he'd seen.

"Yeah, I'm tempted, girl." He came carefully to his feet, his voice low and rough. "Despite your vast admiration of me and what I do, I'm tempted."

Madelyn laced her hands together as if she were about to pray and, wondering if it wouldn't be a good idea, lamely said, "I can get myself another cab."

"If you were Waverly Prince, your car might be sitting there instead of mine. I couldn't let the future president's daughter catch a cab, now could I?"

"If I were Waverly Prince," she retorted, "I'd be your sister, and you wouldn't care how I got to town."

Taylor found the thoughts of her being his sister particularly distasteful, but she was at the door of the car and grasping the handle. He pushed her hands away from it.

"Allow us the few things we poor men can still do, my dear."

Keeping her head down, Madelyn arranged herself numbly upon the pleated leather seat. In a daze, she said: "You've obviously never been liberated, Mr. Champion."

"A rather unfemininist statement, Miss Grey. You've obviously never been married."

For the life of her, Madelyn didn't know why she answered him. It was one of those flippant, meaningless remarks tossed out to land wherever it will. Was it because hidden somewhere inside her she wanted him to think better of her than he did? Or was she effectively burning her bridges so that her lonely mind would have no recourse except to forget this day and go on with her life?

"No," she mumbled as the door came shut. "I've never been married."

The moment Madelyn said it, the lie stuck in her throat like a jagged sliver of bone. *Tell him!* her conscience shrieked as she viewed Taylor walking nimbly around the car and sliding gracefully beneath the wheel. *Tell him it was a mistake! What's the matter with you?*

But each second that passed placed distance between the lie and the truth. Soon it was too vast a gulf to step over.

The new six-hundred-million-dollar face of renaissance Louisville was quickly a shadow behind the haze of the afternoon. As Taylor concentrated on his driving—Madelyn assumed that he concentrated on the driving—she kept her eyes dully fixed upon that outline. Nearer and nearer they came to it. Tighter and tighter stretched her nerves. When the telephone in the car buzzed, she jumped a foot.

Taylor glanced at her with lifted brows. "Easy."

Easy! What did he know about easy? She leaned her head upon the glass window and slumped into a boneless, stupefied huddle.

"Yes," he said into the telephone after identifying himself. He listened for a moment, then said: "Can't you do it yourself? Is Morrison back yet? What about Kelly?''

The newspaper, Madelyn thought. He was probably never far from it. A mother with an ailing child, a doctor on twenty-four-hour call. She stole a glance at his rugged profile against the blur of highway.

He caught her slanted gaze and smiled. ''Well, get ahold of Travis Zimmer in Cleveland,'' he said. ''I'll be there in . . . fifteen minutes. Do you mind?'' he asked her as he placed the remote phone back into its nook. ''A small amount of emergency surgery.''

She minded very much. ''Do I have a choice?''

''I'll get out the stuff on Virginia Prince and we'll get started on it.''

Which was, of course, why she had come in the first place. ''I would appreciate that.''

''But you mustn't get your hopes up.''

''I never get my hopes up.''

He flicked a glance from the interstate traffic to her. ''My mistake.''

''It'll be convenient anyway. I can catch a bus from downtown.''

Again, his look. ''Your mistake.''

Madelyn's shift on the seat betrayed every misgiving she had. The silence that stretched between them was a microscope that enlarged the awkwardness. At length, she touched the dashboard.

''Mitsubishi makes a good engine,'' she said.

Taylor looked over in surprise. She was leaning forward, inspecting the accessories. ''How do you know that?''

''It stands to reason.'' She shrugged. ''They made two of the best fighter planes of World War II.''

Amazement widened Taylor's eyes. Who was this girl? *What* was she?

She smiled. ''The Zero and the G4M1. Both of them flew over Pearl Harbor.''

"I'll be damned." Taylor couldn't think of anything to say after that.

A small bit of forethought on Madelyn's part might have prepared her for the reception she got from downtown Louisville, but she had no way of knowing that in the eight years since Helen Champion's death, Taylor had not been seen in the Times Building with a woman other than the female members of his staff. Now, as they reached the intersection of Fourth Avenue, it seemed that half the people they passed turned to take a second look.

A policeman touched the beak of his cap as they waited for the light to change. "Afternoon, Mr. Champion," he said and stood staring, his big buttery face rippling as he wondered if the Champ were entering his midlife crisis a tad early.

"How are you, Dennehy?" Taylor caught sight of the reflection of Madelyn and himself in a plate glass window and made a vain adjustment to the tie he had reknotted and the jacket he'd put back on. He enjoyed the envy on the traffic cop's face, not the first he'd noticed this afternoon from executively suited professionals to beefy, helmeted construction workers.

"Just fine, sir," crowed Dennehy. "Just fine. And how're you gettin' along?"

"Couldn't be better." As the light flashed 'Walk' Taylor touched Madelyn's elbow and stepped lightly off the curb.

"You take care now," Dennehy called after them. "Don't do nothin' I wouldn't do."

Taylor chuckled, and Madelyn fervently pretended to keep her eyes straight ahead. Everyone thought she was *with* him, of course; Old Woman Hater Champion had come up with a young darling after all these years. Well, she wouldn't deny that it was a good feeling. Let them wonder what seductive feminine wiles she had used to snare him.

Downtown, the summer breeze was beginning to whip up

a flurry. The construction of the Theater Square had people skirting around the scaffolding and wooden construction fence. Traffic was jamming where the utility employees had torn up the street to reroute the water mains, and the whine of cement mixers blended off key with the groan and creak of cranes. Beyond them Louisville's new Galleria glinted through the afternoon haze, and the twin office towers.

The Times Building where the newspaper was housed was a utilitarian structure from the forties, a block long and a half-block deep, a neoclassical study in restraint. Madelyn immediately admired the designer's use of brick arches and pillared ledges. Five of its six floors were newspaper offices, Taylor said. His office was on the third.

They were the only two people who stepped into the elevator when it reached ground level and slid open its doors in invitation. Careful to take the opposite wall from Taylor, Madelyn discovered instantly that that was a mistake; there was little to look at except him, and he was only too willing to step back and let the chemistry simmer on a low flame.

The elevator, old and snail-paced, creaked its way slowly upward. They were suspended between heaven and earth by a system of man-made cables. How dangerous—trapped between heaven and earth with Taylor Champion. Madelyn peered up from beneath thick, apprehensive lashes.

"All better now?" he teased. He had hooked his shoulders to the wall and had crossed his legs at the ankles. His head rested lazily against the wall, his jacket casually unbuttoned, fingertips moving absently over his ribs.

"No," she said with an attempt to keep a healthy resentment between them. "I'm not all better."

The elevator stopped on the second floor of its own accord. Madelyn didn't move as the door, ghostlike, opened. No one was there and just as ghostlike, it closed again.

Not brave enough for silence as they inched upward, she

coughed lightly into her hand and indicated the scar on his jaw. "How'd you get that?"

"Someone hit me with a chair." Taylor touched the jagged line, reliving as he often did the chair in his uncle's hand, the drunken lunge, the impact that was absorbed by his own snapping neck, the breaking of a bone.

"You must have done something terrible."

"I didn't come back with the bottle I was sent after."

Her genuine interest overcame her awkwardness. She tilted her head in sympathy. "I'm sorry. Your father?"

"My uncle."

"You lived with him?"

He laughed. "Only up to a point. Do you live with anyone?"

At first Madelyn shook her head; then she realized what he was really asking and she bridled. Her ponytail swirled over her shoulder and she threw it back. "That's not really any of your business." She coughed lightly into her hand again.

"You're not catching a cold, are you, Madelyn?"

"No," she said through her teeth and grabbed at a subject, any subject. "I don't live in a house."

"A tepee?"

She scowled. "A boat." She sketched a scraggly image in the air. "Technically I suppose you'd call it a barge."

"Why do I get the mental image of an amphibious carrier?"

"It's nice. Tiny, but enough for me now that Mother's in the hospital."

"Large enough for a man, hm?"

Oh, Lord! Madelyn let her glare deflect off the ceiling, then the control panel. This elevator was moving much too slowly. Reaching across, she slammed the button and reddened as she heard him chuckle.

"You really aren't a nice man," she said.

"Okay." Taylor felt the quick sting of relief and laughed.

"That wasn't fair. No man, no live-in. I knew better than that, anyway."

"And you're not getting any nicer."

"Tell me what you do, then. That's being nice."

"Do?" Her jaw hung loosely.

He laughed. "Come on. For a living."

"Portraits." A sigh. "Not photography. Oil reproductions."

His brows came up. "That doesn't surprise me."

"Why?"

As the elevator finally reached the third floor Taylor shifted his weight to one foot. "Your hands, maybe," he answered as the door swished open.

Expecting her to precede him, Taylor waited. The hall was empty, and in the distance was the reassuring promise of the newsroom. Madelyn crossed her arms, shakily remembering their encounter in Owen Prince's garage.

"I've always been sensitive about my hands," she mumbled.

In someone else such a statement would have struck Taylor as vanity. From Madelyn, it was a sweet human weakness that went down much easier than he expected. He wondered just how much he'd regret making a move on her. Very much, he decided.

"It's vanity," she added reluctantly, hating to talk but hating the silence more. "Some women have such lovely hands. You know . . . the manicure, the soft knuckles, the . . ."

He didn't move.

And she didn't move.

The doors of the elevator closed, and it slowly began carrying them upward to the fourth floor. Leaning over, Taylor hit a button and the elevator shuddered to a gentle halt. To hell with his regrets. "They're working hands, Madelyn."

Startled, Madelyn moved back until she felt the wall hard

against her spine. "And you respect working hands, I suppose?"

"Among other things."

She heard it in his voice before she saw it in his eyes. This time he really was going to kiss her, and she couldn't move or speak or explain that kissing wasn't a thing she did a lot of—never lightly and never with a man like him. She had time to say it all; she could've protested a dozen times during the motion of his slow gypsy walk toward her.

"What are you doing?" she asked, shrinking as one of his hands reached out and took her face in its large palm.

"You know exactly what I'm doing." Taylor cupped the other about her jaw and probed the wonder in her eyes. Watching his own hands, he slid them slowly down along the long proud column of her neck, over the fine, boned planes of her shoulders and the tops of her breasts. He returned to study her eyes. "I always finish what I start."

"I thought . . ." She flinched like one of Owen's prize fillies shying at the sight of a bridle.

"That I'd stop?"

Beneath his shirt the hair on his chest was a shadow. Madelyn could smell the heady scent of his jaw, could hear the seductive rustle of her blouse beneath his skimming fingertips. "Yes."

Taylor shook his head. His parted lips grazed her cheek. "I'll stop," he murmured, "but you'll have to tell me to. Just say the word, I promise I will."

In her mind Madelyn rehearsed such words, but she couldn't explain Darrell and certainly not the passion that made her what she was, a sensuality so deep and so unexplored that it felt like part of another life altogether.

"I've never seduced a child." Taylor's breath was sweet and warm in her mouth. Her breasts were fitting to the mold of his chest now, her bones to the angles of his larger ones as his hand splayed wide upon the small of her back. "Tell me not to do it."

There was one point where Madelyn thought he really wanted her to. She opened her eyes and saw his own closing beneath brows that were blunted in some private trouble. His lips were moving upon hers, fastening, as if he hurt somewhere. He had started this; from the beginning he'd been the one moving in. He couldn't stop now.

Something hot emptied into the rush of her blood stream, and she rose up on her toes. "I'm not a child, Taylor." His heat surged blisteringly to the surface. "I'm a woman."

For a breathless suspension the kiss floated high above both their heads—a texture, a taste, circumspect still and not an invasion. Taylor patiently reconnoitered the perimeter that Madelyn had laid about herself from the outset: a sleek stroking, a restrained, careful quest.

"You know what you're saying?" Pulling back, he studied her one last time.

Madelyn didn't open her eyes. "That I'm a consenting adult."

Not believing that she was really doing this, she curled her arms about his neck and slipped her fingers into his hair. It was crisp against her palms, and she suddenly wanted her hands full of it. She wanted his hands upon her breasts, her thighs. Chemistry? In ten minutes she would be out of his life. Yes, chemistry. This one time.

Tipping her head so it would fit neatly to his, she slipped her tongue sweetly between his teeth.

It was all her fault, naturally; she admitted it to herself even as it was happening. Whimpering, she strewed a flurry of kisses over his face, his eyes, the narrow blade of his nose. And when he sought the same in her, her head went back on its axis; she offered him the cool satin of her throat, the shadowy invitation of her breasts.

The fiery passion lying hidden beneath Madelyn's elegant surface made Taylor dizzy. He swore he only meant to press her against the wall, to ease his ache a bit. But when he did, she melted with such willingness that an energy exploded inside him, poured into his veins.

"God, Madelyn."

He hardly recognized his own voice. Her throat was like honey to the taste, a natural sweetness, and he sipped his way down it. Her blouse was no hindrance at all. Her nipples leaped in a tiny promise between his fingers, and her palms were a pressure upon his back, encouraging him. Claiming her mouth anew, drawing in a torn, self-condemning breath, he began blindly robbing it of its sweetness.

He was no boy, no Darrell with his clumsy, hurtful hands. The hard pulse of Taylor's rhythm created a tension that Madelyn found virtually unbearable. He had to see where he was bringing her, to the edge of some killing precipice that both horrified her that she might fall, and terrified her that she wouldn't. It was the grind of it, she thought—the blinding, relentless grind of it, a bone against a bone, the tension of a muscle, everything liquid and straining, a seduction of the mind reacting violently upon the body because his own body was alive and wanted hers. And sweet, merciful heaven, it had been so long since anyone had wanted her!

Yet some instincts refused to change. Madelyn's logic was disciplined to a razor-sharp edge, and now it was slashing across her awakened sexuality. Chemistry or not, this would all end terribly. He was Taylor Champion, and she was . . . Abigail's daughter, Ellwyn Muse's victim, Darrell's ex-wife.

She pushed from him and hid her face so he wouldn't see the desire glazing her eyes. "I'm sorry," she gasped. "Forgive me. Please, I can't. I—"

Her own voice trailed away, and his was sandpapery in her ear as he shifted with her, his body seeking to rejoin hers as naturally as water searching for the shore.

"Don't fight it." He invaded her ear electrifyingly with his tongue. "Let it happen. You know you want it."

But she couldn't. She wouldn't. And she took all the blame.

Taylor stepped away from her and held his breath until the control finally came. He'd never wanted anyone so fast or so totally before, and it drained the strength out of him. Again he wondered who and what she was. Her sensibilities were fastidiously developed, more than his own. He had a reputation for not getting along with women, but most would have to admit he was a skillful lover. He could reach Madelyn on that level if he persisted, he knew; it was the other—the reaching of her soul—that scared him to death.

He took a step toward her, lifted his hands, dropped them. "Madelyn, listen to me."

"I can't listen. And I can't talk about it. I don't know what to say." How had she let this happen?

"It was just a kiss," he said.

"Nothing is 'just' anything with me."

Taylor closed his eyes and drew her lightly into his arms, even though she struggled. "I know it wasn't just a kiss." He pressed his face into the perfume of her hair. "But I'm not going to say I'm sorry."

But she was. She was sorry she hadn't met him at the park or in a cafe. She was sorry that she had ever gone to the Prince mansion so that now he must look at her and wonder if she'd lied about Abigail. She was sorry she couldn't see it as just a kiss.

"I didn't mean to tease," she said as his body made her a moth in his all-encompassing cocoon.

"I didn't think you were a tease. You're making too much of it."

"And I'm not frigid."

He laughed softly, then realized that was a mistake and quickly sobered. "Believe me, I didn't think that."

"And I'm not—"

"Madelyn, sweet, be still."

"But I don't want you to think—"

"Be still. It doesn't matter what I think."

Madelyn slumped against him, groaning. "But it does. That's just it. It matters terribly."

And that was what made her unique. Taylor dropped a light kiss into her hair and wanted to do or say something that would put her mind at rest.

"Madelyn, I'm just a simple, small-town man. I don't have millions of dollars passing in and out of my hands. I do what I'm good at and let it go at that. But even here things move pretty fast sometimes. Men use women, and women use men. No one gives a damn what the other thinks or feels. And even if they do, it costs too much or takes too much time, so they turn off the empathy and keep on using. I think in your heart you know how different you are. But that's what you're dealing with out here in the world, Madelyn. If you don't develop some kind of defense, life'll kill you. I know what I'm talking about. You really shouldn't worry about what I think. Or what anyone else thinks."

Very slowly Madelyn detached herself from Taylor's arms and stepped back, searching for the truth on his face. "Is that what you do? Really? Not care?"

"I . . ." Taylor dragged his fingers through his hair, unconsciously leaving it attractively rumpled. "I don't let myself grieve over it."

"Then how do you care about anything, Taylor? Inside? In your heart? You can't draw a line and say you care about the things that make you feel good but don't feel anything that makes you hurt. There're two sides to every coin. To stifle one automatically stifles the other."

Taylor had the distinct impression that she was much more knowledgeable in these areas than he was. "I didn't say I didn't feel. I said I don't worry so much about what the next guy feels.''

Madelyn remembered times when she'd passed a dead kitten or a puppy on the road and had to stop and weep bitterly. There were times when she empathized so dreadfully with people, she felt ill herself. At times she wanted to open her arms to the whole world; and when it destroyed and hurt itself, something died inside. She couldn't watch people killing each other on the television news, and she often couldn't read about people's suffering in the paper. She would lie to keep from hurting someone's feelings and take blame that wasn't hers in order to spare them.

People who knew her well enough often looked at her with suspicion. They thought she was strange and spineless. And perhaps she was on some things. That was the trouble with that all-glorious IQ she had learned to hate; her empathies, her feelings that were so subliminal as to be uncontrollable. Their indiscriminate sensitivity made her cut across the grain of society. It was making her cut across Taylor's grain. Even now he couldn't understand, and so he thought she was weak.

"It would be much simpler if I could do it your way," she said dully.

Taylor glanced behind himself. The elevator light was flashing, and his sense of inadequacy made him step back to press the button which would return them to the world.

All of Madelyn's shyness seemed to descend upon her at once. She began repairing her clothes. "I'm really embarrassed, Taylor. I'd like to go now."

The elevator creaked. He said: "So now you're going to be all upset about this?"

Madelyn retucked her blouse. How could she tell him how much she wanted to be understood by him? "I will ask one thing of you," she whispered as the elevator began to move.

"I don't promise until I hear what it is."

"Please don't speak to me about this. If, after this day, our paths ever, ever cross, please don't bring it up."

What did he have to lose by lying a little? If there was ever a thing he wanted to pursue, it was this day. "Whatever you say."

"I feel like a fool."

"Well, you are that, but not for the reason you think."

Madelyn hurriedly tugged the clip from her hair and, holding it between her teeth, tossed back her head and caught it in a tight fist.

The elevator carried them to the sixth floor, the top of the building. Taylor jabbed a thumb at the door. "I don't know about you, but I could just as well walk down three flights."

She was scooping up her bag from where it had fallen to the floor. Her cheeks were fiery. She was trembling. "I don't care what we do, just as long as we do it right now."

Chapter Four

$\mathcal{P}$robably no one except Taylor knew just how many different facets composed the *Daily Times*. When Madelyn walked into the newsroom, it seemed to her that nothing sane could ever come out of any of it: television news coming over strategically placed sets, telephones ringing, typewriters chattering, teletypes chugging, and over it all the imperative hum, and occasional yell, of voices.

Taylor's kingdom, Madelyn thought, and shuddered as she recalled Ellwyn Muse showing her around *The Register;* he'd driven the first nail into her palm that day. Here Taylor was monarch, moving with an authority ten times more lethal than Muse's.

Taylor was a stunningly capable man, she saw. He was able to work at several levels simultaneously, and his memory seemed incredibly filled with details available upon recall. He didn't flinch from the questions hurled at him but paused to glance over fluttering sheets of manuscript and a computer screen. Someone waved a telephone receiver at him and he unhurriedly spoke into it as he lifted darkroom prints away from the glare and selected one that suited him. Overriding it all was the one thing which appealed to her more than anything she had seen of him so far: his sense of good taste.

"A black human interest?" he said when someone raised the question. "We just did one."

"Some of the big guns want to display their sympathy for the minority. Election year and all that." The speaker was an older, studious man with the spectacles and anxious look of an educator turned reporter.

"It'll also look like we're trying too hard, Stan. And that's not equal, it's ingratiating."

"Try to convince a first-time candidate."

"Keep it white," Taylor said.

"What about the mudslinging campaign against the attorney general?" called a husky female voice.

Taylor glanced up at Madelyn from what he was reading, and made her realize that he was aware of her awkwardness at being here. "Make sure the public understands it's not the opinion of this paper and print it," he told the woman as he scribbled something on the paper.

"Hank's yelling his head off. We're talking lawsuit here, Taylor."

"Well, that's Hank's problem, Christine." Taylor tossed the papers back to the reporter and turned to address one of the most beautiful, rampantly sexual women Madelyn had ever seen. "Print it."

Madelyn's initial impulse was to hate Christine Hackworth on sight. Who wouldn't? Her dazzling Hollywood smile was surpassed only by her clouds and clouds of glorious blond hair. Her height was made even more disturbing by long, mannish slacks and six-inch heels. Beneath a bubble-gun pink blouse was a bosom that many women would have paid a fortune for in cosmetic surgery.

Above and beyond that—the ultimate of all injuries—she could eat anything she wanted and never gain an ounce.

It occurred to Madelyn to wonder why Taylor bothered kissing her when Christine was around. Then, with a woman's infallible sixth sense, she realized that kissing was the least of what Taylor and Christine had done.

"I'll tell him you said so, Champ," Christine drawled over her shoulder as every male eye in the room hungrily went into shock. "But don't blame me if you have to spend the next week playing racketball with his legal hacks."

As Christine moved down the aisle toward Madelyn, ignoring the battery of sexual jokes that followed her, her look was an assumption of instant intimacy. *I know already I'm going to like you.* "Hello."

"Hello." Madelyn's smile was more fragile.

Christine extended an exquisite nail-polished hand. "I have the distinct impression I should know you. I'm Christine Hackworth."

"It's the face." Smiling, Madelyn casually lifted her shoulders. "It reminds everybody of something."

From the distance which separated him, Taylor covertly watched them. His long affair with Christine had been unlamentably buried, but it gave him a strange sensation to see the two women talking together.

When Christine moved past him she said, with a flaming swing of her hips: "You should make me your executive editor right away, Taylor."

"Really?"

"This place goes to hell when you walk out the door."

Taylor grimaced and gave the editor back his papers. It was no secret that Christine not only wanted him to retire early but that she also wanted his job when he did. "And you think you can hold it all together, eh?"

"I held you together, didn't I?"

"Like everything else, Christine, it's relative." Taylor's irony was lost. Christine was already out of earshot.

"Madelyn!"

Still drowsy from the narcotic influence of Christine, Madelyn smiled when Randy's sandy head popped around the door frame of a flanking office.

"Didn't expect to see you downtown so soon," he said as he dodged around desks to wind up in front of her, slightly out of breath, his arms filled with stacks of newsprint but one hand reaching for hers. "I have the headline all composed: PRINCE-ESS APPEARS TO CLAIM THRONE. I've even seen the clips for the evening news. All I need is your version of the story. Would you have dinner with me? I know this neat little place downtown where you actually get what you order."

Madelyn stiffened as if she'd just been slapped. "The evening news?" she repeated in a daze. "They can't be meaning to run that terrible film they shot at the governor's. I want it stopped. How do I get it stopped?"

He shrugged. "Why, that would violate the sacred freedom of the press. Aw, let 'em have their buzz." He grinned. "I can pick you up at eight o'clock. We can go somewhere informal. You could wear what you have on. As a matter of fact, if you'll wait on me, we can go as soon as I get off work. After dinner we could take in a play or get married. Oh, hi, chief."

Taylor's silences had a way of being more forbidding than most men's words, and though Randy didn't understand the implications of this present one, he knew better than to ignore it. He stepped back to a safer distance and said with a businesslike gravity, "You were saying that nothing happened after I left the governor's, Madelyn?"

Madelyn had to smile. "I'm afraid not, Randy."

"Not even one printable calamity?"

"Life went on," Taylor grumbled as he found Madelyn's elbow and began steering her toward his office. "And would you get Hadley up here? I want him to take a few shots of Miss Grey."

"No!"

So startling was Madelyn's reaction that all three of them stared down at her hands frantically clutching Taylor's. Taylor arched his brows in an amused inquiry, and Madelyn stepped back.

"I mean," she explained with comical deflation, "don't you think the public will tire of me?"

The thick smoked glass beside them bore Taylor's name in gold. He braced a shoulder negligently against it and inspected his fingernails. "It occurs to me that you're awfully camera shy, Madelyn. It makes me wonder what deep, dark secrets lie tucked away behind those pretty brown eyes."

"My secrets are hardly deep and even less dark."

"Ah, but you do have some. Right?"

"Doesn't everyone?" She leaned forward a little at that, almost as if she'd poked a finger into his chest. "Even you?"

"Now, what makes you say a thing like that?"

Madelyn didn't say the word aloud; she formed it with her lips. "Christine."

The only reaction Taylor allowed himself was to let his breath drizzle slowly out. Gradually, his cynicism blending with a crooked smile, he brought his lower lip beneath his teeth. "I think you'd better get in my office, Madelyn, before lightning strikes you dead for a witch. They say it never misses the really bad ones. You'd be a goner."

Randy looked down at both of them from his six feet and four inches. "Before you go, do I get Madelyn's story or what?"

It wasn't that Taylor wanted to deny his reporter the story; at his age, he would've given his eye teeth for it. But now he suffered an unpalatable vision of Randy's endless phone calls to Madelyn, his house calls, then his dates, all in the respectable guise of research.

"I'll see," he said curtly and dismissed him.

Randy's face fell, and his hand came out in a beseeching gesture. "But, chief—"

"I said I'd see!"

Taylor's raised voice was one thing, but Taylor's pettiness was something else entirely. A dozen heads snapped up in amazement, and Madelyn, with a sympathetic glance at Randy, compressed her lips at Taylor as if to say: "That was really unforgivable."

He wanted to yell at her that he didn't have time to deal with people like she did. People had to pay dues in this world, and no one wanted to hear the whining of the next guy. But that wasn't the reason he wanted to lash out and smash something and Taylor knew it. He looked at the two of them—Madelyn with her hands stuffed reproachfully in her pockets and Randy drooping, as if he'd taken a swing at him.

Damn it to hell! Taylor let his shoulders drop in acquiescence to Randy. *"If* there is a story," he said stiffly, "you can have it. Now, if it wouldn't be too much of an imposition on you, would you go upstairs and bring me all the dope on Virginia Prince?"

Grinning, Randy stepped back so hastily that he trod on the mail boy's foot and received a new four-letter word for his troubles. "Sure thing, chief."

"And quit calling me chief."

"Sure thing, Champ. I mean, Mr. Champion."

Sighing, wondering how life had gotten so slippery all of a sudden, Taylor wandered into his office and glared at the typewriter which sat exactly as he'd left it yesterday, an unfinished story on its page. What was he coming to? He savagely ripped it out and hurled the crumbled ball toward a wastebasket, missing by a generous yard. He swore under his breath.

Madelyn followed him and looked about herself. "I didn't know there was such a word."

"I make up my own as I go along."

"Let's pray it doesn't catch on."

It had to be the ugliest office in existence. A coffee maker was crammed on the top of an old file cabinet, and Styrofoam cups and plastic spoons lay littered everywhere. The ashtrays overflowed, and hideous little water rings were emblazoned on the top of his desk and would probably never polish out. Several of his jackets dangled from the coat rack where he'd forgotten them. Hanging crookedly on one wall was a calendar from 1980, two of its pages torn off. March 6 had a red circle around it with 'Christine's birthday' written in its square with a felt-tip pen.

What had he gotten Christine for her birthday? she wondered shrewishly. "Did you see *Cannery Row?*"

Taylor was spinning another piece of paper into his typewriter. Sitting before the keys, he yanked at his tie. "What?"

"*Cannery Row* with Nick Nolte. You know, the Steinbeck book."

"Oh, yeah." He began pounding the keys without removing his jacket.

"Do you remember how bad Doc's laboratory was?"

Taylor didn't miss a beat. "I didn't think it was all that bad."

"*After* the fight scene?"

In a startling cameo of mirth Taylor swiveled around in his chair, both hands coming up to clasp the hair behind his head so that his Adam's apple was a ripple in his throat, his teeth a sparkle of white and eyes a network of merry lines.

Outside, those nearest the office exchanged somber, wondering looks. The Champ was behaving most peculiarly today.

Madelyn's own laughter was purely involuntary; she was too mesmerized with Taylor's. He didn't know what he was revealing of himself, she thought—the yearning, affection-starved boy he had to have been. She pictured him sullen and much more introverted than she, too easily bruised, suspicious of kindness the way some are of a rustle in the dark. What kind of monster could strike such a boy across the face with a chair?

Fearing, then, that he would somehow read her thoughts, Madelyn dipped her head. She nibbled at her lip and walked over to his calendar.

"The truth is"—Taylor was still chuckling as he turned back to the typewriter and punctuated his words with spasmodic hunting and pecking—"this office . . . is a spare set for United . . . Artists. Make yourself comfortable and I'll get coffee . . . in just a minute."

Ellwyn Muse had offered her coffee. Madelyn shivered and said off-handedly: "You should have taken typing in high school."

"I did good to *finish* high school."

Oh, he was deadly, wasn't he? Making an addict of her for that smile and that laugh which somehow managed to balance out his more unlovely faults. He was a dealer injecting heroin into the vein until the habit was there and a person would do anything to get it.

"Do you mind if I open it?" she said and strode frowningly to the closed door.

"Hm?"

"The *door*," Madelyn gritted her words. "Do you mind if I open it?"

Like a child who's been unfairly pinched, Taylor jerked up his head. "In the movie the girl cleaned up the place," he drawled.

Madelyn threw the door back with more force than she intended, and its clatter made several of the people nearest look up, one of whom was Christine. Before she could move, Taylor angled his rangy length around the facing and called, "Hey, Marie. Could we borrow a couple of cups of coffee?"

"Be there in a minute, Champ." The woman's voice was

several decibels deeper than Taylor's, and it struck Madelyn as hilarious.

She turned to find Taylor still leaning forward over his desk, his weight distributed on the palms of both hands. Without the slightest awkwardness he increased the precarious angle of his body until his face was only inches from her own, his narrow, hooked nose precisely level with hers.

He was smiling because he'd just accepted what he'd been going through the last half hour—comparing Christine to Madelyn, wanting Morrison to back off and stay off, laughing at her joke, not so much because it was funny but because he knew she rarely joked and she had complimented him. The words of a popular tune drifted in and out of his thoughts: *"Habits I've had before but never came back so much for more."* So it scared him. So what? It wasn't a crime to be scared.

"Marie," he explained with a nod toward the newsroom. "She's bigger than I am, too."

Madelyn hardly had the breath to speak. She pivoted until she was looking back at him from an angle and she whispered: "What do you want of me, Taylor?"

No laughter covered anything up now. No treacherous teasing. Everything, Taylor thought; he wanted it all. He shook his head with conviction. "What are you willing to give?"

She leaned back against the wall opposite him. He was the kind of man she would've chosen to fall in love with, had she been given a choice. She was probably half in love with him already. But there was so much between where she stood and where he already was: an ocean, a galaxy, infinity.

"Oh, Taylor." Her heart was trying to burst from her breast. "You don't know what you're saying."

"I expect you're right."

"I'm not what you think."

"I don't doubt that."

"I mean, I'm what they call a difficult person, and that's an understatement to test the hyperbole of all time. I overreact. I work 'til I nearly go crazy and I'm never satisfied. I drive people to distraction because I can't accept the superficial, and they hate me for it. I'd make you wish you'd never seen me."

He smiled. "I already do."

She had turned slightly away. Was this how it started? That long, long ritual of love? Did it come creeping up on a person from out of nowwhere?

"I've always lived my life on my own terms, Madelyn," he said quietly. "With the possible exception of Owen. I haven't wanted anything for a long time. I'm just asking you to not shut any doors, that's all."

Confusion pulled at her brows. "But why me?"

Taylor shrugged. It was so simple for him. "Because you make me want to smile again."

It didn't take Madelyn too long to drink the coffee she didn't want and look through the material on Virginia Prince. When Randy returned to dump the file in her lap, she considered its lack of girth and thought, "This is the result of all those searches? This is the total impact of a woman's life?" No matter who Virginia Prince turned out to be, she was immeasurably saddened.

She picked up a pencil from Taylor's desk and carefully arranged the file in her lap. When Taylor began returning his telephone messages, she soberly laid back the cover.

A glossy eight by ten was on top—a stunning Virginia Prince standing beside a horse and handing up a trophy to the mounted jockey so that both their hands were on it. A cheering crowd pressed around them. She was blond; her head was thrown back in vivacious laughter. She was beautiful, and she had a hold on life that was tenacious.

There were other photographs: Virginia's charity functions with Owen, her photographs with Owen when he'd owned the *Daily Times*, after the birth of the twins when Owen had hair; he was announcing that he was going into politics and she was playfully kissing his cheek.

As Taylor hung up, he leaned forward and rested his chin in his palm. "What d'you think?"

Starting, Madelyn pinched the bridge of her nose. She had hoped for so much more. "I think Virginia was quite clever with her makeup. She didn't follow the natural shape of her mouth, for one thing. And she changed the line of her brows. Oh, there're similarities that make me want to say it's possible, but Abigail's been sick for a long time. You can't believe what a prolonged illness can do, Taylor. She hardly looks like she did five years ago, let alone twenty plus."

Randy was straddling a chair, taking everything in. He stared as Taylor moved to the corner of his desk and attached himself to it, letting his back round and the flesh of his abdomen make a neat fold over his belt.

"I'm overanxious," Madelyn said and closed the file. She moved her pencil idly across the surface of it. "I've lain awake too many nights thinking about it—Virginia Prince's brain injury, my mother's condition. I've never been good at comparing people. I can't see the parent in the child like a lot of people do. I look at how people act, and on that basis, Abigail and Virginia aren't the same woman at all."

"Considering what you're up against," Taylor thoughtfully warned, "your proof will have to be indisputable."

"What's she like?" Randy asked.

"My mother?" Madelyn's smile was filled with pleasant memories. "Not what you'd think. She doesn't rant and rave or pace the floor. She just sits there, hurting."

Randy made a sympathetic sound, and Madelyn started moving her pencil again.

"I don't think you're some kind of monster, Madelyn,"

Taylor said. He clasped his hands around one knee to draw it up to his chest. "It takes a great deal of strength to put your own mother in a hospital like that."

His pose was unconsciously arrogant, and Madelyn studied it. "You always wonder if they think you're punishing them."

No one said anything, and she continued to muse. "Mother used to forget things. When I was little, every night we'd sit down and write notes of the things she was supposed to do the next day. We'd tape them all over the house. She was so sweet, like a little child herself. She used to grab me and hug me and tell me the reason she loved me so much was because I was so sweet and she should put me in the sugar bowl."

Hearing the clamor of her own childhood, Madelyn quickly silenced. Presently she said: "I suppose you know Wallace Prince very well."

"I was probably more Wallace's father than his brother." Taylor's smile flickered. "He always worshipped Owen, followed him around like a puppy, but Owen was always too busy. Edwina and I raised Wallace. But when Wallace really gets hard against it, he goes running to Owen."

Madelyn couldn't imagine it. Owen had nothing that she wanted. She moved her pencil again. "There's a feeling between twins, they say. I don't look like Wallace, do I?"

Taylor honestly wished she did, but it would be cruel to let her hope. "There's the same dark hair, general characteristics, the same as there is with Abigail and Virginia. Twins don't always resemble one another that much, Madelyn."

She stirred. "I don't even know where to begin."

"It'll be pretty straightforward. We'll want your birth certificate, of course, everything you have. And Abigail's."

Time missed a dangerous beat.

Madelyn's jaw hung as she perceived the process this

would involve. "Don't you think records would've been the first thing I would have produced?"

Taylor's feet came down hard on the floor. "Are you saying you don't have a birth certificate?"

"Yes. I mean, no, I don't."

He drew his tongue along the edge of his teeth. Randy let out his breath and said: "But everything takes a birth certificate."

Madelyn felt their doubts like a chill on the back of her neck. What had she expected?

The contents of Virginia's file spilled to the floor when she rose, as if they were somehow symbolic of all her hopes in this matter. Stooping, she clumsily swept everything into the chair and jerked her handbag over her shoulder and started making for the door.

Taylor caught her by a shoulder. "What's the matter? You can't go out of here like this."

She was weak with dashed hopes. "I'll get back to you. I can't do this today."

"But you have to."

She turned on him like a fierce, cornered creature. "Look, Taylor, I don't even know who I am. Can you understand? I don't know exactly how old I am. When I started to go to school Abigail picked out a town off a map to be my birthplace. Pine Bluff, Arkansas. She signed an affidavit saying that I was her daughter and they accepted it. Even the affidavit is a lie. I'm a lie. I have to think some more about this!"

But didn't she realize that was actually in her favor? Taylor wondered. Did she think she should have been able to open a drawer and find a certificate with Waverly Prince's fingerprints on it?

His hand shot out for her and missed. "We'll fingerprint you and Abigail. Call in an expert. You're not running away from this, Madelyn. It's gone too far now."

"I'm not running, I'm walking. And we both know this

is hopeless. Frankly, Taylor, I didn't think that it would all be made so public. I don't want my mother dragged through issues of the *Daily Times* for nothing.'' Madelyn let her eyes flutter closed. ''You've been quite wonderful, considering. I'm sorry I took up your time. It was nice meeting you, Randy.''

Without another word, she walked out the door, and as Taylor stood staring after her, Randy bent over her chair. His face was wide with surprise as he lifted the cream-colored folder.

It was a sketch of Taylor, sitting on the corner of his desk, his broad back bowed, his laced hands clasped about the knee that was drawn to his chest. It had captured not only the perfect immediacy of his energy but the implied arrogance just beneath his surface. Incredibly lifelike and true, it had taken her the total of two minutes.

''Can you believe this?'' Randy whistled and thrust it into the hands of his editor.

''I'll be damned.'' Taylor stared down at it. Somewhere in his memory an alarm was going off. He strode to the door.

But Randy was already stepping through. ''Hey, Christine,'' he yelled and waved the file above his head. ''Come here. Lookie, lookie.''

Taylor caught up with Madelyn before she'd gotten twenty feet, and he fell into step as if they had choreographed it that way—one hand slipping with outward innocence to the small of her back, the other clamping down upon her arm between them with urgency.

''Not so easily as that, you don't,'' he murmured through gritted teeth.

''It's not easy.'' Her eyes were brimming with tears. ''You can't possibly know how hard it is.''

Whether or not Taylor would have actually allowed her to walk out of the newsroom, Madelyn didn't know. She thought at one point he would have been glad to. Neither of them saw Christine until the blond reporter was right on top of them.

"Why, Miss Grey," she said and laid her hand upon Taylor's arm. "I was hoping I could catch you before you left." She flashed the sketch and her smile at the same time. "This is good. Very, very good. Where have you been keeping yourself? Taylor, did you see this?"

Madelyn gave a futile shrug, but Christine didn't stop talking.

"Can't you just see it, Taylor? If Miss Grey would do some things for us, it wouldn't matter what—sketches, paintings, watercolors, anything she wanted to—why, there's no telling how much we could make at auction. More than anything we've raised before. Especially if we got some celebrity to be the auctioneer. We could mop up. I'm not kidding."

"Hey, yeah," Randy chimed in as he strolled up and hooked a leg over the corner of a desk. "It would beat the heck out of having a carnival like we did last year."

"I'll be the auctioneer," came a voice from a nearby desk. "I'm not wearing another clown suit, no matter what Christine bribes me with."

Laughter tittered briefly, but none of it was Madelyn's. She felt like she'd stepped into an ambush and found herself surrounded by the enemy. Approximately two dozen people were already moving nearer, and her sketch was being passed from hand to hand. A huge weight was settling in her throat, her middle.

"Auction?" She shook her head, tried to swallow. "What auction?"

By now Taylor was acutely attuned to Madelyn's emotions. All the color had drained from her face, and no facade, even if she'd been clever enough to assume one, could have prevented him from seeing the truth. She was afraid. No, terrified, and the reason for it was beginning to drive him up the wall.

"Right," Randy eagerly explained as he waved both hands grandly. "Christine raises money for the kids at the Holy Grace Orphanage every year. It's kind of a pet charity of the paper."

"And it wouldn't hurt your career any either, Miss Grey," Christine brightly added. "All that newspaper coverage for an artist on her way up. Ah, I said the magic words, didn't I?"

Much more than magic—black magic, a curse, a sacrifice at the stake. Madelyn could almost feel her blood chilling on its way to her heart. An investigation? The evening news? An auction of her work and more newspaper coverage? Where had she gone wrong?

"Well, I don't know—" she weakly protested. Taylor was gaping at her, she knew, dourly adding her up like a column of figures that refused to tally.

"I know it's an imposition even to ask such a thing," Christine rambled on, "but it's not just a charity to me. I think in my heart I've adopted these kids myself. A lot of them have been abused, some of them outright deserted. You really must go with me sometime to visit, Madelyn. May I call you Madelyn? They range anywhere from two months to twelve years, and they need absolutely everything from baby bottles on up. There isn't a more worthy cause in the whole city, and it literally saves lives. D'you think you—"

Madelyn couldn't bear the thought of her work on display. *Strangely boring, tiresome, contemptible.* She couldn't take any more of this.

"I really would love to, Christine," she lied desperately. "And it's no imposition at all. The work, that is. It's just that—"

Christine, even though she was blond, was by no means dumb. She looked from Madelyn to Taylor to Randy and back to Madelyn. And then it dawned. "Ohh," she said with husky awe. "Now I know who you are. It just came to me. Madelyn Grey. You're the artist Ellwyn Muse ripped up so—"

Dear God! It always came from behind, didn't it? Madelyn was rooted into the floor, incapable of everything that had to do with dignified behavior.

Randy Morrison began coming forward, shaking his own sandy head and waving his finger. "I knew it! I knew there was something about you from the very first minute. But I never connected you with her."

"Hey, I remember," someone else said and lowered his voice to explain to the neighboring desk.

"Well," another threw in, "leave it to *The Register*. No style over there, no taste."

"What does Muse know, anyway? He thinks Doc Severinsen's a cellist."

"The jerk."

Madelyn smiled with a skill she'd perfected to an art. Far across the room, the sun was low enough to impose its blinding glare upon the west windows. Someone had risen to adjust the blinds. If she were to paint the scene, she would glaze everything with unworldly hues of yellow and white and gold. She was a student of light; she had studied its effect upon the river for years.

"Madelyn?"

Taylor's voice. Madelyn turned to it in a daze. She wondered if it were possible to escape this place without disgrace. *Help me,* she begged with a look.

Taylor's reaction was instantaneous. "Sounds like a winner to me, Christine," he said. "Right now I have to get Miss Grey someplace. Go ahead and set up a time to confer . . . that is, if it's all right with Miss Grey. What d'you say, Madelyn? You can give me your phone number, etcetera, and we'll work around your schedule. Okay?"

Madelyn nodded mutely. Taylor reached for her arm

without looking, as if it were nothing more than an absent gesture on his part, and gave a few instructions to add finality to the scene.

Madelyn didn't remember leaving. She knew only that the elevator was the most blessed thing she'd ever seen. Hurrying, she pressed the button and rummaged in her bag for a large pair of sunglasses.

"Thank you," she said and kept her head bent low as she turned back. "That's the last thing in the world I expected."

Taylor had crossed his arms and was leaning loose-jointedly against the wall. Her paleness seemed to have soaked to her bones. Her cheekbones strained against the tautly stretched skin. Her transparency, her fragility, aggravated his protective instincts.

"This is Taylor, remember? Muse really did a number on you, didn't he?"

She brushed imaginary hair from her forehead, but her fingers were trembling so badly that she laced them together. Her panic choked off her breath. "It wasn't a number, it was an execution."

"I remember the exhibit. Christine covered it, so I never made the connection. Madelyn—"

"Don't tell me. I don't want to hear the speech about being positive and blowing it off and putting it all behind me. You can't say anything I haven't told myself one thousand times. Nature always attacks the weak, Taylor. It's a law. It keeps the pack strong, don't you know?"

Wishing he had the courage to take her face in his hands right this minute, Taylor glanced away, then back. His shoulders slumped. "You're the most unweak person I ever met. You just feel more deeply than most, Madelyn."

"He killed something in me." Madelyn dropped her head so he could not see how grievously it still hurt.

The elevator bell dinged, announcing its arrival, and

Taylor thought that if she smiled one more time, he would strangle her.

"I owe you an apology," he said as the door slid open.

"I don't want to hear it."

Before she could move, Taylor caught the door and blocked her from stepping in. "I've listened to you. Now you're going to listen to me."

Couldn't she get through to him? "I'm very tired, Taylor."

"You can rest later. Not too long ago we ran a syndicated piece—a study that a Massachusetts psychologist had done. A woman, by the way."

Madelyn wasn't interested. She stared blankly through the smoked lenses at the elevator door, patiently waiting.

"In the opinion of the good doctor," he went on, "the more insecure a person is about their intelligence, the nastier they criticize other people and their work."

For a moment Madelyn didn't move. She could feel her own eyes widening, her mind coming alive. "What's her name?"

"Uh . . . I forget . . ." Pinching the hook of his nose, Taylor flipped through the files of his memory. "Amabile, I think. Teresa Amabile. She's a psychologist and Brandeis professor."

Drawing her sunglasses far down on her nose, Madelyn peered sharply over them. "It would be nice to believe, especially when you're on the receiving end. But how does she support such a statement?"

He shrugged. "Her work began with college students. She wondered what made people so brutally critical of others. So she conducted a whole battery of experiments."

"And?"

Taylor chuckled. Pink was edging up into Madelyn's cheeks, and her eyes were misting with hope. Indefinable sensations began rolling in upon him in waves—happiness, the need to protect, the need to commit. "Her findings were that the negative reviewer is overwhelmingly rated by the public as being more intelligent than the positive one. And he—or she, pardon me—learns that being nasty pays. They automatically go for the jugular because they're afraid if they don't the public will think they're not so bright."

"But—"

"Almost everyone falls for it. But in actual fact the blistering critique says as much about the reviewer as it does about the play or the book or the work of art or the actor or the writer. Supercritics are insecure people, Madelyn. They have a deep-seated need to prove their intellectual muscle. Remember that the next time someone cuts you down. Ellwyn Muse felt threatened by you."

Madelyn felt as if she had just been handed the gift of eternal life. She didn't even try to stop the tears as they welled and trembled on her lashes.

"Dear God," she whispered. "How we waste ourselves."

There were other ways to waste oneself, Taylor wanted to say, but she was involved in some deep, internal struggle with herself. She shocked him when she stepped forward and caught his hands. Lifting them as gently and delicately as moonlight, she kissed them—once, twice, three times and pressed her cheek upon them.

Taylor's lungs felt as if they would burst. There was no way he could have spoken.

"Thank you," she said and pressed them tightly one last time. "God bless you, Taylor Champion." Very quickly she stepped into the elevator.

"But the campaign dinner," he blurted. She couldn't walk away. Not yet, not yet!

There was nothing coy or pretentious about her smile. "I don't have the kinds of clothes to attend an affair like that, Taylor. It would be an embarrassment to me. It's all right. I'm all right. Really. Thank you."

The light glinted off her tear-spiked lashes. The elevator door swished softly shut and she was gone.

For a moment Taylor stood studying the closure where it had been. He imagined her walking out of the building to the bus stop. Just like that she had come into his life, and just like that she'd walked out of it.

He walked back through the newsroom without speaking to anyone. When he reached his office he shut the door. After settling himself at his desk, pausing a moment to study the sketch lying beside his telephone, he picked up the directory and looked through the county numbers until he found the superintendant of Louisville schools.

"Hello, Mike?" he said after a secretary had come on the line and pushed a button on her desk, "this is Taylor at the *Daily Times*. There's somebody I want some dope on. She was a student in the Louisville schools. For a number of years, to my knowledge. Think you could help me?" He gave all the particulars. "Sure, I can hold."

Taylor moved the sketch closer while he waited. He traced the bold strokes of Madelyn's pencil. Incredible! Pinching the receiver between his jaw and shoulder, he searched through a drawer, found another file folder and exchanged them. He gently thumped it on the top of his desk until Mike Spencer came back on the phone.

"Hey, Taylor?"

"What?"

"Boy, you've gotten ahold of a live one here. A real whiz-kid. Listen . . ."

Ten minutes later Taylor laid the receiver carefully in its cradle. Much later, after most of the staff had closed up their desks, shut down their computers, and cut off their lights and gone home, Taylor was still sitting at his desk, staring at the sketch and thinking about Madelyn Grey.

Chapter Five

The marina where Madelyn's houseboat was moored wasn't the Marina Del Rey; it wasn't even a marina. It was an antiquated old dock whose residents had been anchored in its slips so long that everyone knew that Tom Banowitz had gallstones, and that old Bobby Walker gambled his paycheck away, and that Hilda Johnson's grandchild had been born two months early, and that Madelyn had divorced that "White boy" only six months after she'd had her mother committed to a state hospital.

Madelyn's boat was by far the most charming one of the lot. Before Abigail became too ill she had had a considerable amount of work done on it. The windows had all been replaced with oversize ones. Two entire walls were now inserts of pleasing glass panels that looked out over the water to catch the sun. During her nineteenth summer Madelyn had covered the exterior with cedar shakes herself, and they were now quaintly weathered and suited to the roof that Darrell, in a queer fit of domesticity, had redone into a Mansard style.

Beneath the eaves, flourishing from the river mist, Madelyn's ferns spilled lavishly over their baskets, and the airplane plants sent their offspring zooming verdantly down. Geraniums added splashes of effusive color here and there, along with a sturdy red mailbox at the end of the gangplank. The boat looked more like real estate than marine and wasn't so very different from a holiday cottage at a popular lakeside resort.

Hardly a moment passed during the next days that Madelyn didn't think about Taylor and what he'd said about the supercritics of the world. In her first seconds of coming awake his name was just under her tongue and the memory of his words in her ear. When her conscious thoughts succumbed at last to sleep she was holding his face in her mind.

Something was changing inside her; something critical was healing. It was as if she were rousing like Rip Van Winkle after an infinity of sleep. For the first time since Ellwyn Muse, a week wasn't something where daily withdrawals were made on the will in exchange for money; a day wasn't an inert space of time to be accepted until night came and made the wretched thing start all over again; happiness was no longer a bluff so people wouldn't think you were mad. Or even—heaven forbid—negative!

"Oh, Taylor," she whispered when the courage to live again made her dangerously happy. "What if I'd never met you?"

Often during the next days she went to the telephone. She was starving for the sound of Taylor's voice. She wanted to thank him again, to see how he was.

But always she hesitated. Taylor was an enormously strong-willed man. Strength should be complemented by strength, shouldn't it? If she were ever to go to him—and did she want to go to him? Yes!—she must go as a person of value, one who could look at life and say, "I will take you on my own terms." She must go with a dowry of the spirit.

Patience, she told herself, and wondered if Taylor had thought of her. Had he, too, walked to the telephone and considered picking it up? Was it utter madness to pray that he had?

Sandy Robertson always laughingly referred to herself as 'Robertson, Sandy,' which wasn't too far off the mark with her homely face and its too-closely spaced eyes, and her flat chest and aggressive backpacker's knees. She dressed with the attitude that nothing would really help, and today she was wearing flared, lime green polyester pants that struck her above the ankles and a purple button-up sweater whose laundry instructions to 'dry flat' had regretfully been ignored.

She lit a cigarette and waved for Madelyn to come along to the back of McMillan's Studio where the darkrooms and the microwave oven were. "I was about to put a taco in the microwave, honey. You want one?"

Shaking her head, Madelyn followed her along the poorly lit hall. Ralph McMillan, the owner, believed that remodeling was a subversive attempt of the carpenter's union to take over the country, so the photographic studio hadn't changed one board foot since it had been built during the Truman administration. His only redemption was that he was one of the best photographers in town.

"Maybe I can bring you two portraits next time," Madelyn said by way of a half apology and hoped Sandy wouldn't insist that she sit down.

Sandy, her cigarette drooping from between her lips, noisily unwrapped the canvas, which was folded up in the

Daily Times, ironically enough. As she did she chattered about her next trek to the Smokies and threw the newspaper into the wastebasket.

From habit, Madelyn suffered the same horrible, sickening fear in her stomach as Sandy opened up her work. Her sides grew damp and her hands shook. *Strangely boring, tiresome . . .* She clamped off her thoughts. She had vowed to stop that now, hadn't she?

"By the way"—Sandy threw Madelyn a sly, sidelong glance—"I saw the write-up in the paper. Shame on you for keepin' secrets, Madelyn. And Governor Prince, no less. It's not for real, is it? I mean, you don't really think your mother could be Virginia Prince, do you?"

"What article?" Madelyn's jaw dropped. "What're you talking about?"

"You mean you didn't see it? Landsakes, girl, where've you been the last few days?"

Distracted, for she loved more than anything to be the one who told a story first, Sandy moved about the room and riffled through a stack of folded papers and magazines. "I know it's around here someplace. I saw it just yesterday. Yes, here it is. Nice picture too. See? They even mentioned that you worked at the studio. Ralph was real pleased about that. Free advertisement."

Madelyn was no longer listening. Her senior high school photograph smiled back at her—two columns wide beside that of Wallace Prince—and beneath it a short, tasteful article on the events which had taken place at the governor's mansion. In retrospect and on the printed page it didn't sound nearly as bizarre as it had felt at the time. It was kind, low-key, and made no speculations.

She touched the words with her fingertips as if they were threads stretching over the miles to connect her to Taylor. Mumbling something about hoping the portrait was satisfactory, she turned to ask if she might not keep the paper.

Sandy had propped the portrait to the light and was standing back, her head cocked as she took a long drag on her smoke.

"What have you done?" she said and exhaled a cloud into Madelyn's face.

Smothering a cough, Madelyn batted the fumes away. "What d'you mean, what have I done? A portrait, just like always."

Madelyn's supercritical eye scanned the canvas for flaws. She'd recognized her fragility of the last days and had been extremely careful. She placed the photograph beside it and compared. There were no flaws.

"It's different," Sandy said.

Dismayed, Madelyn slumped. "It's not different. I was working quickly, yes, but you know I wouldn't bring you something I was dissatisfied with."

Laughing, Sandy grasped Madelyn's arms and shook them. "Listen, it's not all that bad. It sure does do something for the subject, I'll have to say. Did you ever see a more unphotogenic creature in all your born days?"

The life seemed to seep from Madelyn's pores as Sandy placed the portrait in a huge white package and marched to the front of the studio. She rang open the cash register and counted out Madelyn's money into her palm. She stepped back when she'd finished as if she expected Madelyn to count it again.

Folding it, knowing that it would stretch about half as far as it should among Darrell's creditors, Madelyn stuffed the bills into her purse. Now she almost feared to ask for more work. "Thank you. Do you have more to do?"

Sandy fussed about and found two new photographs. "Things are slow until school starts, you know. But they'll pick up."

"I'll try to have one of them done next week." Madelyn started moving toward the door, heavily depressed. "I'm sorry you didn't like this one."

The other woman waved her away. "We all have our off days. As a matter of fact, it's okay. You just keep on bringin' 'em in, and we'll do fine."

Sighing, Madelyn drew her bag back onto her shoulder. Her feet felt like an old woman's. Maybe Ellwyn Muse had been right, after all. Maybe she should just go out and sack groceries at the supermarket.

She fashioned a thin smile. "Tell Ralph I said hello."

"I will, honey. Sure thing."

Sandy was tempted to bring up the subject of Governor Prince again, but she guessed that there would be no more information forthcoming on that score. "And you take care now, you hear? Try to get a little bit more rest, Madelyn, honey. You're lookin' just a little bit peaked around the edges."

Waving, beaming brightly, and waving again as Madelyn turned from the sidewalk to peep back in, Sandy waited until Madelyn reached the bus stop before she hurried back into the lab where the telephone extension was. With dancing eyes, she dialed Ralph's number at home.

"Ralph," she said with hushed excitement. "You'd better get down here."

"Whatzamatter?" yawned the burly voice on the other end. He'd been watching a soap opera, and it had just gotten to the good part. "We didn't get held up again, did we?"

"It's probably the other way around. Madelyn Grey just brought a portrait in here."

"So?"

"Are you goin' to love me, Ralph. Are you goin' to ever-lovin' love me!"

"Will you get to it?"

"'Course, we'll have one disappointed customer out of the deal, but that's nothin', not when you consider the percentage of profit."

"What're you talking about, Robertson?"

"Listen, Ralph, I don't know what's come over Madelyn Grey, but somethin' sure has. Maybe it's that little to-do with the governor, I don't know. But you should see this portrait. Why, you could take it to any buyer in town and get four times what I just paid for it. And she doesn't know. Do you hear what I'm saying, Ralph? Madelyn Grey doesn't know what she's done. We're sittin' on a blessed gold mine."

The last thing Madelyn needed Friday morning at ten o'clock was a knock at the door. It was her habit to spend the daylight hours at the easel and avail herself of the night to walk L'il Abner, her spoiled but lovable cocker spaniel, and tend to her modest needs.

Today the entire living room—it was actually a combination kitchenette, den, and workroom with a partitioned bath—was draped with old sheets, including the floor. A canvas the size of a wall monopolized everything, but smaller ones were everywhere else, propped on the furniture, tucked under the bed, leaning against the walls, crowded into the corners. Mixing bowls of paint cluttered a small tabletop, together with scrapers and spatulas and jars of brushes. And she looked dreadful; her hair was a snarl that wildly defied the scarf she'd tied about it; her faded jeans and tennis shoes were the speckled and splattered mess they always were when she worked on very large canvases. Her shirt, missing half its buttons, was tied about her middle.

The rapping persisted. L'il Abner set up a ferocious barking and hurled himself at the door like a buff-colored torpedo. Growling, he sat himself down to wait.

Madelyn finally jerked up her head and made an impatient hissing sound between her teeth. "Who is it?"

Between the fingers of her left hand were tucked brushes dipped in different colors. In her right, she held a putty knife. Laying it all down, she began peeling off thin latex gloves.

"Who's there?"

No reply, only another knock.

"Darn!" She strode irritably to the door. "Pearl knows better than this."

Pearl and John McGrath, the older couple next door, had adopted themselves as Madelyn's pseudograndparents. Pearl considered the safe-guarding of Madelyn's health to be a quest for the Holy Grail itself, and several times a week she dropped by to check on Madelyn's eating habits and see if she had run out of vitamins or chickweed tea.

Calling to mind a half-dozen excuses of why she simply could not go shopping for raw veggies and herbs, Madelyn snatched open the door. She peered up, wide-eyed and openmouthed, at Taylor's grinning face, while L'il Abner, overcome with a rush of protective fervor, happily took a bite of his trousers.

"Ouch!" Taylor's grin dissolved. He glared down at the dog wrestling with the leg of his best pair of Jas. K. Wilson's.

Horrified, Madelyn dropped to her knees. "Let go, you little beast! Taylor, help me. I'm sorry. L'il Abner!"

Though it wasn't exactly the welcome he'd hoped for, Taylor gamely dropped into a sprinter's squat and applied a crucial bit of pressure upon L'il Abner's windpipe. Between that and Madelyn's frantic efforts to drag the dog into her arms, L'il Abner made a quick decision that cowardice was the better part of most anything. He scrambled desperately out of her arms and raced up the gangplank to drop in a shaken and exhausted bundle to collect his wits and try to figure out where he'd gone wrong.

Still too stunned to speak, Madelyn leaned back on her heels. Taylor looked wonderful in his collarless open-throated shirt, his pleated navy slacks, now slightly mangled. He remained, half-kneeling, and stared at where her tail-tied shirt had crept high beneath her breasts. Her jeans, strained to the limit, had unfortunately dropped past her navel in the other direction.

Since she'd already made love with him a hundred times in her mind, Madelyn turned quite red and came clumsily to her feet, pulling and fussing and adjusting.

He chuckled. "Hello, Madelyn. How've you been? I must say that you're looking very . . ." He paused. "Ahh, very good."

Her brows arched steeply. "They're not ruined, are they?" Bending down to look, she groped through her mind. What could she say that would make her at least appear to be clever and in control? "You'll probably set a fashion. By next week every man in Louisville will be trying to buy slacks with those little eyelets in the leg."

"You know, Madelyn"—he studied her with an intensity more intense than the circumstances warranted—"I seem to lose an article of clothing every time I'm around you. At this rate, I'll soon have to go to work in my shorts."

"That's not fair. I offered to wash your handkerchief, if you'll remember, and you gave me one of those Tarzanish rebuffs." She dropped her voice a mocking octave. " 'Offers to do the laundry usually come a bit later in the relationship, Madelyn.' "

His bow was one of repentance. "It was completely unforgivable. Allow me to make amends. I'll take off my pants and you can wash them this very minute."

She dragged the scarf off her head and frivolously picked at the knot. "It's your mouth that needs washing, Taylor."

"Well, I'm game for that too." He tried to catch her eye without success. "But I'll fight. I warn you."

She tipped up her head. "That's supposed to scare me?"

"I fight dirty." Chuckling, he caught sight of her living room over her head. "You're really a terrible hostess. Aren't you going to ask me in?"

Madelyn was feeling better about herself but not nearly enough to allow anyone the intimacy of seeing her work, not even Taylor. Stepping back, she pulled the door closed with an abruptness that made them both aware of just how delicately this attraction hung between them.

"Well"—he didn't attempt to disguise his disappointment—"at least you're well protected."

From his vantage, L'il Abner was memorizing the tall trousered creature, and Madelyn shaded her eyes as she squinted at him. "You hurt his feelings, you know."

"You're not going to call the ASPCA, are you?"

With her arm uplifted, Taylor could see the outline of her breasts against her shirt. She wasn't wearing a bra, and when she bent at her waist and clapped her hands for the dog, her shirt innocently gapped open. The sight of her breasts, as tremblingly white as he'd imagined them and so sweet with their tight blushing nipples, made him instantly, achingly aroused. She straightened, for L'il Abner cocked his head at her as if she had to be insane to suggest he return. He bounded across the dock without so much as a guilty glance backward.

"He's the trial of my life," she said with a sigh. "He has this addiction to potato peelings, especially Mr. Nutley's."

And I'm addicted to you, Taylor thought and murmured, "A potato junkie. How lovely."

Since Helen's death, Taylor had built a safe and incomprehensible world around himself, no impassioned hopes left over from his youth, and a declared truce with the pain that had spawned him. And why not? he'd often rationalized. If one's life has no love, no joy, no happiness, then one prostitutes oneself to success—basically put, money. Plus the hollow respect that came with it. But then Madelyn Grey had stood beside the elevator, her eyes swollen and her spirits crushed, needing him as no one had ever needed him before, and he wanted to shake his fist at Fate. How could he return to his safe world after that?

He leaned back against the redwood railing that ran around the boat and let his legs sprawl wide. He'd never minded risks before—the more dangerous the better. But he'd had nothing to lose then. Now he was all but shaking when he reached out the hook of his arm and captured Madelyn's neck. His breaths were shallow when he drew her into the snare of his legs.

Yet she let him fit her into the nest of his crotch. She kept her eyes fixed upon the second button of his shirt and murmured: "Aren't you supposed to be writing bylines or sending reporters off to chase ambulances or cover robberies for page one?"

He fixed his gaze on her face. "Lou Grant does that for me. Lord, I've missed you."

She dipped her face into the slope of his neck with a sigh. How good they felt, his strong arms. From habit, she wanted to prolong the moment, drain it of every good sensation, store it up as a reserve against bad times. "I thought about you."

"Did you?" Nothing could make him as reckless as her shy honesty. He laid a hand along the side of her hip, slid it upward to the satiny expanse of bare midriff.

She caught her breath, but she didn't move away. "How did you find me?"

"Newspaper people are born bloodhounds." He pressed a cautious kiss upon the curve of her nape, and when she made a sound back in her throat he knew a sharp desire for more. "Why don't you want me to come in, Madelyn?"

She could never have explained it to him. "Things are a mess."

They engaged in a tiny duel for the knot of her shirttails, but Taylor won and the shirt spilled over his hands to make everything beneath a discreet secret. He promised: "I'll close my eyes."

"And the turpentine—it just permeates everything. I open up all the windows, but still it takes hours—oh!"

"Shut up, Madelyn." Taylor closed one hand upon her breast with a deep sigh. "Please, will you just shut up."

He kissed her for what seemed to Madelyn forever, his mouth shifting, moving upon hers, experimenting, his tongue asking tiny flickering questions. At first she felt as if she were drifting on some unreal current that would surely lead to anathema. And then she was kissing him back, unable to taste enough, to touch enough. There didn't seem to be any short-term embraces with Taylor Champion. She collapsed upon his chest.

"You make me faint," she whimpered.

"D'you promise?" Blisteringly aroused, Taylor wrenched his shirt free of his trousers and placed her hands upon his chest. "It's all I've thought about for days. I think I'm in a crisis."

"You'd better do something fast." Had she actually said that?

He had locked his legs about hers, and now he was kissing her eyes shut. "I'm trying as hard as I can, sweetheart." Without the tease, then, he added against her cheek, "If it matters, Madelyn, the last time I asked a woman for anything was when I was married."

"Taylor—"

"Don't say no."

Far down the river the *Belle of Louisville* was tooting her whistle as she steam-paddled her way up. Behind them, two boys whizzed down the dock with noisemakers clacking in the spokes of their bicycles. This was too exposed, too spontaneous to be safe.

Not realizing her perfect cruelty until it was too late, Madelyn leaned back against the gate of Taylor's legs. "Is that the only reason you came?"

That she could ask such a question wounded Taylor to the quick. If she could think that, he didn't know what he was doing here.

A bit desperately he released her and retied the tails of

her shirt. "The fact is, I have an old house out in the country that I work on in my spare time. I thought you might help me with some color selections. Since you're such a famous young artiste."

Madelyn was painfully conscious of having ruined the fragile moment. She tried to redeem herself by teasing him. "That's the worst excuse I ever heard."

He refused to diffuse the tension. "I agree. I put some samples in the car to try and make it sound legitimate. I thought I might at least get you as far as Sherwin Williams."

The small boy was showing in him again, still sullen, still mistrusting. Madelyn grimaced. "Will you go away for a few minutes and let me clean up?"

"My patience span is notoriously short."

She thrust out her chin, feeling her own stored-up pain. "Is forty-five minutes too much for you to bear?"

He scowled at his wristwatch. "A half hour."

With a few steps he was halfway up the gangplank. Turning, he let a moment of silence stretch between them, then said: "Hide all the little secrets you've got in there, Madelyn. Unless you want me to come through all that plate glass when we get back, you're going to open the door."

A half hour wasn't nearly long enough. Madelyn flew rabidly about the place, shoving canvases face down against the wall and carefully covering the wet one. She showered in record time and twisted her hair into a topknot, and holding its sliding mass in place with one hand, she searched frantically for hairpins with the other. No sooner had she found two and poked them into the twisted coil then she heard the whine of the Mitsubishi outside.

"Oh, great!"

She hastily smoothed on some lip gloss and worked her lips, sprayed a dash of 'Anaïs Anaïs' on her throat and made a final scrutiny of herself: black slacks, a big shrug shirt

caught fluidly at the waist with the one great belt she
owned, a Graziano silk cord, and her old dependable
low-heeled pumps that she'd paid an exorbitant price for
five years before.

She caught Taylor at the door before he knocked and
slipped through the sliver of space like a shadow before he
could insinuate his way in.

"I did everything you said," she said and winced as he
inspected her. "Do I get an A?"

She could have worn a burlap sack and he would still
have wanted to drag her off to bed. "You're an overachiev-
er, Madelyn Grey." He motioned for her to precede him up
the gangplank.

"And what were you, Mr. Champion?" she lightly
countered.

"A dumb jock."

They had reached the flat part of the pier, and Taylor's
small, silver car was parked only a few feet away. Madelyn
turned back to catch him in an unguarded moment. He was
pale, and the expression on his face was that of a man who
had grabbed a tiger and didn't know what to do with it.

"You're not dumb, Taylor Champion." she said softly.

He peered down into her eyes for a long, pulsing
moment. "That, my darling, remains to be seen," he said
and opened her door.

Madelyn never shopped at the River City Mall. To her
the Galleria was for browsing only, and Stewart's
Drygoods was the department store with Coffeetrees,
where works of Kentucky artists were featured. Her own
works, needless to say, were not on the agenda for the near
future.

Taylor pulled into a parking place, and Madelyn crawled
out her side as if their relationship had long since dispensed
with formalities. Once they emerged into the sunshine, he
automatically took the outside of the walk. As they waited
for the light to change between Liberty and Muhammad

Ali, he moved subtly nearer, his hand a fleeting and possessive movement beneath her elbow.

"Do you ever look up at those buildings and wonder if they'll fall on top of you?" she asked, hurrying along beside him.

He grinned. "Do you ever wonder if your boat will sink?"

"I used to. When I was little." Her sidelong look was one of monumental gravity. "I checked out the displacement of this boat myself, Taylor. The chances of it sinking are so small as to be nonexistent."

To her astonishment, Taylor caught her up in his arms in the middle of the sidewalk, made a complete turn, and set her down with a kiss upon the top of her head. Blue eyes twinkling, he laughed and said: "I knew I could depend on you to cut to the heart of the matter."

By the time they had window-shopped through the Galleria and argued over paints and color combinations, textures and patterns, Madelyn's senses were overflowing with him. She smiled as he bought ice cream and then decided that he liked hers better and ate them both. She studied him from the corner of her eye as they munched on giant peanut butter cookies and shared his exasperation when they walked into the wilderness of a small shop where the choice was an overkill that made them want to run out screaming.

How easily he was drawing her into the flow of his life! His shoulder was always so casually there, his fingers so inclined to twine with hers. He told her about breaking into Owen's house and his adoption. She told him about Abigail and her lost dreams. By the time he motioned her into Evan and Lord's, Madelyn was so used to his familiarities that she gazed up at him and thought: *Please know that I'm falling in love with you. Please don't break my heart.*

Evan and Lord's was one of the most lavish department stores in the South. It housed the most expensive clothes, the most aloof salespeople, and the most ostentatious interior between Kentucky and New York. Madelyn hesitated as Taylor nudged her forward. Here the smell was expensive; even the sounds were expensive.

Giving a small shrug, she followed aimlessly alongside him, but when Taylor told the clerk that he wanted to see something in women's formal evening wear it finally struck home: the governor's campaign dinner!

Madelyn rebuked him with a half-turn and a downward twist of her mouth. "Oh, no, Taylor, you're not going to—"

He caught her arm none too gently as she was moving away, his brows darkly insistent. "There aren't any strings attached to this."

"Strings?" She nearly choked. "You're talking ropes, Taylor. Thank you, but no."

Madelyn's whisper attracted the disapproval of the clerk as she walked toward them and peered at them from over a bosom that didn't belong in the twentieth century. *Lovers,* Madelyn imagined her thinking; *bringing their quarrel to a public place.*

"Oh, hell, Madelyn, it's just a dress. Now, will you behave yourself and bear it gracefully?"

Owen Prince could have bought her a dress and it wouldn't have mattered; her boss at McMillan's, Randy Morrison, the taxi driver, for crying out loud. But not Taylor Champion.

"Mr. Champion," cooed the clerk from over the bridge of her imperious nose. "How very nice to see you again. It's been some time since you've been in to see us. How is dear Edwina?"

"She's fine, Miss Ackerman. This"—he indicated Madelyn—"is Miss Grey. I think we'd like to see something . . ." Taylor gave Madelyn a look that warned of unspeakable things if she embarrassed him. "In green, I think. Very dark and very clear."

At that moment Madelyn hated him. Did Miss Ackerman think that she was the next in the string of Taylor's lovers?

Miss Ackerman, after a second inspection of Madelyn, nodded her approval. She walked briskly off and left them to trail along. "As always, your taste is impeccable. Would you come this way, please."

Madelyn resisted Taylor's hand as she stumbled numbly alongside him. "You are ill-mannered and unforgivably rude," she whispered hotly.

Drawing her into the circle of his arm against her will, Taylor pressed his mouth against her drooping hair in a way that warned Madelyn he meant to win. "I'm also very stubborn. Now be quiet."

The clerk turned to bestow an imperial look. Madelyn pasted a silly smile upon her face.

Through a maze of racks and manikins wearing Anne Klein and Liz Claiborne and Bill Blass and Jones of New York, plus an endless array of breathtaking Diors and de la Rentas and André Laugs, they were led to an area divided into a half-dozen indecently private compartments. Each nook possessed its own dressing room of mirrors, a place to wait with lush, slightly masculine furnishings, more mirrors, ashtrays and magazines, a telephone and a coffee machine.

Madelyn couldn't imagine anything in this store costing less than a thousand dollars, and judging by the opulence of things, she didn't know whether she was supposed to try on clothes or be seduced.

Taylor promptly sprawled out on a settee and braced a trousered leg upon a knee. Stretching both arms across the back, he then amused himself by watching Madelyn fidget beneath the deft and professional ministrations of Miss Ackerman.

"You're quite slender," Ackerman said in a tone that Madelyn was sure she practiced to mean: You're skinny.

"You know, of course, that the length of the gown will not be true in *those*."

Three pairs of eyes followed Miss Ackerman's accusing fingertip to Madelyn's low-heeled pumps.

"Be back in a minute," Taylor said and came to his feet and disappeared.

Madelyn belatedly wished that she'd never picked up the telephone to call that cab. "I'll stand on tiptoe."

She tried on three gowns. What a cruelty it was, she thought, to close her eyes and feel the cool linings slither against her skin and hear the swish of taffeta when she walked out, at Taylor's insistence, to model each one. He had returned with a pair of black high-heeled slings that fit perfectly (another thing she found intolerable), and she could hardly meet his eyes as he laid a forefinger sexily across his mouth and considered the pros and cons of each garment. He gave the impression that he'd been buying her clothes for years.

"Turn around," he said at one point, coming to his feet and turning her by both arms. "Let me see the hips."

Feeling her pulse crazily in the tips of her fingers, Madelyn obediently pivoted. Her eyes, when she caught his, were razored.

"Hmm."

Taylor stood behind her in the three-way reflection. When she looked up, he grinned and pinched the fabric on both sides of the zipper at her back. Releasing it, he deftly took in a seam's depth on each shoulder and studied the reflection of the deep cowl draping across her breasts.

"Hold in your stomach, darling," he murmured.

Madelyn's throat blazed scarlet, and her teeth clenched furiously. "I *am* holding it in."

He shook his dark head in a chuckle. She had no idea how he enjoyed taking care of her. "The first one, I think," he said. "The Halston."

The clerk beamed. "I think so too."

Madelyn's whisper was grating. "The neckline of the Halston is too low, Taylor."

He peered over her shoulder and pondered her reflection as if he were fondly imagining cleavage. He grinned. "It'll do just fine."

Having no reply whatsoever, Madelyn lifted her gaze to the ceiling.

Miss Ackerman was efficiency itself. She swept up the discarded gowns and hovered over Taylor as he reached for his wallet. As Madelyn grabbed up the long skirt of the one she was wearing and escaped to the dressing room, she heard the woman say, "Will there be anything else today, Mr. Champion? Lingerie, perhaps? Underwear?"

Oh, God! Madelyn dragged the gown over her head, totally destroying what remained of her hairdo. Standing in her plain white bra and cotton panties, both of which looked hideously ugly now, she held up the dress and stared at it: a dark silk charmeuse with a pleated surplice front and luscious dolman sleeves, a belt that caught her waist snugly and made her prettier than she had thought she could ever be. A person never craved the taste of cake until they'd tasted it. How could she return to the drabness of her life after Taylor had played husband for a day?

Miss Ackerman's steps sounded outside the drapery. Madelyn thrust the dress out at her. She was aroused by the sensuousness of luxury and the memory of Taylor's possessive mannerisms. Her legs were hot, and her breasts were alive; the lobes of her ears burned and her heart beat too rapidly.

"Is there anything else I can get you, Miss Grey?"

Starting, swiping the tears savagely from her lashes, Madelyn arranged her face. She scooped up her slacks and began shrugging into them. "No, no. I'm fine, thank you."

"Very well. May I have the shoes, please?"

Madelyn threw them out the door.

"Will you want these to go with the gown?"

"Please see Mr. Champion about that," she managed to croak.

"As you wish."

No, not as she wished! If she did as she wished, she would sweep it all up in her greedy little arms, slip her feet into Cinderella's glass slippers, climb into the coach and four, and let the devil take tomorrow!

Chapter Six

You know," Madelyn said with waning brightness as Taylor ducked his head and took several lanky strides through her door, "Pearl and John are probably standing at their window this very minute, making a match between us."

What she said was not what she was thinking: that for six months Darrell White had lived in this houseboat and despite feeling invaded by him, sometimes overpowered by him, the place had never failed to accommodate him or any number of her casual friends—Pearl and John, David Hirschfield, a few dates, an occasional repairman. Now Taylor dwarfed everything with his maleness, and she felt out of place, as if it were his place and she was the outsider.

She dropped L'il Abner to the floor and placed her mail on the table while Taylor placed the box from Evan and Lord's on her sofa like an honored guest.

"Matchmaking," he murmured. "The pastime of happily married folk. Oh, to have such a problem."

Madelyn covertly watched Taylor strolling to her windows and opening the drapes. The accents and shadows changed, and he moved to the other wall of glass, which looked out over the river, and pulled those drapes too. He looked too perfect here, too at home, too habit-forming.

Swollen rainclouds were rolling in from the north, slicing the sky in half—brilliant blue shining on one side and dark, angry gray boiling on the other. Taylor stood with his hands slipped in his back pockets, studying it.

Madelyn thoughtfully moved to stand beside him. "It's going to storm."

"Mmm. You afraid?"

"Of storms?" She shook her head. "No. Do you know this river carries twice the tonnage of the Panama Canal?"

From his height above her, Taylor smiled. Could he go the rest of his life without these unexpected, jarring little moments? "Not exactly."

She flicked a mildly censuring smile his way. "Stop laughing at me. This river's been good to America."

"I wasn't laughing, I was admiring. And I was thinking how this country hasn't always been so good to it." What he'd been thinking was how much he would like to pull her down on the divan and kiss every curve, every hollow of her from the top of her head to the soles of her feet.

"The first steamboats appeared on this river," she went on, unaware of his designs. "Now they're having to filter the water around Cincinnati. The earth is our best friend, Taylor. It's never selfish. It doesn't even ask to be loved, only understood. Do you know what I mean?"

Which was why he desired her above everything. She was absorbed with the drops starting to hit against the wall of glass with ringing, staccatoed pings, and he grew absorbed with the shape of her cheek.

The steel curtain drew nearer. The bright sunshine was

suddenly swallowed up, and when the curtain dropped it was straight and heavy, coming against the boat in a pounding roar. Sheets of wet sluiced over the windows, covered the deck and made the river as gray as the sky. Thunder was alive in the distance. They were isolated now, while the sky quarreled with itself.

Madelyn glanced fleetingly at Taylor, as if to say, "And now what?"

Taylor had no suggestions. He followed her about, chatting easily about work and other storms and ruined office picnics as she turned on lamps and fetched glasses, stooped to peer inside her bare refrigerator.

The furniture was all old and makeshift, Taylor saw, but she had made it attractive with a professional flare: bright checked slipcovers for the divan and chair, a chic mosaic screen to shut off the bedroom and bath. The lamps all had charming shades. The bedroom, what he could see of it, was feminine, cream and wine colors. Over a frilly dressing table was hung an antique fan. Her plants, potted in small glazed pottery, ran riot everywhere—down the crowded bookshelves and over the refrigerator to spill across the walls. On the side that caught the light stood her easel and a whole bevy of canvases whose fronts he could not see. Yet nothing was an accident; economical and exceptional.

She should have much more room to work, he thought. Space and high ceilings and room after room of light. Stooping, he extended the peace pipe to L'il Abner by scratching his ears and said, "I know a half-dozen people who'd trade places with you on the spot."

She smiled. At least he was self-conscious too. "Looks romantic, does it?"

"You don't think so? All this water and atmosphere?"

"It's always a good conversation piece. And myself, of course. You'll find I'm quite knowledgeable about navigation and weather, Taylor. Even plumbing. Ask me some questions. I'll tell you everything."

Taylor was uncomfortable with the distance she was keeping between them. She was nervous, but it was silly to pretend that nothing had happened. She fretted with her mail, held up an envelope to the light, and placed the rest on the table.

"May I get you something?" She was aware of his displeasure and had immediately played hostess.

He nodded. "Only so you can't turn me out in the rain."

"Beast." Madelyn laughed but avoided looking at him. "I've got an extra Coke taking up space in my pantry."

"Never let it be said that I'm hard to please." He bowed mockingly.

He gave her the time to fix the drink and walked, sipping, to her tape deck as she read her letter. A cassette was in place, and he pressed a button and a haunting soprano melody drifted across the room.

"Beim Schlafengehen," she said absently, feeling his question before he asked it. "Strauss."

A number of canvases leaned against the wall nearest him, some of them quite large. On the easel was the portrait of a smiling face—a good technique, he thought, commercial, but stylistically fascinating. He glanced over his shoulder to ask about her work at McMillan's and found a frown wrinkling the space between her brows as she read. She was chewing at the edge of her lip.

"Trouble?"

Glancing up with a start, she smiled too quickly. "It's nothing." She immediately dropped the letter.

A tiny alarm went off in Taylor's head. He indicated her canvases. "D'you mind if I look?"

"Yes, I do mind."

To his surprise, she moved across the room and, with a carelessness of a rich woman flinging priceless jewelry aside, flipped the canvas off the easel and leaned it, back out, against the wall with the others.

A heavier piece was sticking out into the room, and after giving it a second thought, she leaned her weight against it. It was heavy; her face pinkened with the exertion, but finally the canvas scooted along the wall and lodged firmly in the corner. Her action—toes buried gingerly into the carpet, hips and legs straining like a prideful young man—made her at once unbearably desirable.

"How long have you lived here?" he asked more gruffly than he intended.

"In the boat? Ever since I can remember. We moved around a lot when I was small, but we always lived in the boat."

"Kind of hard, wasn't it?"

"Changing? My friends weren't the kind you minded leaving very much."

"My friends were the kind you wanted to leave. Street kids." He watched the grace of her hands as she swiftly made order of her work table. "I grew up in Butchertown. That's where I got this." He touched the scar on his jaw. "And a police record a foot long."

Glancing up, she smiled. Butchertown was now being restored. The shotgun and row houses were being turned i nto elite boutiques and profitable antique shops. "Then you and Butchertown made it. Butchertown got tax money and you got Owen Prince."

Madelyn had meant the remark to be casual. She wasn't prepared for Taylor's dark intensity when he stepped toward her. Gooseflesh suddenly raised along the surface of her skin.

"Don't throw that in my face anymore," he said and stared meaningfully at her mouth. "I pay my dues for being Owen's son."

Something along her spine quivered. "I'm sure you do."

Taylor picked up a scraping tool from the table. How damnably pretentious she was. He could feel the passion in her, could feel the heat rising in her. Yet here, inside her own home where there was privacy and some of the most beautiful music he'd ever heard, her resistance was stronger than it had been that first day.

Quickly, before she could realize his intentions, he strode to her canvases and separated the top one from the others. He heard her gasp, but he refused to turn; he would only see that hurt innocence in her eyes, and then he wouldn't be able to do it.

The nearest canvas wasn't too large. Lifting it, he brought it up to balance the bottom edge across the tops of his thighs. It was a landscape, extremely elegant in texture and almost dangerously restrained. The colors were muted and consciously void of accent—a lovely, subtle piece and one that made Taylor wonder if her reluctance to let him see it had been some charade in the first place.

He chanced a glance over his shoulder then. The color had drained from her face, and her teeth were buried into the cushion of her lower lip. It was no charade. Unshed tears sparkled in her wide, frightened eyes, and both her hands crossed over her breasts as if she feared life would leave her body.

As heartless as it must seem to her, he knew he must see the rest of the works. "I have to, Madelyn."

He exchanged the first canvas for a second. It was another landscape, relatively like the first in texture and style. But the third was a wild, raw experimentation—something hinting of the prehistoric with exuberant brushwork, unbelievable and almost supernatural light.

Taylor sucked in his breath and, literally forgetting about Madelyn, walked across to the opposite side of the boat and turned back to study it. It was afire. He removed another canvas, different still. And several smaller pieces, all aggressive. The fifth was a moody self-portrait that seemed almost to weep by its texture. He determined to have it for himself.

The last, not the largest canvas but one that he had to

wrestle around to lean back against the wall, was a contemporary of the violent *heftig* coming out of Italy and Germany. It was littered with danger and expressive of the most incredible pain, yet at the same time brashly, wildly hubristic. Here, on this canvas, was the fire of her alter ego, her great depth of intelligence, and an artistry that was staggering.

"My God!" he whispered, dumbfounded.

He had known she was a genius, but it was more than that. Madelyn Grey, with all her converging contradictions, was some once-in-a-generation rarity, buried down here on the river and having suffered . . . no one would ever know what people like her suffered, the Mozarts, Scriabins and Goyas of the world. How was it possible in the enlightened eighties that someone hadn't seen what Madelyn Grey was before now? He couldn't have expected it from her mother, but what about her teachers? Her friends? Pearl McGrath?

Taylor didn't hear Madelyn's weeping; he felt it. Turning, he saw the rivulets coursing down her cheeks, golden ribbons in the lamplight. His resentment of the last moments melted, and a great wave of tenderness washed over him.

"But they're wonderful," he said inadequately and took a step toward her. "You shouldn't . . ."

Her crying was unlike any he'd ever seen: a silent, blind grief that poured out of unblinking eyes. "Ahh, Madelyn." He couldn't possibly say what lay in his heart. "Don't cry." He took her into his arms and buried his face in her hair. "Shh, don't cry."

He only meant to hold her until she could recover, but her hair was spilling over his arms, its perfume an intoxication that went straight to his head, her smallness a miracle that excited him beyond anything he'd felt in his whole life. When he stroked the lines of her flank, her shudders incited shudders of his own. Whether it was his clumsiness, he didn't know, but she suddenly struggled in his embrace and in attempting to wrench herself free triggered a reflexive action that made him hold her tighter. The angles of her body meshed powerfully with his, and his needs erupted into raging flames.

"No, no." The hoarseness of his own voice shocked him. "Please. Just for a minute."

She shook her head. "Let me go."

Didn't she know he couldn't do that? That she was searing into his flesh like acid? "Sweetheart—"

Thunder crashed outside, and as she arched back in his arms, one unguarded moment passed between them: a moment Taylor knew that neither of them could ever hope later to deny, a space where either of them could have pulled back and both knew it. He thought that Madelyn looked at him with two pairs of eyes—one searching for an escape, frantic, virginal eyes, and the other the eyes of a temptress who was deliberately seductive, challenging.

He shaped his hand about the femininely fashioned bones where her legs parted. She was warm and alive and in that moment was turning her face to his. Where she had been struggling, now she was standing on the tips of her toes, straining upward, moving against him.

All the collected risks that Taylor should have taken in the past and never had, bore down upon him now. He dragged Madelyn to her knees with an urgency that he knew had to bring pain. He heard the rending of cloth as he wrestled with her blouse and she with his belt. It occurred to him to ask her forgiveness for what was happening, but she tore her blouse free of its buttons. He closed his mouth upon her breast, and she groaned like some tortured thing.

By some means that was half-nightmare, half-ecstasy, he managed to unzip his trousers enough to make the next step inevitable. Their sounds were primitive, guttural, moaning. He struggled with her slacks and the damned pantyhose, but they clung and she kicked them off. As he pulled himself upon her, she reached for him and urged him into her with a sobbing that both confused him and compelled him on.

"I'm sorry," he managed to choke, but her hands were upon his hips, gathering him to her.

Over and over she repeated, "Please, please," until he, unable to bear it any longer, silenced her with the frenzy of his mouth.

It was very short and very violent.

She arched blindly upward, and Taylor brought it to its end with a sharp swiftness that he would have said was impossible. And then, midway between ecstasy and the return to reality, he lifted his head from where it rested in the curve of her neck. Her eyes were shut and her face twisted like that of a child. He wondered if, in the delirium of his desire, he had killed her.

If it had been dark, Madelyn thought, it would have been easier. Or even planned. If they had slept, one of them could have escaped and left an hysterical note for the other. But there was nothing to do but lie still and listen to the rain and feel the gradually slowing heartbeat of the other. How to do this gracefully without hurting either of them?

When Taylor lifted her hair from between them, Madelyn closed her eyes as if she could protect herself just a few moments longer. It would be a wasteland now, wouldn't it?

"Not just yet," she whispered and struggled to guess the final end. Would he think now that he had made a mistake, that there were hundreds of women infinitely less troublesome and easier to bed than she?

"I know what you're thinking," he said.

She turned her face away. "You couldn't possibly."

He dropped back to the floor, and she didn't turn to see him staring at the ceiling. He was reasonably clothed while she was completely naked.

"You think I'm Attila the Hun," he said.

"Only a distant relative."

"Are you sorry?"

She shivered. No one, past or present, sexual or platonic, had ever made her feel as whole as his lapse of control had done. He had seen—at whatever level—*her;* on the canvas; with respect. For that she would never be sorry.

"No." She shook her head and crossed her arms to protect her nakedness. "No, I'm not sorry."

Her gesture of modesty caused Taylor to roll onto his side and brace himself on an elbow. "You look sorry." He gently, and in slow motion, uncrossed her arms. "I just want to see you, sweet. Nothing more."

Madelyn took a quick breath as he made a slow sweep from her head to her toes, as if to compare his visual impressions with an imaginary one. He seemed fascinated by his own hand as he smoothed it across the valley between her breasts, her waist, her triangular sculpture of bones. She watched his chest expand quickly, and knew that she wasn't disappointing him.

"You're so rare," he mused softly. "I can't seem to put all the pieces of you together in my mind."

She could hardly make her voice work. "So many pieces?"

"Not so many, perhaps, just so . . ." He traced the line of her brows, the line where her hair began to grow, the orb of her ear. "You intimidate me, I think. I know you're smarter than I am, and—"

"Shh!"

She hushed him with her lips, and as his kiss quickly deepened, as his tongue searched for hers with something very near desperation, he came to his feet and reached down for her hands. He didn't release her mouth even as he pulled her up and swept her into his arms. The room was almost completely shadowed now, and the tape had played itself out. There was only the quiet, steady hiss of rain and the melancholy, faraway hoot of a barge coming up the river.

He walked with her to the bedroom and finally lifted his head. "Now," he said softly as he laid her down, "let's do it right this time."

Books lay on the rumpled coverlet from her earlier haste. He brushed them to the floor with a thump and parted her legs with a knee and fit his length between, still clad in socks and half-zipped slacks and a shirt whose tails fell over her belly.

"What do you want, Madelyn?" he asked, studying her intensely. "From me? I've never asked anyone before. I've never cared before. But now that we've . . ."

"Done it?" she supplied unhelpfully when he hesitated. "Or were you going to say 'made love'?"

"Oh, damn!" He rolled off her, and Madelyn immediately regretted her lightness. He didn't speak for a moment. Then: "It used to be easier, I think. Back before sex got free, they used to keep things separate. Men were men, women were women, sex was sex, and love was love. People didn't make 'love' without the commitment and all that went with it. No one expected anything from sex except what it was. But a person always knew where they stood."

"Is that what you're trying to say to me?" She twisted her head so she could see the truth in his eyes. "All right. I don't expect anything from this, Taylor. I make no demands. I know where I stand."

"I didn't mean that." His eyes hardened to agate. "You know I didn't mean that."

What did he want? The satisfaction of hearing her make a commitment while he did nothing?

She slumped deeper into the bed, and her voice sounded strange and faraway when she said, "Have you ever known anyone from the slums? Not from this country, but from somewhere like Asia, where there is never, never enough of anything?''

''No.''

''I knew a woman once who'd raised a Korean girl. She gave the child everything, good schools, nice clothes, all the physical comforts. But for years she would find little pieces of food that the girl had hidden away in her drawers and in the pockets of her clothes in the closet. It hurt her. But the girl never got over being hungry.''

When Madelyn grew quiet the only sound was the rain, the only movement Taylor's thoughtful stroking of her hair.

''I've gone hungry all my life, Taylor. Not physically, but . . . you know. I've known from the beginning that you wanted to get me in bed. It was a turn-on. I won't lie about that. But then you saw my work, and the look in your eyes was different from Muse's, from Hirschfield's, from any-one's, and I wanted to take parts of you and hide them away like that girl did.''

Taylor pulled himself upon her until his face hovered only inches above hers. His forehead was creased with concern. ''What are you so afraid of?''

Madelyn turned her face away, unable to bear the solemnity of that look. ''Of missing you.''

A shiver went through Taylor, even through his legs, and she instinctively brought her hands to his back. His mouth found her ear as if he needed to whisper the words rather than say them outloud. ''I want to tell you things, but I'm afraid too. Not only because I said them once and got my heart ripped out. I'm afraid you won't believe me, and then I'll feel like a fool.''

His heart was pounding hard against her breast. Madelyn couldn't promise him that she would believe, but she tried to memorize the way he swung himself off the bed and stripped off one sock, then the other. Where his shirt fell open was a sprinkling of wispy curls on his chest—

tapering, thinning into the line that disappeared beneath the loose band of his slacks. He dropped his shirt onto the floor.

When he stood only in his slacks, he reached down and buried his hand in her hair, tipping up her face so she was forced to look at him. "Madelyn, why don't you ask me if I'm falling in love with you?"

Because she was terrified, she moved beyond his reach and sat up, letting her hair protect her nakedness. She drew up her knees and rested her head upon them.

"It's bad luck to want too much," she said.

His zipper was a whisper. He was such a beautiful man, but then she thought she'd always known he would be. She could paint him—that strong, tanned back and lean flank, the dip of waist and swell of calf. She wanted to touch him, but touching was different from painting.

"Ask me." His voice was grating now, and he stood above her like a monument. *"Ask me."*

She could scarcely say the words. He was turning toward her, and she could feel his desire stirring, see it, and she wanted to touch him there. She tipped back her head, compelled herself to look him straight in the eyes.

"Do you love me?"

He took her hand, guided her to him, closed her fingers. "Yes. But it's not just this, you touching me this way or my being inside you. If I had to choose between this and the need in your eyes outside the elevator that day, I would say there was no contest. No contest at all."

"Oh, Taylor." Madelyn wrapped her arms about him and brushed her parted lips across his belly until the flesh quivered uncontrollably. She drew her tongue along the line where his tan stopped, knowing she was pleasing him. She wanted so utterly to please him and be pleased.

Before his control lost its fragile thread, Taylor took her by the arms and pulled her to her feet. He fell with her to the bed, keeping her above him, coming up into her like a sweet, piercing blade. She drew in her breath.

"I want to give you everything," he said as he lifted his head for her kiss and pulled hers down at the same time. "And I want to have it all."

Madelyn willingly gave, and she thrilled to Taylor's languid moves—as he turned her yet again, stroked the length of her legs, softly, expertly, seeking where it was softer still, and silky. His need was furiously assertive against her thigh, and Madelyn moaned as his fingers came up into her and his thumb explored a downy and sensitive place. She taught him all the intricacies of herself, and he refused to stop watching her. She turned her face away with a groan.

She didn't understand the pleasure Taylor found in just touching her, and she was embarrassed for him to see passion rise to such a peak in her. She could hardly keep still against his relentless stroking, and she moved, turning her head from side to side, whispering his name. He parted her knees, and when his mouth sought and found her, it happened almost immediately.

Her cry brought him immense pleasure but cost him pain too, for she buried her fingers in his hair and closed them hard in those seconds that had to be the most totally selfish and self-centered of any in existence. *This is madness,* she thought as he slowly, gently, entered her. *How can I bear more?*

He was more beautiful to her than she could have imagined—muscles ripping through his back, his buttocks. She almost resented him for opening her eyes to how it could be. Again and again he moved in her until some deep tension slowly began surging from the inside of her. *Self-hypnosis,* she thought until it grew and gradually began turning her inside out. She felt as if he were pulling it from her by force, and she was emptying, emptying. She thought: *I'm lost, I'm dying.*

But she wasn't dying; she was being reborn, and she was clinging to him for what seemed to be her very life, trying not to weep, not to cry, not to scream. He made a sort of half-tortured sound and filled his hands with her hips. He lifted her up to meet him as if she were a sacrifice he was bringing to lay at the feet of the gods. In a surge of potent, loving force, he came spilling into her.

The world returned as they slept in each other's arms—darkened now, dripping peacefully with rain and the hushed murmurs of love. Taylor knew that nothing in his life would go back to what it had before, and Madelyn lay warmly dreaming of how wonderfully 'unlonely' the future would have to be.

After belting a robe about her waist, she occupied herself with the pleasant domesticity of brewing tea while Taylor dressed. It was like what she imagined marriage with him would be, the quiet security of being cared for and loved well, the happy performance of rituals, knowing that he was only a room away.

When he returned, he moved easily about her kitchen. He kissed the back of her head and passed his hand over the slope of her buttock, knowledgeably and intimately but without desire.

"You're too big for everything," she mused over her shoulder as he struggled to fit his long legs beneath her table and she fetched napkins. "Do you want something sweet with your tea?"

He chuckled. "I just had something sweet."

"Then you're sated, of course."

"Absolutely. For an hour, at least."

She smiled and took pleasure in the sound of tea gurgling into the cups, the spoons clinking delicately against the china saucers. Before she placed the readied tray on the table she stooped to kiss his temple. Taylor's hair was damp and sweetly fresh. She loved it. She loved him.

She had already taken her chair and was lifting her cup

when she saw the damning letter. It was lying open upon the stack of mail where she'd left it: notice of a lawsuit being filed by one of Darrell's creditors for the amount of four thousand dollars. And then she knew the huge and costly mistake she'd made.

The blood suddenly withdrew from her arms and legs, and she shivered with cold. Could she even yet steal it away, keep him from seeing it?

But he'd already seen. She sat frozen, her cup held midway between the saucer and lip. Taylor glanced politely from the folded paper to her face. Then slowly, without speaking or acknowledging her dismay, returned to it and slowly read.

Madelyn thought his expression changed with every word. When he lifted his head, betrayal had blanched his color until it was gray. Her throat spasmed painfully. She wanted to cry out that it wasn't what he was thinking, but all she could do was lower her cup and listen in shock as it staccatoed upon the saucer.

"Mrs. Darrell White?" Disbelief drew out Taylor's words until they were hardly more than a whisper. "Madelyn Grey is Mrs. Darrell White?"

"You're jumping to conclusions about that, Taylor," she said stupidly.

He didn't even answer but dropped the letter like a refused bribe. "Don't make it worse."

"I'm not Mrs. White anymore." She wasn't sure he even believed her. He simply sat there—mute and hurt and angry. Then he leaned across the table and cut her to ribbons as only he could. "Is this why you came to ask Owen Prince for money?"

Oh, the bloodletting! Madelyn didn't think she could ever forgive him for that. Her self-blame was spreading upward into her breast, crushing the life out of her. Everything—her love, the future—looked ugly and brown. She had the sensation that she would fall out of her chair.

She could feel the hair upon her head, its roots, and all the pores of her body.

She said: "You know better than that."

Taylor lunged up from his chair, squeezing his head between his hands as if everything beneath his skull were in pain. "Do I?"

In his misery, he saw himself reading the headline of his own paper about Helen being killed with her lover. He saw himself standing over her grave, vowing never, never to leave himself open to this again. He spun on his heel. He loved Madelyn infinitely more than he'd ever loved Helen. So that meant he would hurt infinitely more.

"I have to go," he said numbly.

Madelyn sat in center of the rubble she'd just brought down around her. Oh, she'd known better than to love him!

"Go then," she said in a low, too-quick breath, wanting to hurt him the way she was hurting. "There's nothing to keep you here."

The lines beside Taylor's eyes and mouth deepened bitterly. He started to walk over to her, grab her up from her chair and slam her against the wall. Damn her! Damn her! But he walked toward her door like a blind man, and all the while there was a hushed voice inside his head whispering, *Stop me. Don't let me do this. I don't want to leave you.*

Madelyn sat at the table, her hands beneath it clenched until her nails were drawing blood in her palms. *Don't go, don't go.*

But he opened the door, hesitated a moment as if some breath she'd taken had alerted him. Without looking back then, he stepped out into the dark drizzle.

Madelyn's feet stumbled upon themselves as she rushed to the shut door. She leaned against it, her fingernails scraping on the surface as she prayed that the engine of his car would never start, that she would hear his steps growing louder and louder as he returned.

The Mitsubishi fired to life, and Madelyn's legs slowly buckled and she went sliding, sliding into a heap on the floor. He was gone. And it was all her fault. He was gone, and she would never love another man as she had loved him. As she still loved him. Ah, that was the cruel irony of it, wasn't it? She would always love him.

There are only so many tears a person can shed. After Madelyn's heart had emptied its ocean of grief, as had happened with Ellwyn Muse, a sort of lethargic automation set in and she was able to stumble through the days, dazed but operating.

Each morning at dawn she rose, showered and dressed and sat numbly down to a breakfast that looked and tasted like sand. She stared at it until she was nauseated, then she carried it to the sink. Still, she had almost come to the point where she believed she would go back to work. Then the letters began arriving.

Only one letter at first, a pleasant chatty note from someone named Harriet Schwartzengen who had seen the article in the *Daily Times* and whose penmanship made Madelyn imagine her watching television all day while she crocheted crafts for church bazaars.

"You must persevere in your quest for truth, Miss Grey," Harriet admonished and enclosed the clipping. "A person has the right to know who their parents were. Take it from me, my dear, truth is the only thing that endures in this age. Keep at it, Miss Grey, keep at it."

What truth? That a pain had been gnawing in her stomach for days? That she had fallen in love with a good man, then destroyed that love with her own two wicked hands?

The next day more letters came, and the ache in her middle stayed with her all day. The third day, over fifty. Most wished her well in her search for her identity and that of her mother. A few, those who called her an opportunist, said the world would be a much better place without people like her.

Madelyn felt sick to her stomach. She ached all over. *Self-pity*, she told herself. *I won't have it. I'll outlive them all—Muse, Taylor, these people who don't understand and don't care. Work is the answer.* And if she couldn't work, she could at least smear paint on the canvas until she could.

"You're ill!" Pearl McGrath had banged relentlessly on the door until Madelyn was forced to answer it. Madelyn stood there, looking her neighbor full in the face: tear-stained, sallow, lined.

There had been times during Abigail's breakdown when Pearl thought she couldn't bear the small braveries she saw in Madelyn every day. She wanted to go to her then, to wrap her about with stout arms and say that she would be her second mother if Madelyn ever needed her.

But Madelyn had chugged tenaciously on, day after day, striving. Then her marriage had blown up in her face and divorce was in the works. Pearl was the one who got the Valium prescription filled. John had warned his wife, "Be her friend, but that's all you've a right to be. Stay out of it, Pearl."

And now Pearl looked at Madelyn with her fine maternal eyes, and Madelyn went straight into her arms. "Get dressed, Madelyn. I'm taking you to the doctor."

Madelyn shivered. "It's a virus or something. It'll wear off in a few days."

"Virus, my foot. It's that miserable newspaper. I'm going to call that editor and give him a piece of my mind. Irresponsible, I don't care what you say."

"No!" That would be the ultimate humiliation—having Taylor know that she was going under. Madelyn stared at her hand trembling upon Pearl's arm and tried to smile.

"What I mean is," she mumbled, "it wouldn't be proper. After all, I went to Mr. Prince with Abigail's allegation, not the other way around. Mr. Champion's only doing what any good newspaperman would do.''

''So that's his name.'' Pearl moved about the place, picking up things, tossing a few crumpled napkins into the wastebasket. ''Champion. Well, he doesn't deserve your loyalty, Madelyn. Does he know you're ill?''

He *was* her illness! ''It's the mail. It wouldn't be so bad if I had something to keep them from hurting me. But it takes money to be that safe, Pearl. Power. There's nothing I can do. There never has been.''

''They're just people, honey.'' Pearl identified with how they felt. ''They're bored with their lives, and they're hungry to be involved in something that might turn out happily in the end. Try not to think about them. I'm here.''

''I know, Pearl.'' Madelyn couldn't tell her about Taylor. She wanted to, but she couldn't.

''Crawl into bed now,'' Pearl said. ''On second thought, sit here while I change the sheets. I'll launder them and bring you back something to eat at the same time.''

An old habitual smile found Madelyn's mouth. How could she refuse Pearl anything? When Pearl brought soup and gelatin and fruit juice, she swore she'd eat it, but in the end she poured it down the sink with the rest.

The next day she roamed restlessly about. She brushed a film of dust off the tape deck and flipped open the ejector for the tape. ''Beim Schlafengehen,'' the Strauss that Taylor had played from *Four Last Songs*. She pushed a button. The poignant German words filled the room.

> ''Now the day has wearied me.
> And my ardent longing shall
> the stormy night in friendship
> enfold like a tired child
>
> Hands, leave all work;
> brow, forget all thought.

Now all my senses
long to sink themselves in slumber

And the spirit unguarded
longs to soar on free wings,
so that, in the magic circle of night,
it may live deeply, and a thousandfold.''

Chapter Seven

*I*t didn't hurt Pearl McGrath's conscience in the least to ignore Madelyn's protest and call the editor-in-chief of the *Daily Times*. "You don't know me, Mr. Champion," she said baldly the moment his voice came on the line. "I'm Madelyn Grey's friend."

It was nine o'clock in the morning, and Taylor wasn't ready for this. Since he'd walked out of Madelyn's house in all his righteous furor, he'd been in a funk the likes of which he'd never known before. Every night he drank himself to sleep—the finest whiskey, the most grand determinations. At two o'clock in the morning he'd sit up in his bed, lost, alone, life not worth the effort without Madelyn. What words could he say? What act of contrition would make it go back to the way it was before?

Now he slumped over his desk, exhausted, the taste of

stale coffee and sorbic acid furry in his mouth. He'd cut himself shaving. His hands trembled from caffeine. He hated everything and everyone.

"Yes, Mrs. McGrath," he said, coming fully awake. "Madelyn mentioned you. What may I do for you?"

Pearl wondered if she didn't detect a bit of remorse in Mr. Champion's tone. Strange, she thought, and told him about the mail pouring in upon her young neighbor. He explained that they were swamped with it themselves, twice a day.

"Actually, it's a healthy sign," he said. "Whenever violence is scarce people get hungry for a good human interest story. Is Madelyn taking it all right?"

"I don't know if you know Madelyn very well, Mr. Champion. She's—"

"I know what Madelyn is."

"Things like this are hard on a person of her sensitivity. Oh, I know she doesn't complain. She never does. But it eats at her, wears her down." Pearl thought she heard the faint chink of an aspirin bottle, the gurgle of water being poured.

Presently he said, "Mrs. McGrath, I'm wondering if you would do me a personal favor."

She hesitated. John would have her head for becoming involved like this. "If I can."

"If Madelyn needs anything, I mean the slightest thing, would you let me know?"

"As long as John and I are alive, Madelyn will never suffer for anything, Mr. Champion. But, if you really mean it, I'll tell her you made the offer."

"No!"

From where Pearl stood, she could peer out her window at Madelyn's neat little house floating in the slip beside hers. Something had happened between Madelyn and this man. What, for heaven's sake?

"Whatever arrangement we have between us, Mrs.

McGrath," he was saying, "I want kept strictly between us. Madelyn's . . . you know how proud she is."

"But do you?"

He sighed heavily. "Believe me, I do. Day or night, I want you to call me."

Yes, something had definitely gone on with this man, was perhaps still going on. That would explain a lot. "As you wish, Mr. Champion," she said wearily.

"Keep in touch."

"Of course," Pearl's tone distinctly said: *But if you do something to hurt that girl, I'll have your hide, Mr. Newspaperman.*

Madelyn dragged her last large canvas from under the bed. Sunshine flooded the boat and sunshine always made her guilty. Craft intent upon summer pleasures were plying the river, yachts and skiers and fishermen, sightseers on the *Belle of Louisville*.

She forced herself to go through the motions of mixing colors and readying brushes. How was this for carrying on? Great, huh?

"What a pair we are, L'il Abner," she said with a self-mocking glance at the dog as he lay with his paws crossed meekly over his nose. "You go after Mr. Nutley's potato peelings, and I destroy myself. That's the way it's always been, always will be. Accept what is, I say, and go with it. Pretend to the world all you want to, but never to yourself."

L'il Abner's stubby tail wagged in devout agreement.

"Most women would chalk Taylor up as a one-night stand and go on with their life. Me? I'd be kicked out of the club. Well, okay. If that's the way it is. The truth is, I've never had things equal, so I don't know what I've been missing. I would give enough for both of us. Very unpopular these days, martyrdom. Should I throw myself in the river, do you think?"

She paused to pull on a pair of thin latex gloves. "It's not like I don't have things to do. I could do McMillan's work blindfolded. How many people don't have that much? If I just didn't want to be good, I'd be fine. But I have this hangup about achievement, you know. Money's all right, but if I had respect . . ."

She stood perfectly still for a moment and twirled the tip of a brush. It was time to stop joking. "I could see Taylor again. There's always the campaign dinner. If I had an ounce of pride, I wouldn't consider going, but sometimes pride costs an awful lot. I could make him happy, L'il Abner. Can't he see that?"

Glancing at the telephone, Madelyn laid down the brushes. If she could only hear Taylor's voice say "hello" before she hung up, perhaps it would inspire her, trigger some magical nerve that would get her going again. The number fell from her fingertips as she dialed. She pictured someone at a switchboard. But what would happen when she was finally connected? Would she hear that distance in his voice?

Before the number could ring she slammed the receiver back into its cradle and jerked her hand away. Her breaths were harsh and painful, and she dropped to her knees and rocked herself, hugging her middle because she was hurting so badly she wanted to die, and it wasn't because of wanting respect or success or anything else. She just wanted Taylor.

L'il Abner padded up beside her, whimpering, nuzzling. Madelyn wrapped her arms about his little neck and slowly stopped her sniffling. Faithful little beast.

Get up, she ordered herself. *Get up, you fool. Do you think you're the only person alone in this world? There isn't anyone to make everything all right. There never has been. There never will be.*

She dragged herself to her feet and threw cold water over her face. So Muse had chopped her up. So Taylor had misunderstood her. So she had made a mess of everything.

So what? If she thought that anyone was sitting around counting her mistakes—or her good points, for that matter —she was crazy.

She set up the canvas and picked up her brushes, shook her head to clear out some of the cobwebs. "Now do something," she demanded out loud. "Do *some*thing, Madelyn Grey, or you're dead."

It took her a week. The painting was one of the best, most spontaneously complex things she'd ever done—full of tension and impressionistic textures and balance; a study of the river, but not a pretty reflection, rather what it spawned in her imagination: violence and heat, tenderness and breathtaking surrealism. It was seen through a man as he stood, his legs astride against the light like a monument; a hard, scarred man. And, coming out of the river, almost out of another age so that it was an unwilling part of the painting, was the suggestion of a woman. Her face was the frailest and most disturbing of profiles.

Besides this canvas there were other new ones—oils and acrylic blends that revealed heroic imagery, painted at odd moments and with incredible swiftness.

Collapsing onto a kitchen chair, Madelyn stretched her jean-clad, paint-spattered legs. She was drained, utterly exhausted; she had no idea of what time it was or how long since she'd eaten. She hadn't gone to visit her mother, and she hadn't talked to Pearl or gone by McMillan's. She'd slipped outside to bring in the mail; the laundry basket was now spilling over onto the floor with unopened envelopes.

She walked to the phone and dialed a number, her face a mixture of emotions. On the fourth ring David Hirschfield answered.

David Hirschfield had a lower jaw like a backhoe and a voice that sounded as if it were coming from the bottom of a gravel pit. Rarely was he seen when a cigar wasn't poking out from under his drooping mustache and dribbling ashes down the front of his clothes. His high-speed optimism wore Madelyn out, but his sense of what composed good art was exceedingly keen and left him almost without peer.

Now he clumped among her canvases, mumbling to himself as he studied one, then another. He heaved sigh after sigh in a way that made Madelyn think she would go mad.

"Are you going to tell me?" she demanded of him, terrified. "In my lifetime? And the truth?"

Hirschfield promptly forgot the canvases and faced his even more difficult protégée. He rocked back and forth on surprisingly little feet. "Would I lie to you?"

"Hirschfield, there is no one on God's green earth who could predict what you'd do."

Laughing, he strode to the glass wall. Darkness had fallen now, and boat lights twinkled daintily upon the river. Louisville was a glow of candlepower against the sky.

Turning, his head wreathed with cigar smoke, Hirschfield said: "I've always believed that you had this inside you. I told myself that when you had an experience of the heart it would happen. Didn't I say that? Now it's happened. So I must assume you've had the experience."

"The experience?" Madelyn had no intentions of sharing Taylor with anyone.

His frown didn't allow for cop-outs. "A meeting, my child genius, of minds. And you know exactly what I'm talking about. I won't ask you who he is, but don't try to pretend with me. Deal?" If another Darrell White was in her life, he would personally, and with relish, strangle him.

Madelyn moved to her table of paints and began a ritual of tidying. "He's very mature," she said quietly. "A fine man, an honorable man. I think he even loves me in a way, though I don't see why." Peering up, she smiled unhappily. "Is that enough?"

He took her into his great, comforting arms. "Ah, my darling Madelyn, the artist is both blessed and cursed. And, sad to say, greatness almost always has its roots in the deepest depths of his pain."

His words required no discussion or confirmation. Madelyn had lived their proof more than once. "Do you think these paintings are good?"

His brows resembled little devil's wings. "Do you?"

"I feel they say something, but I don't know if they're good." When he twirled her around the room, Madelyn squealed with surprise.

"Acid!" he roared. "Pure, unadulterated acid, child. The best, most original stuff I've seen in years. Someday, if you want to be, you will be better than good. Will you believe that now?"

Madelyn's first impulse was: *What will Taylor say?* Idiot!

She stuffed her face into the front of Hirschfield's shabby jacket and clung with all her strength. "I look at other people's work and I know mine isn't like theirs. But theirs looks so good to me. People say such nice things about them. It scares me, Hirschfield. I try to be like them. I try to think like they think. I try—"

"How do you know they're good?"

"Good is what goes over."

"Pornography goes over." Hirschfield tipped up her tortured face. "You aren't like anyone else, Madelyn. You aren't even like you used to be. What you did in the past was good, sweetie, but it wasn't this."

She laid her cheek against Hirschfield's buttons. "He's everything I want, Hirschfield. He's lived a lot, some of it very hard. He knows about my loneliness and rejection. I hurt him. It's breaking my heart."

Hirschfield had read about Madelyn's incident with Governor Prince. He wondered if this were all connected. In time she would tell him, perhaps, but he knew better than to press her. She would shut him out again.

"What if I arranged something?" he said energetically and drew her back to the canvases.

Studying them, she wiped her eyes on the backs of her hands. "What d'you have in mind?"

"I want to take some of these."

Her out-tossed hand was negligent. "Whatever."

"There's someone I want to see them. If he sees what I see—well, perhaps a few of the local galleries at first. Then Young Hoffmann, perhaps. Maybe even Annina Nosei."

Apprehension grew wide in Madelyn's eyes. "That's too much. It's too soon."

"Trust me."

"But what if I can't do it again? What if people start looking at me with expectations? What'll I do then? Then they'll say, 'What's the matter? Are you a flash in the pan?'"

He caught her hands, shook them. "Listen to me! You've been alone all your life, Madelyn. Maybe that's what makes you good. But it's time to share it now. It's your duty, a sacred duty, if you will."

Would Taylor be happy for her when he learned? Would he feel a little pride? Or would he see only that damning letter? Hear that accursed lie?

"All right," she said with a gloomy sigh. "Take them. Do whatever you think is best. I'm very tired. Tomorrow I must go and see my mother."

Taylor loved the days when adrenalin ran high and there wasn't a single free moment to think. His brain was supercharged; just staying alive was a furious race with the clock. Today was definitely not one of those times. Pushing away from his desk, he strode to his office door and jerked it open.

"Morrison!" he barked.

"Sir?"

"Get in here!"

Shrugging, Randy received and accepted glances of sympathy as he headed for the editor's desk with an unenthusiastic shuffle. Everyone had trodden softly the last days. One brave soul had even dared tape a swastika to Taylor's door, but Randy had luckily spied it and ripped it off before the Champ came in that morning.

"Yes, sir," he said as he shut the door and braced against it, nervously chewing his gum.

"Sit down, Randy. You look like an exclamation point." He waved him to a chair. "Did you come up with anything on Waverly's fingerprints?"

"It was a small private hospital. They're balking."

"What the hell for?" Taylor rubbed his face with both palms. In order to prevent gossip about the 'premature' babies, Virginia had hired herself an elite woman doctor with a clinic near the Smokey Mountains. On one occasion she had sent them Waverly's footprints, but Owen had 'lost' them.

"What about Abigail's birth certificate?"

"Technically," Randy said, "Abigail Grey doesn't exist."

She existed, all right. Unknown to Randy, he'd gone to the hospital and seen Abigail for himself. She did resemble Virginia in a vague sort of way, but then . . .

"Virginia has no fingerprints anywhere," Taylor said with a sigh.

"Would blood tests prove anything?"

"They might prove who Abigail isn't. We'll go that route if we absolutely have to. See about what kind of releases we'd need. I don't want any trouble from this, Randy. I'm dead tired. I guess we might as well go about getting Abigail fingerprinted. Find out what it'll take."

Randy watched Champion shrug into his sport jacket and blurted, "You think Madelyn really could be Wallace's twin, don't you?"

"I'm certainly not ruling it out." Taylor clapped a hand to the back of his neck. "What d'you think?"

"It's more . . . what I feel, sir."

"And that is?"

Randy's freckled face crinkled with thought. "Little things, maybe. Abigail's mental condition. The lack of records. Madelyn's an artist, Wallace is, or would've been, a pianist. Or maybe it's the things we don't have. Everyone else came with some proof they claimed was irrefutable. Madelyn came with nothing except what Abigail said. I guess I do think she could be Waverly."

So did Taylor, but he was too tired to work anymore. He closed up his desk and was about to walk out the door himself when he glimpsed Christine Hackworth coming down the long center aisle toward his office.

"Hi." Christine waved at him through the glass door and pushed it open to slouch invitingly. "I saw you leaving. You look terrible, Taylor. Why don't you let me finish this piece and I'll buy you a drink?"

She waved a sheaf of papers that Taylor knew signified a criminal suit between two trucking agencies. He secured the knot of his tie. "What d'you mean, terrible? Doesn't this tie go with my suit?"

Christine's navy sharkskin skirt revealed one of her legs beneath its deep gash, legs that Taylor remembered well. She arranged them to advantage as she perched on the edge of his desk. The lace edge of her panties winked at him.

"Devil," she purred. "You know what I'm talking about. I've watched you for years, Taylor Champion. Do you really think you can fool me?"

"Aw heck, Christine." Once Taylor had preferred her kind of brisk aggression. Now he found it surprisingly distasteful. "Why would I want to do that?"

One of the things Christine liked best about Taylor was his ability to elude her. She grinned like a cat cherishing the anticipation of cream. "My sentiments exactly. Give me a minute?"

He'd give her a minute. He'd give her a hundred minutes. Taylor jerked up his attaché case. What was Madelyn doing right now? He remained standing for so long with his hand curved about the handle of his case that Christine's voice jerked him back with a start.

"Taylor," she chided, "is it yes or no?"

"I'll wait for you outside the rear door."

"See you in five."

Even before he reached the exit, Taylor regretted what he had just agreed to. He stepped outside and leaned his shoulders back against the brick wall. The late afternoon was warm. Louisville: the Gateway to the South, where violins could equal the pounding of hammers as the city put on its new face. His city because he knew both faces intimately.

He wondered how despicable it would be to stand Christine up and just start walking. For some reason he'd like to stroll along the old streets by the river. What was it with him? Madelyn wasn't interested in something lasting. He was a fool to turn down good sex when Christine offered it with no strings and in such a pretty package. Yet he felt—crazily—like a husband about to cheat on his wife.

"Ah, you waited."

Christine's voice caught Taylor up short. "Did you think I wouldn't?"

A whiff of expensive perfume filled Taylor's nostrils when she looped her arm through his. Suddenly, Christine was pressing into him, pushing him back against the building and bringing her mouth up to his.

"Wait a minute," he protested, holding her at arm's length. "What's the hurry?"

She combed through his hair with long, painted nails. "Starvation diet, baby. You don't look too well fed yourself. Come on, loosen up."

Unable to stop her without causing a distasteful scene, Taylor submitted to being kissed. There'd been a time when he would have hurried Christine to the car and dragged her down into the seat. Now he found himself counting the seconds until it was over. Ending it, he avoided her eyes.

Christine cocked her head in disbelief. Ever since Helen had been killed, Taylor had been there for her. Their affair had been spasmodic, interspersed with other people, but in the end one had always come back to the other. Now something was different; Taylor had never pulled this far back before.

"I don't believe this," she said. "What have you done?"

"Nothing."

"Liar. You've gotten involved with a woman, haven't you? And you don't have the guts to tell me."·

Taylor gave her a look calculated to protect his privacy. "Do I look like I'm in *love?*" He rolled the word about in his mouth as if it left a bad taste. "Look, do you want to have that drink or what?"

Damn him! "Well, well, well."

"Come off it, Christine!" Taylor's eyes blazed resentment.

"Who is she, Taylor? Who's the woman who's done what everyone said could not be done? Hmm?"

Taylor could smell the fragrance of Christine's skin from where he stood. He looked down at her straining breasts, the lusciousness of her hair. His body stirred in spite of himself, and he clapped a hand to the back of his neck. Cruelly he said, "I don't broadcast the details of my life like some bloody second-rate piece of street talk."

Christine drew back as if he'd slapped her. "You're a cruel man, Taylor Champion."

She turned on her heel and began to walk away. Taylor felt like throwing himself out into the street. Christine was a valuable woman for the paper, and he didn't want to lose her.

"Hey, hey." He went after her. "Wait up."

The silence wavered somewhere between hostility and consideration of truce. Christine moved beyond Taylor's fingers and held her hair down in the wind, eyeing him in puzzlement.

"I did it once, you know," she said quietly. "Fell in love. It was awful. I wanted to kill myself."

"Don't put ideas into my head." Taylor grimly fumbled with his pocket change. Was it that obvious to everyone? "I promised myself it would never happen."

"Who is she?"

"It doesn't matter."

"You give up everything we've ever had and say it doesn't matter?"

"She's no one." Something tightened in Taylor's throat, threatened to cut off his breath. "Just a girl."

"Madelyn Grey."

Taylor's head jerked up. "I didn't say that."

"You didn't have to, you fool." Christine shook her head. "Taylor, when are you going to join the rest of the world and be human? Look, I'll buy you that drink some other time. By the looks of you, the day may come when you'll need it even worse than you do now. Go home. Go to sleep. Accept what is."

Taylor was glad when Christine swung off across the parking lot with that walk of hers. She even turned when she reached her own car, waved.

Folding himself into the Mitsubishi, he forgot that he'd been meaning to pick up something to eat. He drove for hours and ended up at the river. It was quite dark when he steered along the dock where Madelyn's boat was moored. For a long time he just looked at it. No lights twinkled from the windows, no L'il Abner, no sign of life anywhere. She was out with someone, probably. To hell with it! He hoped she was as miserable as he was.

When Taylor slammed the door of his modest two-story

house on Shelbyville Road, he threw his jacket to a chair and walked immediately to the telephone. He punched in Madelyn's number, let it ring forever. Where was she, dammit? Or had she unplugged the telephone?

He punched in another number he knew from memory. When it didn't answer he drew back the cuff of his shirt and glanced at his wristwatch. Jesus, it was past midnight.

"Hello," a groggy voice finally growled. "Whoever you are, this had better be worth a contract put out on you at dawn."

"It's Taylor, Gorman, and I don't know whether it's good or not. I didn't realize it was so late."

"Don't they have clocks on your side of town?"

Gorman Dillon was a Bottom Line Man. He was on the board of governors for the Kentucky Center for the Arts and owner of an elite and chic little museum on Upper River Road. He controlled an endowment fund and was consultant on a half dozen of the city's most prestigious committees. Taylor never questioned his knowledge when it came to art.

"Well," Gorman droned, "since Eleanor and I are both wide awake now, what's on your mind?"

"*Who*, Gorman," replied Taylor. "*Who's* on my mind. Have you ever heard of a young woman named Madelyn Grey?"

A pause simmered on the line.

Gorman coughed. "What is this, a conspiracy?"

Taylor dropped down into a chair and started unbuttoning his shirt. "She's someone I want you to look into, Gorman, that's all."

"You and the rest of the world. I got a call from David Hirschfield today. Do you know him?"

"No." Taylor shook his head.

"He wanted me to arrange a show on the spur of the moment. I told him absolutely not, and he bet me a thousand dollars that I would regret it before dark."

A dozen thoughts went spinning through Taylor's mind, all of them bristling with excitement. "Go on, go on."

"He brought me some things to look at. I've spent my entire afternoon giving your Miss Grey the most coveted space the gallery has to offer. So, what's your angle?"

Laughing—had he actually laughed?—Taylor slid down on his spine. "Just tell me one thing, Gorman. I've seen some of her work, but I'm no critic and I want to hear it from the horse's mouth."

"I'm not overfond of that metaphor, Taylor."

"Is she good?"

"Or is it simile?" Gorman mumbled something aside, then apologized for talking to his wife.

"Is she good?" Taylor repeated, coming forward, his elbows finding his knees.

"There is no good and bad, Taylor."

"Dammit, Gorman, don't give me one of your semantic rituals tonight."

"Well, I'll say this, she's reckless. She could go in any number of ways from here, but if she goes at all, she'll probably put the fear of God into more than one artist in this town."

Taylor felt the same sensation as when he'd waited outside Owen's house that night, long years before, and had decided to grab life by the horns and blindly hang on. It was possible that Madelyn wouldn't even want him in her life, but that didn't mean he couldn't help her, behind the scenes and without her knowledge. If that was as near her as he could get, he'd settle for that.

"Taylor, are you still there?"

He laughed. "I'm not going anywhere, Gorman."

"You're behind this girl, I take it?"

"Two hundred percent."

Gorman was no novice to the business. "She should

make it, Taylor. Big. But she's got to have time and space. Are you going to see that she gets it?''

"She'll have it." The excitement was clearing his head. "Good night, Gorman. By the way, when will the show be?"

"In two days," Gorman retorted dryly. "Don't you read your own paper?"

"I've made a mistake."

Madelyn's misery literally robbed her of the strength to move. Hirschfield had just called for her. In two hours the Gorman Dillon Gallery doors were scheduled to open to the public, but she was in a time machine, hurtling back to the Chancellor Gallery where Ellwyn Muse was slashing her work into confetti.

She stood in the doorway of the boat, holding herself as if her insides were all independent of each other. "I can't go through with this, Hirschfield. I don't know what I've been thinking. I can't, I can't."

Taking her by the arms, Hirschfield steered her back into the room. He had dinner reservations at Bristol Downtown, and he'd worn as formal an attire as was possible for him: a pair of dotty old slacks from the pre-Korean era and a jacket that didn't seem to belong to any particular age. He had knotted a tie about a shirt whose collar had never seen an iron—nonmaterialism at its worst—and the unsmoked cigar clamped between his teeth dribbled tobacco upon his tie, which was no big deal because the other stains on it were so blatant that they disguised it.

"Madelyn, darling, are you going to suffer crucifixion all over again because of one stupid critic? When you come to the end of your life and look back upon it, you'll be forced to admit the truth."

"How?" she groaned. "I don't know what truth is anymore."

"It is this. When Ellwyn Muse is drawing unemployment, you will still be painting."

Madelyn walked drearily across the room. The hem of her gown rustled with an elegance that was totally incongruous with her mood, and she dragged her fingers through her hair, leaving it wildly disheveled.

"You love me, Hirschfield," she mourned. "How can I trust what you think?"

"But Gorman Dillon doesn't love you."

Which was true. Hirschfield was bending over her latest canvas propped against the wall. Madelyn wandered over, glanced furtively at him. "I don't mean to act like a tragedy queen."

Hirschfield's sharp ears heard a strange new note in Madelyn. He stared at her. "You want to talk about him?"

She shook her head.

"Well, whoever he is, he's made you better. Your expression is better, your point of focus is better. You know, Madelyn, I once fought you over Darrell White because he didn't do that for you. He dragged you in the opposite direction. But I'm not fighting you now. You've progressed, matured, and I can only believe that it's because of what you feel for this . . . someone."

She brought her hands up to her face, hid behind them for a moment. "You'd think that I would know what to do with my life, Hirschfield. I'm not a stupid person. But I'm constantly going awry. There aren't any blacks and whites."

"You think your genius—I call it that for lack of a better word—will keep you from making mistakes? If the truth be known, my darling, it will cause you to make them more easily. This mysterious thing in you is a highly delicate piece of machinery. No, left to yourself, you will make many mistakes."

"I need a keeper."

Tipping back his head, Hirschfield roared. "From the mouths of babes. There is more truth to that than you realize. There are two few rare flowers in this world, and despite what people will tell you, the gardeners are even more scarce, sometimes even more in demand. Not everyone can grow orchids, you know."

"That's not a comforting analogy, Hirschfield."

"What's uncomfortable? You're selling the gardener short. You think he'd like to be an orchid? No, his deepest pleasure is to tend the orchid, give it room to grow, make it more beautiful that it ever dreamed it could be. Believe me, the gardener gets his own reward, different from yours and every bit as satisfying."

A key turned somewhere inside Madelyn. Was it possible that Hirschfield was right? That she and Taylor were hurting each other because of superimposed roles that shouldn't conflict at all?

She lifted her hands to her disordered mass of hair. "Will you give me five more minutes to do my hair?"

"Do you think all I have to do is waste my time with you?" Hirschfield shooed her away and leaned on her bedroom door jamb.

"I once knew a violinist," he called. "He up-chucked ten minutes before every concert he ever played, and his wife was the only person who could go near him all day. He was probably one of the most sane men I ever knew. Our reservations for dinner are at seven-thirty, so you'd better get a move on. If you throw up, I want it to be the finest food money can buy."

Madelyn touched her eyelids with a restrained smoke color and placed a copper tint upon her lips. She brushed her hair furiously and twirled it up into a topknot, anchored it with pins. Then she scrubbed down her makeup so it looked as if she didn't have any on. Her black floor-length dress was one she'd made herself, but she'd taken part of the money she should've spent on Darrell's bills and bought a silver belt.

Stepping out into the living room, she curtsied. "How do I look?"

"If I didn't have this face and this body and wasn't as old as I am and have such a lousy disposition, I'd try to make you fall in love with me."

"Do you think I'd be foolish enough to fall in love?" she said lightly, took his arm and walked him to the door.

"Of course not." He motioned her through. "Just like you'd never be foolish enough to try to pull the wool over my old eyes."

Madelyn wasn't soloing tonight. Two other artists were sharing the billing with her, and the *Daily Times* had published biographies of all three. Ellwyn Muse had given the exhibit passing note with time and place. Luckily, neither paper made mention of her encounter with Owen Prince, nor did the *Daily Times* delve so elaborately into her biography that Abigail's hospitalization was disclosed.

What had Taylor thought when he'd seen the mock-up? There she went again, mentally plucking the same old petals again: he cares, he doesn't care. A very real pain radiated in the vicinity of her stomach.

Hirschfield was a terrible driver. He drove them to the restaurant, then to the gallery in his Volkswagen. He looked everywhere but where he was going, and his hands were in a constant and elaborate state of motion. Clutching the sides of her seat, Madelyn wondered if the crumpled fender on her side weren't some kind of omen.

"You're exhibited on the first floor," he told her as he slammed into the curb and bounced back. "Gorman Dillon gave you his most costly wall space."

"I hope it's by the restrooms."

"Frankly, I wasn't sure he'd do it for me. My name must punch more of a wallop in this town than I thought."

She had to laugh, despite her tight nerves. "Which is why I adore you, Hirschfield."

Chortling, he removed his cigar to get out and open her door because it required a special kick.

The Gorman Dillon Gallery was one of the most discriminating in the city and regularly lent support to regional artists. It displayed some of Louisville's finest antiques. Metal works and wood had an occasional showing, and more prestigious sculptures. As Madelyn and Hirschfield entered from a side door, dozens of guests were already filing into the dome-shaped mezzanine. Cocktails were underway. Glittering gowns, pants, and tailored evening suits mixed healthily with caftans, ethnic regalia, and jeans.

The hum drifting across the floor was the pseudo-intellectual chitchat that always accompanied such events. More than one critic browsed about, chatting with gallery 'regulars.' Pearl and John were there, Sandy Robertson and Ralph McMillan, Christine, Randy. They all hugged her and said she was wonderful and that she would continue to be wonderful, neither of which Madelyn believed at all.

Madelyn's works were displayed in the red rooms. "I hate this," she kept whispering under her breath as Hirschfield dragged her there. "I hate this, Hirschfield."

Hirschfield kept her hand imprisoned over his arm as they proceeded through the display area. Light wood floors gleamed with polish. The finest paneling was offset by inserts of brilliant crimson in the red rooms, blue inserts in the blue rooms and on and on. In the center of each room was a four-sided structure with lights trained upon it from all angles. When a person walked into the red rooms, Madelyn's river painting dominated everything.

"The place of honor," Hirschfield said with pride rattling deep in his chest. "Your self-portrait is on the opposite side."

Now Madelyn understood why some actors never went to

see their own movies. When an artist worked from the center of himself, objectivity was an obsolete word.

"It needs more work," she grieved in a frail child's voice. "I should have been more aggressive with the blue. I've got to find the ladies' room, Hirschfield. Go on without me."

"But you must—"

"I'll find you later. Please."

With a sigh, Hirschfield let her go. She would simply have to get used to it; after tonight, success was a cross she would have to bear.

The restroom Madelyn found was more plush than a house. She huddled on the edge of a chaise with her hand clamped over her mouth, fearing the few bites she'd eaten would come bouncing up. After deciding that they weren't going to, she washed her hands, despaired over them a moment, and smoothed in a lotion she always carried with her.

The raised jacquard design of her dress caught the light. The dress zipped up the front, and the deep V reached to the center of her breasts. A long strand of onyx beads hung there. They gave her something to worry with, that and her tiny beaded evening bag.

People had no idea that she was one of the artists as she walked back into the hall. They laughed and chatted about movies. Like a victim drawn by a hypnotist's spell, she wandered back to her exhibit.

"Well, she's radical, I'll say that," one observer said as he studied some of the smaller works. "I don't know if I like this or not."

"America is shifting," said another. "You wouldn't have seen this stuff five years ago."

"I like it."

"Seems hyper to me. Compared to the other artists they're exhibiting."

"You say everything is hyper if it's not Michelangelo."

"It's sheer genius."

"There's some reporter from *Excalibur* walking around, I heard him say his magazine is going to do a spread on Ms. Grey. You know what that means. Stardom."

"This young woman is going to shake up a few things in America. You watch what I say."

"Awesome, darling. Simply awesome."

Madelyn felt herself grabbed from behind by Hirschfield's meaty fists. "Where have you been?"

She peered up through a tortured haze. "What?"

"You shouldn't be here by yourself. There's a man looking for you. I told him you'd do an interview."

"What?"

"I'll be with you every minute. It's perfectly painless. One of the prices you must pay for being good. Whatever would you do without me? Come along now."

Madelyn was a puppet being propelled across the main plaza and out into the reception area which wasn't so busy. Vivaldi drifted softly from speakers somewhere. Low-slung benches formed a border along the walls. Private nooks. Greenery.

She lifted her skirt so she wouldn't walk on it. Nothing felt real. "Who is this man I'm supposed to meet?"

"A reporter for *Excalibur*. I'll have to be honest and admit I didn't arrange it. Dillon said one of the local newspapermen flew him down."

A little stitch of warning needled along the path of Madelyn's logic. Her fingers tightened upon the silk of her dress, and she looked up to glimpse two men skirting the mezzanine. One was a short balding man whose prim steps looked as if his shoes were a bad fit. The other, strolling effortlessly beside him, his height and his lithe, sure-footed grace setting him apart from everyone else in the room, was Taylor.

Chapter Eight

In every person's life there are asterisks—starred points where turning back is not possible: one step too far on a cliff; one drop too many in a cup; one second too late for an antidote. As Madelyn stood staring at Taylor, her skirt spilling from her hands to the floor, she knew this was one of those times. Whatever remained in her future, good or bad, it would be forever marked by this man.

He was momentarily turned from her: his tan trousers flawless, his blazer one that none could fault, a shirt of a superior cotton stripe, tie perfect, hems correct, though a lace was coming loose on his shoe. Outward excellence: princely, noble.

And then he turned, his tired eyes passing along to jerk to a stop of recognition, a sweep back, a widening, a softening. *Hello,* his sad smile said.

Madelyn hoped she was smiling back, but her lips were quivering, so she wasn't sure. *Hello.*

Taylor murmured something to the man he was with without so much as a glance in his direction. He began walking with measured and determined steps toward her. An energy charged into Madelyn's limbs.

Now Hirschfield understood who the 'someone' was, and he knew, instinctively, that it was right for Madelyn. "Go to him," he urged her with a gentle shove. "Go, dear heart!"

When only yards lay between them, Madelyn stopped walking. Taylor stopped. They were both uncertain, searching the other for an answer to how much remained of their pain, how much they even wanted to remember.

One of Taylor's hands reached for a button on his blazer. "I wasn't sure you'd come."

"I didn't want to." She thought all the parts of her body were disconnected. "Hirschfield never takes my excuses. Have you been well?"

"Well enough." His smile was briefly there. "And you?"

"I've been working hard."

"I've seen some of it. It's very good."

"There's a lot to be finished yet."

"Yes," he said and wanted to get her somewhere alone. But he couldn't. This was her night. He looked quickly over her head and cleared his throat. "This . . . this is Hirschfield?"

She'd forgotten all about Hirschfield! And the small man waiting with patiently folded hands behind Taylor.

"Oh. I'm sorry." Madelyn waved Hirschfield forward. "Let me introduce you. Taylor, this is . . . That's not right, is it?" Hands to cheeks, she grimaced. "Mr. Hirschfield, this is Taylor Champion. Taylor is—"

"I know who Mr. Champion is." Madelyn was so charmingly chagrined that Hirschfield boomed with laughter and drew his protégée against his side. "He won't remember, but I certainly do. He was just a youth, and I was . . . well, younger. He was covering a fire at an apartment building I once lived in. Why don't you call me David, Taylor? Madelyn's the only person who ever calls me Mr. Hirschfield.''

As Hirschfield rattled blissfully on, Taylor observed Madelyn with an intensity that was much more typical of him—searching her over, up, down, up again. She was different, though he wasn't sure how. She looked taller in her black dress. She was dangerously thin but very, very alive, chin up, eyes quick. He could see the inner curve of one breast beneath the discreetly zippered neckline. He wanted to kiss that curve. He wanted to kiss every curve she had.

''Madelyn's very old-fashioned,'' he murmured to Hirschfield and smiled down at Madelyn, his eyes touching everything now, saying everything.

Hirschfield sighted down his cigar. ''Madelyn lives in two worlds—her art and an occasional excursion into reality with the rest of us. Her art is beyond my ability to understand. More often than not, her reality is too.''

''A publishable understatement there, Bill,'' Taylor threw over his shoulder. ''Madelyn, I want to introduce William Diehl from *Excalibur* magazine. Bill, Mrs.—''

Ah! There it was! Such a tiny little flick and such a great stab of pain. Such blood!

Little ridges of offense sprang up beside Madelyn's mouth. She spun around, but she could feel Taylor's eyes burning into the back of her head. How many times must he disappoint her before she learned?

''It's *Miss* Grey.''

Taylor had spent an entire day putting together the pieces of Madelyn's marriage. He probably knew more about Darrell White than Darrell White did.

''Wait!'' he said and grabbed her wrist.

Only once had he ever apologized—to Edwina, for stealing her jewelry. Now he swung Madelyn around, and didn't lower his voice to keep the men from hearing. "I'm sorry, Madelyn." His tone was a caress. "I'm so very, very sorry."

Hirschfield became extravagantly busy lighting his cigar, while William Diehl pried his glasses off his face and began furiously cleaning them. Before Madelyn could say anything, Taylor inclined his head to Diehl. With that, he turned on his heel and walked away.

Diehl hooked his glasses behind his ears as Madelyn watched Taylor leave her, her lips softly parted, her thoughts spinning out like a thread.

"Your river painting, Miss Grey," he said kindly and waited until she looked back at him. He motioned toward some distant chairs where they would be comfortable. "Would you tell me why you did it?"

The interview was amazingly painless. Hirschfield hovered like an anxious fairy godmother as Diehl asked his questions and took scrupulous notes. Taylor settled himself at a distance by the windows. Madelyn looked at him often, at his strong arms spread easily along the cushions as he chatted with Christine who stopped by, and Randy, plus a number of people she'd never seen before. Sometimes he stood, his back to her, his hands clasped behind his back. But occasionally she found him sitting alone, contemplating her the way a detective ponders a case when he's pressed for a solution when all the evidence is not yet in.

Finally William Diehl came to his feet and replaced his gold pen into the breast pocket of his suit, along with his small spiral pad.

"I'll be taking some pictures during the course of the evening," he said. "But there's no need for you to be nervous. Go right on as if I weren't even here. Everything's just fine."

Hirschfield shook with laughter. "Nervous? Why, Madelyn wouldn't dream of being nervous."

They all laughed, and Madelyn covertly glimpsed Taylor unfolding himself. He motioned to a man she'd never seen before.

Mr. Diehl was taking her hand in his. "Dear Miss Grey, when Taylor called me last week I thought he'd probably exaggerate your talent. But when I saw for myself . . ." He smiled. "Well, you must never doubt yourself again. You work from the heart, my dear, and that's probably the only voice left on this old earth worth listening to."

Madelyn gaped at him in amazement. When *Taylor* had called *him?* Taylor was responsible for all this exposure—publicity that a lot of people would consider committing murder to get?

She spun around, eyes searching in disbelief, but Taylor had disappeared. Her look darted from man to man, each one who stood above the crowd, every broad back, every dark head.

"Don't thank me, Mr. Diehl," she said, hardly aware of her words. "I was born with it. The people who deserve the thanks are those who have to work for it."

William Diehl bowed with old-fashioned gallantry. "Rarely have I heard it put so graciously, but in more cases than not, my dear, it isn't the talent that makes the artist. It's his strength to survive all the garbage lying between it and him. Forgive me . . ." He coughed apologetically. "I mean, her."

Smiling, Madelyn couldn't agree with him more. "That I will accept thanks for. I work hard to survive."

Hirschfield swiftly planted a kiss upon Madelyn's cheek and indicated to Diehl that he would walk with him the length of the mezzanine. He whispered to Madelyn: "Behave yourself. I'll find you later."

The two men made a comical duo as they trudged off side by side—Hirschfield's mooselike shuffle, Diehl's delicate mince.

"Miss Grey?"

Off-guard, Madelyn came around. "Yes?"

"I'm Bruce Fitzgerald from Memphis, Miss Grey. Mr. Champion of the *Daily Times* said you might allow us to take a few pictures for *Kentucky Monthly*."

"He did?" Strobelights flashed. Someone asked her to turn to her left if she didn't mind, please ma'am.

"My name is Zebrowski, Miss Grey, from *Illustrated Life*," a voice called as a small crowd began to gather around. "Could you answer a few questions before you leave?"

"Miss Grey, I do a syndicated column. Gorman Dillon says he would list you in the top five innovative artists in the country. Would you comment on this statement?"

They kept her there for some time—four, perhaps five different publications that would print reproductions of her works to be seen by people all over the United States. Randy Morrison joined the circle and smiled at her from the fringes, and Ralph McMillan snapped pictures to his heart's content, the roll around his middle quivering happily as he explained how he had 'discovered' Madelyn, that some of the portraits she had done for 'him' would be worth thousands in the years to come.

Madelyn wanted to laugh at the predictability of human nature. Her smile was still intact when she spotted Ellwyn Muse.

Muse had been watching her for some time, she guessed as she grew suddenly chilled. His blond mustache was laid as elegantly as ever across his upper lip, his mouth tipped up at the corners in a perpetual, humorless smile. He lifted his shoulders as if to convey his bewilderment that she wasn't including him in the interview.

"I beg your pardon," she said hastily to the woman from *Woman's* magazine. "What did you say?"

"That we'd like to know something about your work habits," the reporter repeated. "Do you know before you begin what you will paint?"

Muse grimaced at that question, and Madelyn felt blood rising to her face. After two years—the most painful of limbos on her part, thriving success on his—he had the gall to flaunt himself before her. Yet even in the imbalance of their positions, she sensed something different; he wanted to end it.

A smile from her would be enough, she guessed. That way he could save face and she would be minus one thorn in the flesh. Give him the smile. Be practical. Compromise is the twentieth-century game, didn't you know?

It wasn't that simple. People had no right to go through life running roughshod over other people. It wasn't right!

She glanced across the room. Taylor had returned. He saw her, and he saw Muse. He closed one eye in a slow wink.

That wink triggered a series of memories. *"Supercritics are insecure, and they have a dire need to prove their intellectual muscle. People who are insecure go on the defensive. Faulty premise . . . misinformed public . . . the querulous could actually be more stupid. . . ."*

So why should she be the one to bend the knee? Because she was younger, a woman, *smarter?* Everything in the room seemed suddenly sharp and clear.

Ellwyn Muse was only a man. He had to sort his smelly laundry, scrub the ring out of the bathtub, blow his nose and brush a film off his teeth like everyone else in the world. She might not have the courage to stand up to him, but she didn't have to pay token tribute. Damn him. Let him smile and end the cold war!

"I've said all I know," she said to the reporters with an abruptness that startled them. "Thank you for finding something worthwhile in my work. You've been wonderful, but I have to go."

"Miss Grey . . ."

"Thank you, thank you very much."

Walk slowly, she told herself, *slowly and regally. And*

don't look in his direction or you'll turn into a pillar of salt like Lot's wife. Behind her the reporter from *Woman's* magazine was watching. Madelyn heard her say, ''Well, I don't know. I'm not sure she's the genius they say she is.''

''Not sure?''

''She didn't insult me, Ellwyn. My goodness, she didn't insult anyone.''

''That's part of a cleverly constructed facade, darling. I know Miss Grey quite well. Did you know her mother's in an insane asylum?''

All through the interview Taylor had felt a little like the parent tossing the child into the water and yelling, ''Sink or swim!'' It had taken all his control to keep from hovering over Madelyn. He had gone to great lengths to make everything perfect for her tonight, behind the scenes as usual, but he hadn't found anonymity as gratifying as he had in the past. Even Muse, the vulture, was closer to her than he was.

Tonight would be the turning point for Madelyn, he supposed. She was handling herself like a veteran with the reporters—sparkling, smiling, playing the game, and that hint of reticence only made them adore her. Like himself, they sensed her utter lack of malice. After tonight Madelyn would emerge from her shell and realize that the world was much more ready for her than she was for it. The day would come when she would outgrow him. What would he do then? Could he love her enough to step aside?

Only when Madelyn started her slow walk toward him did Taylor take his first easy breath. There had been a moment when he was certain that Muse had intimidated her. But she'd taken a step he hadn't been sure she would. She didn't put him in his place, but she didn't buckle either. Good girl.

Her dark eyes danced as she covered the floor with that

stylish walk of hers. She slipped her arms about his waist and hugged. "I've got to talk to you. Now."

"Such a famous lady?" Taylor leaned back in a mixture of amusement and intimate approval of her. "Gee, I'm not sure—"

"It's either that or death by hanging, Taylor."

He laughed. "Never has anyone cut so quickly to the heart of the matter, my dear."

"You're a clever man, Taylor Champion."

Grasping Taylor's hand, Madelyn began blazing a trail through the shoulder-to-shoulder crowd. After several minutes of hard work and a considerable shifting of Taylor's hand to encompass her waist, they emerged into one of the quiet corridors that led to the smaller galleries upstairs.

Once there, however, Madelyn was at a loss. She stood with her eyes fixed upon her bag and failed to find an easy way to express her gratitude for what he had done. "It feels like a year since everything went to pieces. I hardly know where to start."

"Well"—Taylor deliberately misread her—"this room over here's pretty good. 'Course I haven't seen them all. I'm going mainly on—"

"You aren't going to let me do it, are you?"

The tease was no longer funny. Taylor felt bits of himself coming unglued. "I don't want your apology, Madelyn. You don't owe it. Never, not to me."

"Well, you're going to get it." Madelyn opened and shut her beaded bag, looked down again. "That lie about my never having been married was an accident, Taylor. I don't know why I said it except that I was terribly impressed with who you were that day. I thought I looked stupid compared to everyone you knew."

"You thought wrong."

"Now all this." Madelyn threw out her arm to include the gallery. "Thank you."

Taylor took her hand and spread it upon his larger one, outlining her fingers. "I don't want that, either."

He was as vulnerable as she was, wasn't he? "Why does it embarrass you to be thanked?"

"That's silly."

"See how easy it is to lie?" She decided to try a different approach. "Hirschfield thinks I should make a tour of Europe."

"Really?"

"I probably will. Go, I mean."

A pause. "When will all this business take place?"

"This fall. Maybe. I don't know."

"And I suppose it will all take a great deal of time?"

Ah. Madelyn heard it now in his voice. The silence hung, waiting for the end of the sentence, the drop of the other shoe. A group of people wandered into the hall. They were planning a party for later on.

"Well," she shrugged prettily, "I don't think you really get the feel of Europe unless you live over there a while, do you? I'd have to at least stay the winter. But I'd write you, every day."

Scowling, Taylor drew himself up to his full height. Madelyn was pricking at him, with a very sharp needle. She was stringing him out, forcing him to a point where he'd throw caution to the wind and lay his cards on the table. No, he couldn't step aside!

Like some pagan warrior suddenly determined to claim a bounty that was rightfully his, Taylor flicked open his blazer and covered the steps between them. "Turn you loose on an unsuspecting world? Like hell."

Before Madelyn could protest or agree, he swept her up in his arms in a flurry of protesting silk and brought his mouth down hard upon hers. A low thunder rumbled in Madelyn's head. This was where she wanted to be.

Taylor's tongue sparred with her own as if it were the most important battle he would ever fight. Her legs dangled limply over his arm, and one of her black slings slipped from her foot to the floor with a *clunk*.

Over the kiss, Taylor opened his eyes and met the enthralled stare of a middle-aged woman who was walking past. Without a word, she bent for the shoe and hooked it wonderingly over the finger Taylor poked out from beneath the skirt of Madelyn's gown. He was positive that she was still staring when—by some fortunate inner radar—he managed to clear the nearest corner and drop back against the wall.

"What d'you do to me, woman?" he mumbled as he let her slide languidly down his length. "You plan it, don't you? You stay up nights brewing potions to put me at your mercy?"

Every inch of her was fitting to the matching inches of him. Madelyn wanted it to work this time. "If I could have had you at my mercy, Taylor Champion"—she gazed up at his eyes as they devoured her—"d'you think I would have waited until now?"

The weight of her hair was pulling loose over Taylor's arm. She half-heartedly caught at it, but Taylor brushed her hand away. It tumbled down in a dark, shiny fall.

"You want this to boil to the crisis point so badly?" he growled. "Then tell me. Say it."

He had taken the lead in a race she had begun herself. Some self-protective instinct procrastinated. "I missed you terribly. It was awful. It made me sick."

He bent over her, making her arch farther and farther back: a slender bow reversed upon itself. "Not that, and you know it."

"A minute," she pleaded. "Just a minute. I want to be very sure. I want—"

But his teeth captured the lobe of her ear, and his refusal to wait any longer was in his breath. His hands were moving over her. Gooseflesh was rising.

"Time has run out, my darling."

Madelyn let her eyes close. There she was. She must run the risk of every person who had gone before her. There was no other way.

"I love you." She was unable to weep and unable to prevent it. "I love you, Taylor. Take me home. I love you."

Home was not where he took her. Taylor paused long enough to scribble a message to Hirschfield on the back of a business card and whisked Madelyn out of the gallery beneath the noses of Christine and Randy and, miracle of miracles, Pearl McGrath. He couldn't even surrender her long enough to get the key in the lock of the car door but opened it by feel and slid across the seat, drawing her with him into the thickly shadowed interior.

"Did you plan all this?" she gasped as he, turning, slipped his hands into the mass of her fly-away hair with a soft groan.

"I only hoped."

"Lusted."

"Same difference."

"Only to a warped, evil mind."

"Ain't it wonderful?"

"Only to another warped, evil mind. When do we begin?"

If life went no further than this moment, Madelyn thought she would have been happy. She was in love with Taylor's fingers as they gripped her skull. She was in love with his breaths that filled the small space. The streetlights were diamonds in his eyes, and she loved that too, slipping her hands beneath his blazer and hugging his waist.

Taylor's heartbeat quickened beneath his shirt. "Ah, Madelyn, my love. You're so fine. There's no one in the world as fine as you."

He leaned back against his window and bridged the space

between the seats, wincing and dragging her down on top of him. "Listen while I talk to you."

"I'm listening."

He kissed her.

"Hey, that's some talking."

"Hush. I want to make all the promises that the book says a person should, Madelyn. I want to marry you, and I'll admit it scares me stupid. I swore I'd never bring a child into this stinking, lousy world, and tonight when I saw you walking toward me I wanted it more than air to breathe. I don't know where I am anymore, Madelyn. I don't even know how to plan for next week."

"I wasn't sure I'd even live until next week."

He inched himself up and drew her closer. She lay her cheek upon his heart and said, "I know this isn't a one-night stand, Taylor. You don't have to make plans for me. I don't feel cheated. I'm okay."

The lack of space was frustrating, and Taylor shifted and swore and shifted again. Finally he pushed her to her own side of the car. "Stay there," he ordered. "Don't say a word to me until we get there."

One of her arms was still draped around his neck. "I just wanted to kiss your jaw."

She pressed her parted lips to his scar, and he lifted his chin in a greedy gesture for more, which she willingly gave until they were again locked in a frenzied embrace. The gear shift caught him in the back.

"Damn it!"

Taylor dragged himself free, and Madelyn dropped back in a dreamy daze. The engine fired and air conditioning poured over them the moment he started the car. And music from rear speakers. The streets were dark and tree-shadowed, the streetlights a necklace of rough-cut diamonds.

"Where're we going?" she murmured from her cloud.

"Did I say you could talk?"

"Do you think I'm afraid of you?" She laughed.

"I'm taking you to my place. Do you mind?"

Madelyn caught his hand upon the steering wheel. "Taylor, I—"

She considered not telling him and just taking the pregnancy risk. She opened her mouth, closed it, then said with eyes lowered, "I was going to get some pills. Then I didn't think I'd ever see you again. I—"

He brushed her lower lip tenderly with a fingertip. "Not every man sticks his head in the sand about that. I'll take care of it. You're not worried, are you? About before?"

What his solution would be if she got pregnant, she didn't ask. He would marry her, she was sure. But she didn't want it to be that way. He was already swinging the car onto the interstate that would whisk them out of the city.

What kind of a house would he live in? A pretty corner brick, she figured; a shrewd real estate investment that would be worth three times what he paid for it back in '65. Beside it would sit a two-car garage with a brave little prewar Karman Ghia for a touch of conversational chic. A hammock would droop between two trees in the backyard. He would pay a neighbor boy to mow his lawn once a week.

From the interstate, Taylor drove until the city was a pale memory. Properties were sparse now, and the verdant Kentucky summer flaunted its charm of ancient fences smothered with exuberant honeysuckle and lazy creeper, majestic oak trees a person couldn't reach around, hills and hollows with their secrets of blue and gray uniforms winding along its floors, moonshine whiskey brewed by the light of the same moon that was splashing this night with a glitter as fragile as a sigh.

Whipping off the blacktop, he sped down a gravel road. A spume of dust roiled out behind them like smoke. Madelyn asked no questions, but when he slowed to a crawl and turned in a drive that was little more than ruts and weeds that slapped the underpinning of the car, she peered into the night.

The house had to have been decaying for at least a decade. Low to the ground, the new foundation was as visible as a fresh bandage. Verandas sprawled on all sides—a mixture of old and new lumber. Plywood was neatly stacked in the yard, and a ladder leaned against a tree. Braced against two of the veranda's outer walls were at least a dozen huge sheets of glass.

"She's a very old lady," he said softly and cut off the engine. "Needs a bit of work."

"Resurrection from the dead would be more like it." All that glass! Madelyn had an excruciating need to know when he'd begun planning to install glass windows. Because of her? "It's wonderful."

He grinned in the darkness. "I thought . . . I was almost certain you'd like it."

"You don't live here, though."

"I've been working weekends for a couple of years."

As they got out, Madelyn rotated beneath the great trees that cast the yard into deep ebony shadows. Her heels sank into the ground, and she lifted her gown to slip them off. "My best pair of shoes."

Taylor peeled out of his blazer and tossed it carelessly back into the car, along with the predictable tie. He flicked loose his cuffs and rolled them back. Madelyn peeled off her stockings and wriggled her toes in the dew-moistened grass.

"There aren't any conveniences inside," he said. "Cold water but not hot. Electricity but no heat."

"Back to nature."

The night was a concert of sounds—the wind and the katydids and tree frogs, the distant lowing of cattle and, somewhere in the inky sky, a jet on its way to Atlanta.

Taylor lowered himself to a step, leaned back on his elbows, and let his legs sprawl wide. Shadows played across his face.

He didn't look at her. "Do you know about my wife?"

Madelyn compelled herself not to show surprise. He'd never mentioned Helen Champion before. "I heard how she died."

"I was two years older than you are now." He leaned forward to rest his head in his hands.

"Did you love her?"

"I needed her."

"I'm sorry."

Straightening, he glanced out at the timberland on both sides of them, shook his head. "It wasn't her fault. I couldn't give her what she wanted."

"So you blame yourself. I thought that was my line."

"I think I'm ready to forgive my youth a few mistakes now."

Madelyn wondered if their love had played any part in that decision. "At least you can hit a center. I have trouble with centers."

"Was Darrell a center?"

Ambling to one of the trees, Madelyn picked at the bark. The night was mistily sympathetic and caressing. "Darrell didn't deserve me."

"Deserve is a hard word."

"If you asked Darrell which he'd rather have, a hundred angry creditors or a life with me, he would say he'd come out better with the creditors." Before she thought, she tasted the bark. It was bitter, and she spat.

Taylor chuckled. "That, I take it, is your opinion of marriage?"

Her hem caught on a snag, and she plucked it loose as she considered the serious turn of the conversation. "I don't want to make any more mistakes either, Taylor. When I was fighting so hard for Abigail, I was invincible. I really was.

And then I had to put her in the hospital and was faced with fighting for myself for a change. I found I couldn't do it. Muse already had me beaten down, and Darrell just about finished me off. I couldn't even have done this night if you—''

"That isn't true.''

She met his eyes without hesitation. "I did the paintings, that was all.''

Taylor leaned forward to grasp her hand and pull her into the V of his legs. He locked his hands across the backs of her hips.

"That's all you were supposed to do, my sweet. Let some of the rest of us share with you. It's our pleasure. I could help you with Abigail. I could give you a nice place to work.''

"You could marry me?'' Madelyn relaxed, and he locked her in with his legs. "Have a project?''

"That's not fair, Madelyn.''

"But honest.''

"Are you too proud to be a human being like the rest of us? Yes, I want to marry you, provide for you. You can't do it all. Does it upset you so much to admit you're not perfect, that you need someone?''

From her human prison, Madelyn covered her face with her hands. "You don't know how easy it would be for me to just say yes. But I can't let myself get into the habit of thinking, 'Taylor will fix it.' ''

"Then you don't love me.''

"I do! But it's imposing.''

"It's the privilege of love to impose, dammit.''

"At least give me time to make myself equal.''

"Equal!'' His voice was a whip. "Don't give me that femininst bull. Nothing in this world is equal. Absolutely nothing!''

When Madelyn stood very tall, lifting her head until the moonlight made her face an ivory carving, she stared down at the stubborn fringe of Taylor's lowered lids. She touched his head, smoothed back the rebellious locks.

"I wasn't thinking of the inequality being on my side, but yours. It's not fair to you, Taylor. I'm a mess right now. Let me work it out."

"That's like saying a person has to become perfect before he's good enough to get religion."

She drew his weary head to her belly, stroked the back of his neck the way one would caress a child. "I love you, Taylor."

"I know you do."

"You scare me."

"Join the club."

In the darkness, wings fluttered and carried an owl swiftly away. Taylor's breath was blistering Madelyn through the silk, and her heart began a too-quick cadence. When he slid the zipper along its track to her waist and slipped his thumbs beneath its slash, she thought her heart would stop altogether.

The moonlight turned her skin to silver as Taylor drew her gown over her shoulders. Standing as she was, it caught in dark folds low on her hips. She was at once a statue discovered in some Grecian cave, a bare-footed peasant girl in a Renaissance painting, a high priestess about to perform mysterious and sensual rites in another age.

"You always do this to me," he whispered as he explored the back of her legs through her gown. Her nipples roused at his slightest touch, and he cupped the almost impudent curves of her buttocks to draw her close. "I could keep you here forever."

He closed his mouth upon her breast, and Madelyn folded her arms about his head, moved against him in slow, pulsing circles.

"And I . . ." She could hardly breathe. He was doing terrible things to her will—making her dizzy and greedy and demanding. She let her head drop back and crooned low, throaty sounds not unlike the hushed sighs of the night which surrounded them.

"I can close my eyes and see . . ." She couldn't say what she saw. Her fantasies were blurring with reality and she was being dragged across a border in her mind where sensation was consuming.

Her gown slithered into a black pool about her feet. Taylor knew exactly where to touch her, how to move with her, how to insinuate himself into her secrets. She felt tension building like a band stretched too tightly against itself. She forgot dignity; she forgot pain, and the past and the future. Nothing existed but Taylor and what he was doing to her. She lost track of time and searched only for the inevitable release against him. His pleasure was in her pleasure as it began—separate, yet linked together until she finally collapsed against him and bent her head to let it come slowly to rest upon his own.

Excited beyond his ability to stand it any longer, Taylor caught Madelyn up in his arms and climbed the steps. Her gown was left forgotten upon the grass like some carelessly errant shadow.

She whimpered against his chest. "I don't want to lose you, Taylor."

"Then marry me. Doubts and all." Taylor kicked open the front door and caught it with his knee. He stood in the portal, gazing down at her in the remnants of the moonlight. "The night of Owen's dinner campaign affair, I'm sending a limousine for you. Be ready. And have your answer ready. That's as long as I can wait."

The room was large and empty, undraped but with soft new carpet. Now it would no longer be empty. It would be filled with memories.

"How could I deny you anything?" she whispered and pressed her lips against the scar on his jaw.

Chapter Nine

$\mathcal{I}$t was said of Owen Prince that Southern hospitality found its ultimate consummation in him. This statement was concocted by a very expensive publicity man and was completely false. The truth was, Edwina's mother, the wife of a Supreme Court judge for the last twenty years of her life, had farsightedly trained her daughter in the fine skill of entertaining.

Edwina knew, because anyone who lived with Owen Prince must know, how to take most any affair that Owen could ruin and make sanity of it. To his credit, Owen knew this; he would sooner lose television time to a Republican than walk into a room of politicians and their wives without Edwina by his side.

As Madelyn stepped out of the limousine Taylor sent for her, Edwina was standing beneath the chandelier in the foyer of the mansion. She was shaking the hand of Howard Page, the handsome senator from Georgia whom a number of her female guests knew only too well. Howard was telling one of his memorized jokes, and as Madelyn reached the bottom step, the lights of the portico caught her beauty vividly. Howard did a doubletake and completely forgot his punch line.

When Taylor had bought Madelyn's gown his instincts had not been amiss. Its green was so deep and so clear that Madelyn's white skin was iridescent by contrast, as luminous as the finest mother of pearl. She seemed to float with the dress, and to add to the near-mystical illusion she had caught her hair upward to the crown in a loose Gibson-girl fashion. It gave Howard the impression that the touch of a loving hand would bring it lusciously down again. His should be that hand, he decided on the spot, and a familiar tension began in his groin.

Edwina was caught by surprise too when Madelyn arrived, so much that she forgot to laugh at Howard's joke, which she would have done in any case, with or without the punch line.

"Well, well, well, Edwina," Howard murmured. "Such secrets you've been keeping up here in Kentucky. Who *is* that gorgeous creature?"

"She's Owen's young guest." Edwina kept in mind Howard's infamous ardor. "The question has been raised if her mother isn't the long-lost Virginia Prince. Please do be good, Howard. If she turns out to be who she says . . ."

Chuckling, Howard smoothed back his hair like a man preparing to enter a bevy of photographers. "Such a delicate affair. Tsk, tsk. Is it true, do you think? About her mother?"

"We don't know." Edwina shrugged. "She says that she doesn't either. There've been so many false alarms in the past."

"Owen suspects her of lying?"

"Owen waits until all the evidence is in, Howard. You know that."

The second hung with the fragility of a cobweb, but the senator's smile was too practiced and Edwina's too tactful. "Well, if that girl's a liar, who wants the truth anyway? Oh, I'll behave. Introduce us, Edwina."

Madelyn's days since Taylor's proposal had been the most pleasant, truly secure days she'd ever known. Taylor was religiously frugal about her daylight hours, but each evening was a surprise where nothing was predictable and everything an irresistible challenge.

Once they dressed up in their finest togs and went to a barbecue pit with sawdust on the floor. On another warm twilight she heard a shout outside her bedroom window, walked out on deck to find Taylor throwing her the line of an outboard motorboat. He had a bucket of fried chicken and iced-down drinks and they traveled far upriver and listened to the radio. They sat on the grass at the park once and ate a gallon of ice cream out of the carton with two iced-tea spoons. They went fishing. They attended the ballet. They listened to records and made love on the divan. Her sketch pad went everywhere, and her folio of Taylor grew deliciously fat.

But each night ended the same. With his long, leisurely good-night kiss he said, "I don't like my empty bed anymore. Have your answer ready."

Now Edwina extended her hand to Madelyn with a smile. "I was afraid you wouldn't be able to come."

The formal receiving line had been dispensed with. "Am I the last to arrive?" Madelyn asked breathily.

"Saved the best 'til last." Howard Page confidently wedged himself between the two women and slipped an arm about Madelyn's waist. "A fine old custom I never appreciated much until now."

"Madelyn, dear"—Edwina's look at Howard was not altogether a mock exasperation—"this is Senator Page from Georgia. I must warn you about Howard. Naughty Democratic blood flows in his veins. Don't believe a single word he says.''

There was something trustworthy about Owen Prince's wife, Madelyn thought fondly. Her lavender dress was kind to her waist and discreetly covered her upper arms. (Edwina's mother had also taught her that no woman over forty should wear a sleeveless dress.) It enhanced her dainty loveliness so that she looked silvery and fragile, completely approachable.

"Don't pay any attention to Edwina." Howard laughingly admired Madelyn's neckline in a way that made her lift her hand to her throat. "She thinks all men from Georgia are Rhett Butler."

"Now, Howard."

"I notice you are without an escort, Miss Grey," Howard persisted. "Would you allow me the honor?"

Giving a nod to the part of the house where the party sounds were reverberating, Howard extended his arm. Madelyn shrugged and gamely placed her hand upon Howard's arm.

"My mother and I once lived in Georgia," she said as the three of them walked together. "I liked it, but I never understood how Scarlett O'Hara stood all those petticoats."

Howard burst out laughing. "That, my dear, is Margaret Mitchell's problem. May I call you Madelyn? Let's find some champagne, shall we?"

The room Madelyn walked into was enormous, resembling a giant glassed-in gazebo projecting out from the house: high, exposed rafters that angled to the center where a cupola reached skyward, great jalousies on all sides. Madelyn guessed that it glowed like a planet for miles and all the sparkling gowns of the women must look like colored rings about its twinkling moon.

A band with a string ensemble backup had been hired out

of Louisville for the evening. The female singer, whose fabulous floor-length gown was red sequins, was kicking the cord of her microphone around her leg and throatily crooning some of the dreamy country ballads Kentucky was famous for. Red, white, and blue streamers sectioned off part of the waxed floor for dancing and a gargantuan blow-up of Owen Prince revolved from the ceiling like a mirrored ball.

With an intuition that was as true as the needle to the pole, Madelyn's gaze moved over it all. Where was Taylor? Had he arrived first?

The dining room stretched out at a distance on her right. Waiters were moving between white-clothed tables and checking centerpieces of little American flags smothered with red roses. There, beyond the bandstand near the bar, was Taylor.

He hadn't noticed her yet. He stood talking with two women, one hand gesturing wide as he made his point, the other holding a drink near his waist. He wore his tuxedo with his usual gypsy flair, giving the impression that he would be equally capable of meeting the president or jumping onto a motorcycle for a moonlight ride.

Men like him didn't age or go out of fashion, Madelyn thought. They grew a bit leaner with the years and grayed around the edges. He would be in his fifties when their children came to adulthood. What kind of man would he be then? Still possessing that fine, honed edge? Earning the adoration of his daughters and demanding the respect of his sons?

One of the women, a striking blonde, obviously someone's well-versed and well-used wife, flaunted her wealth of rings. As Taylor laughed she patted his cheek, and Madelyn's brows went up.

She turned to the senator just as Taylor spotted her. "You flew in, did you, Mr. Page?"

Howard winked. "Now, now, now. You're a much more interesting subject than I am. Tell me, Madelyn, how long have you suspected you were Waverly Prince?"

A puppeteer could have been controlling her ragdoll's limbs; her head slowly turned around, and her gaze invariably flicked over her shoulder. Taylor was staring hard at her back, devouring her in an up-and-down appraisal. The devil!

She turned back, frowning. "What did you say, Senator?"

"Please, call me Howard."

Now the woman was half in Taylor's arms. Was he asking her to dance? Good grief, yes!

By the time Madelyn looked back to Howard, he was sweeping the room to find the object of her distraction. His gaze fixed upon Taylor. The newspaperman? Hell, what on earth did she see in him?

"Let's dance," he said and caught Madelyn so close that the breath was crushed out of her. "What's a party for?"

Not for this, Madelyn thought dizzily but tried not to disappoint Howard. He was quite good with a skilled, strong lead, but as he moved her around the floor the edges of her glances persisted in returning to Taylor.

Are you planning to spend the evening with him? Taylor scowlingly demanded when he maneuvered his partner nearer.

Madelyn's lips pursed into a tight smile. *If I don't, at least I won't have to be pried away with a crowbar.*

The dance had to be a disappointment for Howard. Madelyn stumbled over his feet a number of times and kept losing her train of thought. She was about to plead a phony headache when an elbow in her back sent her stumbling. A run popped into her stocking and zipped up her ankle.

That did it! Turning, promising herself the vengeance of a glare at least, she peered up at Taylor's grin.

"Oh, I beg your pardon," he drawled sweetly. "Didn't mean to do any damage. Well, I'll declare, if it's not Senator Page from Georgia."

"Champion?" Howard dourly acknowledged.

"And my word, Miss Grey. Fancy meetin' you here. I didn't step on your sweet little foot, did I, Miss Grey?"

Taylor made a few sympathetic sounds between his teeth as Madelyn began to glare, and the blonde, finding herself suddenly neglected, threw her weight to a hip.

"As a matter of fact," Madelyn said coolly, "you did." She poked out a foot where a one-inch run was laddering whitely up her shin.

"Hmm." Straightening, Taylor appreciated Madelyn's décolletage even more than Howard had. "I'm very sorry, Miss Grey. Very sorry indeed. Please accept my deepest apologies. And may I say"—he peered innocently up at Howard—"that is a stunning gown you're wearin'. You look stunning too, Howard. Oh, dear, the music's over. I guess I've ruined your dance. I *am* sorry."

Indeed, thought Madelyn. Taylor's partner, though she smiled, didn't seem overly impressed with him; her sultry, shadowed lids lowered, and she braced a fist against a pair of pants so tight that Madelyn feared for them.

"I'm Diane Leyman, Senator Page," she murmured with an outstretched, beringed hand for Howard. "Isn't this a divine party?"

"Oh, my," Taylor muttered. "My manners."

He commenced upon introductions so confusing that Madelyn wanted to laugh. Poor Howard was making a swift decision that Diane showed infinitely more promise than Madelyn herself. He flashed his debonair smile. "Diane, that is absolutely a remarkable pair of pants. Would you like to dance?"

"Why, thank you, Howard." Diane gave Taylor a look which said: *You didn't compliment me on my pants.*

Howard spun Diane away with uncontested fervor, and Madelyn and Taylor were left in the middle of the floor, staring after them.

Turning, Madelyn patted Taylor's cheek and crooned, "Isn't this a divine party?"

"Cat eyes," Taylor retorted and caught Madelyn against him so that her head was thrown back and her skirt billowed out in a cloud. "I don't suppose you'd care to dance?"

"After that display, I'd sooner trust a Revenuer with a bloodhound."

Taylor's laughter rang out over the music and turned more than one head, including that of his stepmother, who exchanged a speculative glance with Owen that distinctly said, "See? It really is serious."

A half-dozen pivots left Madelyn dizzy. She pressed against his chest, panting, and his face lowered to hers until their noses touched.

"Blink," he said.

"Everyone's watching us, Taylor."

"I've wanted to do this since the day you ran me down in the taxi."

"I did not run you down." But Madelyn laughingly obliged him, and when his lashes collided with hers, she giggled. The musky scent on his jaw made her reckless. "Have we discovered a new way of kissing?"

"It'll never catch on."

"I don't know. You have an inventive mind. Improve on it."

The lines at the edges of his eyes crinkled. "Do you realize just how much experimentation is necessary for a thing like that? Literally years and years."

Beneath his banter, Madelyn knew what he was asking. She flushingly tucked her head beneath his chin and felt his body move wonderfully with the music. "Would a lifetime be long enough? If we got started right away?"

Taylor came to a dead stop and narrowed his eyes. He got nervous when things were too easy. "Say that again. I want to look in your eyes when you say it."

Her eyes were twinkling, shining with love. "Yes, Taylor. My answer is yes."

"When?"

"Whenever you say."

A passing waiter caught Taylor's attention, and he signaled him to stop. He filched two glasses from his tray and placed one in Madelyn's hand, sipped the other because he suddenly felt in dire need of it.

"I'm going to slip out," he said. "Wait the decent interval and meet me in the library. D'you think you can find it?"

Madelyn peered down at the glass. "What is this?"

"A love potion. Are you coming?"

She teasingly pretended to be shy. "But it's my first assignation. I think it may be beyond me."

He grinned. "Nothing, but nothing, is beyond you."

But Norman Bullard was beyond her. The moment she saw him—small, shiny, toupeed, walking toward her with Governor Prince—Madelyn knew that life was about to make one of those killing turnarounds where you dared not grab ahold of anything but would lose everything if you didn't.

Over her shoulder she searched nervously for Taylor, but he was probably stretched out on the Chippendale sofa by now.

"Well, I wish you'd look who's here!" the governor called as he charged up. Instead of shaking her hand, he patted her on the back as if she were a child with a bone lodged in her throat. "Edwina told me you'd arrived, little lady. Now, if you're not the prettiest thing, I don't know what is. Norm and I have been lookin' for you."

Madelyn carefully set her glass of champagne down on a

table and looked around for cameras but saw none. She smiled. "Yes, sir?"

"Now, now, none of that sir business. May I present Norman Bullard, Miss Grey? A friend of mine since the bad old days. Taylor's wandered off somewhere, has he?"

You know perfectly well that he has, Madelyn wanted to say. "Shall I go find him?"

"No bother, no bother. In fact, it was you Norm wanted to see." Owen patted his girth and beamed at Norman. "Taylor did a great job with the profile of Miss Grey in the paper, don't you think, Norm? Great job, great job. Always did think that Taylor had the keenest market sense I'd ever seen."

Norman nodded, and his toupee caught the light. Madelyn could see where he'd tried to match it to his hair. He should've gone to a professional.

"True in every aspect, Governor. And I'm so happy to meet you, Miss Grey. You're a lively topic of conversation these days, but that's only natural, isn't it?"

Madelyn received an overpowering whiff of cologne as Norman Bullard bent over her hand.

"I was wondering if I could have a few minutes of your time, Miss Grey?" He was an ingratiatingly polite man. "There are a few questions I'd like to ask you."

"Very good, Norman," Owen said approvingly as he scanned the ballroom. "Well, I'll leave you two alone to chat. I'm sure you can do as well without me. Have to run. Someone's waving at me."

A chat with Norman? Madelyn turned to protest, but Owen was already weaving his way through his admirers toward his wife. Taylor was probably pacing the floor by now. "What questions could you possibly have to ask me, Mr. Bullard?"

"Absolutely nothing to worry about," cooed Norman. "Just a few minor matters. Could I get you some more champagne, Miss Grey?"

Norman removed a handkerchief from his inner breast pocket and meticulously blotted the back of his head, then his forehead. He inspected the handkerchief before replacing it, and Madelyn wondered what he had expected to find.

"Champagne?" he repeated.

"No! No, thank you."

"It's lovely weather we've been having this spring."

"Oh, yes. Very nice weather."

"I love summer in Kentucky. Have you ever spent much time in the mountains? The Smokies?"

"I've never spent much time there." How long had Taylor been gone now? Five minutes?

"How long have you lived in Louisville?"

"Hmm?" Madelyn jerked up her head. "Oh, about eight years."

"Your mother was living at home with you then?"

Something very bad was happening here. Where was this heading? Why would this man mention Abigail? Why had Owen Prince brought him over?

She fixed him in a direct stare. "How do you know about my mother?"

Norman drew his lips back from his teeth. They were small and very white canine teeth behind an effeminate, rosebud mouth. "I probably know everything there is to know about you, Miss Grey," he said and pursed his lips. "I know everything about everyone."

Madelyn felt her own face tightening with apprehension. "Who are you, Mr. Bullard? How do you know about me?"

"I'm the IRS, Miss Grey. I've been going over your tax returns for the past six years. I found them very . . . shall we say, *interesting*."

Chapter Ten

*E*very horror story Madelyn had ever heard about the Internal Revenue stabbed into her like a needle and broke off. This was precisely how the terror was supposed to begin, wasn't it—a misunderstanding, then an explanation that the IRS didn't accept? After that another investigation and a discovered error? Then another investigation and another and another?

"I noticed that you carried your mother as a dependent when you were seventeen years old," Norman Bullard was saying around his terrifying smile. "Extraordinary, I thought to myself. I also noticed that you filled out the form yourself. Again, extraordinary for a seventeen-year-old girl, wouldn't you say?"

Not when you've got a brain cell working, Madelyn wanted to yell as she frantically searched through possible reasons for this. Had she made an error? Couldn't she pay it back?

"I haven't cheated the government, Mr. Bullard. At least not intentionally."

Norman recoiled. "Did I accuse you of fraud, Miss Grey? Why, you misunderstand, my dear."

"Then—"

"Tsk, tsk, tsk." Norman woefully shook his head. "Is it any wonder that the public has such a perverted opinion of the IRS?"

She didn't say anything for fear of whining. This was another of those Ellwyn Musian games. She mustn't let him see that she didn't know how to play.

"On the other hand," he mused, "if I did have cause to wonder . . . for instance, if I heard a report from some source that you had defrauded someone . . . let's say, the governor of Kentucky, for example, why then it might be in my mind to wonder if you hadn't defrauded on your taxes just the tiniest, tiniest amount. But I'm sure everything is in perfect order in your case, Miss Grey. One look at your face, and anyone could tell you're as honest as the day is long."

Ah! So that was it. The governor, with all the glamor surrounding him, the culture, refinement, intellegentsia, and unmeasured wealth. The man who she once hoped and prayed was Abigail's husband. *Mother, you don't need this man. You don't want this man!*

"What does the governor want of me?" she asked coldly. "A public retraction or what?"

"It sounds so ugly when you say it like that."

"That's because it is ugly, Mr. Bullard. It stinks."

Something about the way she was holding herself attracted the attention of those guests standing nearest. Norman felt a trickle of sweat along his spine. The governor had insisted upon smooth transitions, quiet moves. Dumb cluck, why couldn't she be discreet?

He drew Madelyn into the curve of his arm. "I would

like very much to dance with you, Miss Grey," he said with icy sweetness. "The waltz is my forte."

"Well, ask the governor," she snapped and jerked away. "I think dancing is his forte too."

Conversation stopped on their side of the room. Couples lifted their brows and began speculating behind their hands. Norman hurriedly maneuvered Madelyn against a wall so that his body was at least positioned between hers and theirs.

"Be still, Miss Grey. If you don't want Taylor Champion's name dragged through something very, very sticky, lower your voice."

Taylor? Sticky? She should have known. Things had been going too well. She'd been happy, which was the surest sign of all.

He smiled like she imagined a weasel would smile. "That's better. See how easy it is? Now, let me put this a bit—"

"I think I have it straight, Mr. Bullard." She bit off her words savagely. "The governor wants me to retract that I might be his daughter. And if I decline to do so, Taylor will be hurt—the time, place, and manner left to your discretion, of course."

She'd played right into their hands, hadn't she? Given them the perfect weapon by falling in love with Taylor.

Norman stretched his neck against the knot of his tie. "That's a little crudely stated, but . . ."

"All right. You've got it. Right now. I'll get up on the bandstand and make an announcement."

Her heartbeat was a dull thud in her temples. Without giving Norman time to think, Madelyn began moving toward the singer who was getting a deafening feedback and was holding her microphone out from herself while looking helplessly at the guitarist. It was a calculated bluff; the last thing she intended to do was get up on that podium, but if she could only make him think so . . .

The singer lifted her arms apologetically to the audience, and Madelyn caught her attention. "I beg your pardon, Miss—"

Norman grabbed her so violently that he nearly bowled her over. His grimace at the singer must have passed for a smile as he half dragged, half danced Madelyn as far away as possible.

"There've been enough public statements, don't you think?" he gasped, out of breath. "Just a quiet, dignified exit would be much preferable. In fact, if it's dignified enough, Miss Grey, I venture to say that you might receive a few coins for your inconvenience."

She wanted to hit him.

"The best thing for you, Miss Grey, is to leave town. If your mother's hospitalization poses a problem, those arrangements can be made."

"By the governor?" she sneered.

"By someone. Listen to reason. Don't come back, don't see Taylor, don't pass 'Go.' Don't do anything in this town again, Miss Grey, ever. Just . . . go."

In that frozen moment of indecision, Madelyn saw herself from a distance: Look at Madelyn in her splendid rage, her hand raised back and connecting with Norman Bullard's mouth. See how he bends double, holding his face as he glares up at her from his crouch, seething but impotent. Now the governor and his wife are appearing on the scene. They hear what has happened and the governor throws out his Great Arm of Justice and banishes Bullard from his house forever. Edwina has everyone applaud Madelyn's courage now. Taylor announces their engagement and declares to everyone how proud he is to be marrying a woman so brave and strong.

But what would happen to Taylor if she refused to go along? His life was wrapped up in Owen Prince. This would kill him. Betrayal by two fathers in one lifetime? And between them the uncle. It wasn't fair.

"Well?" Norman said, his small eyes dancing around from the guests to her to the guests.

Madelyn mumbled something about needing time to think it over. Keeping her head down, her hand uplifted as if she were holding a hairpin in place, she started weaving her way toward the door that opened onto the front foyer.

"Where in heaven's name have you been?"

Taylor's fingers were bruising as he grabbed Madelyn by the shoulders and swung her around. She blinked dumbly and he looked surprised and glanced down at his hands, frowned slightly and loosened his grip. "Sweetheart?"

What lie could she tell? What smile could she smile? "I—I got too . . . warm," she blurted. "I was coming. I was trying to get out of here for a few minutes."

"Really?" Taylor inspected her as if he were looking for wounds.

She must have looked ghastly enough for him to believe something was wrong. He drew her into his arms and, holding her tightly against his side, walked her across the room.

"Let's get you some air." Suddenly Taylor stopped dead in his tracks, and he tipped up her face with a finger, his brows defying her to give him anything less than the truth. "You're not pregnant, are you?"

Hysteria tickled in her throat. Was he hoping? Dreading? "I don't know. No. No, I can't be."

The music followed them as he took her hand and pulled her behind a flower-disguised rack of bottles near the kitchen. It was cool there, dark.

"Then you're either suffering from low blood sugar or a warlock curse," he chuckled. "Maybe it's prewedding jitters. Breathe deeply. And relax."

"Actually"—her laughter was a well-timed bluff—"I saw myself fainting and going down in history as the fainter painter."

"Gad, for that I should have left you out there."

A large air-conditioning vent poured out a stream of almost icy air upon them, and the whole end of the room smelled like roses. Only yards beyond, through the glass, was the starlit night and the lawn where drivers huddled around the cars and smoked and threw dice while they waited for the owners.

Madelyn's skirt brushed against a spray of peonies and loose petals showered to the floor like the tail of a comet. Had Norman seen her return to the room with Taylor? She glanced furtively over her shoulder, caught Taylor studying her, and smiled wanly.

Taylor didn't understand what was happening. She was, for a reason he couldn't fathom at all, drawing into a shell. With any other woman a man might dismiss such a shift of mood, but to ignore it in Madelyn was to invite disaster. Besides that, he loved her; he didn't want to ignore it.

He leaned back against the bottles so that a club soda poked him in the ribs like a shotgun barrel. "I want to tell the family tonight. Is that all right with you?"

She bent to brush the clinging petals off her dress, which was an absurd gesture considering what he'd just asked.

He caught at her hands and compelled her to look at him. "Madelyn?"

"I guess."

Then she simply stood staring down at their joined hands. Presently tears spattered wetly on them, and Taylor, for the hundredth time, had the sensation of being left behind by her.

"Tell me what's happened," he coaxed.

"Nothing." This in a shrill, strangled voice.

"This is me, remember? Don't do this."

Her head came up. "I just think we should wait on getting married, that's all."

"What's so complicated about telling me that? Why are you crying?"

She smiled blearily. "I'm not crying."

He took her in his arms and kissed her. A desperate little shiver rippled through her, and she clung to him in a way she never had before, as if—this was a highly paranoid line of thinking, birthed of his own guilts with Helen, no doubt—as if she were saying good-bye.

"Hey," he whispered and pulled back to peer down at her. "It's all right." He smoothed a wisp of hair into its trembly pompadour.

"Don't make general statements."

"What's general? What d'you mean, general?"

Something snapped in her, and she jerked away from him, threw her weight to one hip. "Do you know you do that to me all the time? Answer a question with a question?"

Taylor felt unfairly attacked. And not because of her words, which were so unjust as to be ludicrous, but that she had just agreed to marry him as soon as possible and was acting as if it were nothing, nothing! She was like a too-expensive machine that worked perfectly for the mechanic yet always failed at the crucial moment. He saw himself shaking her until she was senseless.

"I don't understand you." His voice was quivering with anger. "Sometimes I don't understand you at all."

"I warned you this would happen."

"Come off that!"

His finger was aimed at her face as if he were a high school principal, and when he realized it he lowered his arm, turned helplessly away, then back. "I swear, Madelyn, if you don't level with me, I'm going to walk out that door and never look back."

She was such a picture of stunned misery—like some victim who had just crawled out of a wrecked automobile and hadn't figured out what had gone wrong or where the blood was coming from.

Taylor cursed himself. He took her in his arms against her

will. She was like an iron poker, and he forced her head down on his shoulder. "I didn't mean that." He rocked her. "Shh, tell me what's the matter. You can tell me anything, little one."

Norman's voice was moving back and forth in Madelyn's mind: a needle on a flawed recording. *Don't come back, come back, come back, come back* . . . She was used to fighting things with her own limited resources. But it was different now, wasn't it? She and Taylor were together: strength in numbers. Couldn't she trust blindly, for once in her life?

"It happened just after you left," she said and, sniffing, wiped her eyes with the backs of her hands.

Edwina was much too experienced a hostess ever to congratulate herself that things were going well at a party. That was the surest way to invite disaster. And tonight something—perhaps it was the sight of Madelyn Grey talking to Norman Bullard—had already set off a series of tiny alarms in her head, though nothing seemed to have come of it.

Conditioned reflex, she called her worry and went to check with the waiter on the pâté. When she returned to the ballroom, she came through the kitchen door.

If it had been just anyone striding across the dance floor, his hand trailing slightly behind him and clasped with that of a woman, Edwina would have forgotten about it. But her Taylor? With those wide, angry shoulders which she knew only too well spelled trouble?

Edwina took a grip on her nerves and scanned the room for sight of her husband. As she found him, Taylor walked up to Norman Bullard and said something. Madelyn Grey stood beside the two men, looking absolutely wretched and touching Taylor's arm. He brushed it aside as if she were a worrisome child.

A calamity was in the works. Edwina knew it in the way

some knew the weather. "Owen," she said, coming up to shake his arm, "do something."

Owen Prince was deep in contemplation of the two out-of-state checks in his breast pocket amounting to four hundred and fifty thousand dollars. He grudgingly focused his eyes upon his wife. "What's that? What're you all in a dither about now, Edwina?"

"That." Edwina indicated Norman Bullard with his back pressing against a distant wall and Taylor towering over him.

Owen pretended to study the scene, then said: "They're just talking. Everyone is talking."

"Oh, don't do that to me. I saw Norman talking to Miss Grey only a few minutes ago. And now Taylor . . ."

"For God's sake, Edwina, Taylor is thirty-five years old. If you're not ready to cut the apron strings, at least let him!"

Edwina gasped, not because she'd just been insulted—she was used to Owen's insults—but because of a growing silence. It promised to be one of those contagious pauses that precipitates disaster.

She lifted her skirt in her hands. "I'll be right back."

The governor's hand on Edwina's arm was like a wrench, biting into her tender flesh. Dumbfounded, Edwina stopped. Owen hadn't handled her like this since she'd threatened to walk out on him after Taylor had come to stay.

"Let it be," Owen commanded in a low, hard voice.

"Owen!"

"You heard me, Edwina."

Edwina had never openly crossed Owen. She didn't agree with most of what he did; he offended her with almost every breath that came out of his mouth, but she had married him, and he needed her. Edwina believed in paying her dues.

But she refused to pretend ignorance. "What have you done, Owen?"

He turned away and clapped the attorney general on the back as if she hadn't said a word. "Russell, how's it going, old boy, old boy?"

Laughing, Russell winked at Edwina over his shoulder. "Some kinda guy, isn't he, Edwina?"

"Yes," she said, smiling thinly. "Some kind of guy."

"Wonder what's wrong with Taylor Champion," Howard said to Diane as they danced by and noticed the newspaperman working his large hands, one within another. He was anxious for this to be done with. Diane was having him over to her place for the night. "He looks like he could knock that man's block off."

Diane peered back over her shoulder, then fluttered her ringed fingers. Wasn't it lucky that Bill was out of town this week? "A fight? At one of Edwina's parties? You've got to be kidding."

"You can't go in there, Wallace," Serina Prince said as Wallace thrust her hand off his arm and carefully balanced himself in the doorway. "You're drunk."

"It's a party," Wallace slurred and stepped into the room. "'Sides, I don't give a whit for bein' disinherited. That's what Father said he'd do if I didn't make an appearance. Ever'body's drunk. Look, even Taylor. God, he hates these things too. I'm in good comp'ny. Where's th' bar?"

Serina followed the direction of Wallace's beautiful brown eyes which she loved more than she despised those of his father. "No," she shook her head, "Taylor's not drunk. He's angry. We'd better get Edwina."

Generally, no one was better at carrying on a conversation while thinking about something else than Edwina was. Tonight, she simply didn't care. She moved near Howard

Page and Diane Leyman who were cooling off with a drink. From here she had a clear view of Taylor and Norman.

Diane smiled and waved the neckline of her dress to cool herself. "It's hot."

"Isn't it though?" Edwina agreed.

"But it's a lovely party. About time for the speech, huh?"

"About time, yes."

Diane exchanged a questioning look with Howard. What's with her?

"White House, here we come," Howard teased and spotted Wallace weaving somewhat unsteadily toward them. "Ah, Wallace. Have a drink."

"I jus' did."

Wallace laughed, bent to kiss his stepmother, and excused the smell of his breath with a giggle. Edwina's eyes were daggers, and Serina gave her a helpless shrug. Howard was immediately off on one of his tasteless drunk jokes, and Edwina didn't disappoint him by failing to make the proper response, but she never looked at him. And Serina didn't stop staring at Edwina; her mother-in-law was looking at the side of Madelyn Grey's head as if her life depended on it.

Please look up, Edwina was repeating in her mind. *Please look up, Miss Grey, and please, please don't make me out to be wrong about you.*

In high school Norman Bullard had been the short, unpopular class brain with the glasses who sold his notes to the desperate on the eve of class exams. He'd never done business with Taylor because Taylor ran around with the "bad boys" who never paid for anything and who still managed to get through somehow. He despised that crowd; they got all the girls and had all the fun. He suspected that they still did.

Then Taylor had latched onto Owen Prince, and Prince, fool that he was, had poured a small fortune into making him respectable. Now Taylor was coming down upon him. Madelyn Grey had talked, the bitch. He would make her pay.

"Well, Norman Bullard," Taylor drawled as he made a swift turnaround that placed him not only in front of Norman but positioned him so that Madelyn would be pressed safely against his side. He settled one hand upon her waist and extended the other in a handshake to Norman. "It's been a long time."

The last thing Norman wanted to do was shake hands with Champion. He forced himself. "Yes, indeed. A long time."

"Let's see." Taylor's hands remained firm and inflexible as he pondered. "It was that terrible convention in Lexington, wasn't it? Unless my memory fails me. Ah, now I remember. You and one of the girls from the hotel—"

Damn! Norman jerked back his hand, nursed it a moment. A pain was creeping into the bottom of his stomach: his ulcer. "I remember the convention perfectly. Well, it was nice seeing you again, Taylor, but as a matter of fact, I just got a high sign from the governor over there. He's really worked up about all this fund-raising, isn't he? Damned if he might not just pull it off. President Prince. Heh, heh."

To her shock, Madelyn felt herself pushed lightly into Norman's path. Before she could grasp what was happening, Taylor had positioned himself before the little man. In order to escape, Norman would have to go through both of them.

Madelyn watched Norman's expression change from irritation to dread.

"Now," Taylor said through his smile. "Now we're all comfy and cozy. I do like it when things are comfy and cozy, don't you, Norm? Perhaps you'll finish your little chat with Madelyn now.'' He flicked his eyes up and down, and his face darkened dangerously. "Before I break every bone in your sweet little face.''

Sweat began to drizzle from beneath Norman's toupee, but he didn't mop it away. "Taylor . . ." he said in his most reasonable tone, "there is no need to resort to barbarianism over this.''

"Barbarianism!'' Taylor threw back his head in a laugh, then looked back with a lethal gravity. "Well, Norm, you always did know how to get to the nitty gritty of things. What's the matter, Norm? You're not looking so well.''

Taylor leaned forward to adjust the lapels of Norman's tuxedo. "You really should take more care, Norm," he murmured and brushed the shoulders as if he were removing dandruff. "Owen likes for his top men to look the part.''

To Norman's horror, Taylor reached for his own handkerchief and blotted at the runnels of sweat streaming down Norman's temples and onto his neck. "You know what's the matter with you, Norm? You're sticky. Isn't that the word you threatened my future wife with? Sticky? There's only one cure when a person's sticky, Norm. You have to peel the skin off, just like you'd skin a polecat, y'know? Like *pain*, Norm. Really bad pain.''

Oh, Christ, Norman thought wildly. Future wife? Why hadn't Owen told him about this? Taylor had grown up on the streets. Street brawlers did unspeakable things to the human body.

"I was only obeying orders," he whimpered.

For the first time, Madelyn saw the true violence beneath Taylor's surface. His eyes were like two chips of slate. His lips were twisted with murderous fury, drawn back over his teeth as he lifted his hand. Madelyn knew that Taylor meant to bring the back of it brutally across Norman's face.

She flung herself against Taylor's back and wrapped her arms tightly, pressed her breasts hard, holding on with all her strength. "Please, Taylor," she begged. "Let it go. It'll come to nothing. Let it go."

The moment could have been a frozen time frame. Madelyn fixed Norman Bullard with a look that said: *Now your fate hangs in my balance, sir.*

Norman had no doubts about that. He was shaking all over. He felt toxic. He wished he'd never seen Owen Prince and never heard of Taylor Champion.

Taylor broke the spell by removing Madelyn without looking at her. "Get us some champagne, darling. Blackmail works up my thirst something awful."

"Taylor," she pleaded with him. "He won't do anything."

"Talk to me about Owen, Norm," Taylor was demanding quietly as he flicked a glance out at people who pretended they weren't gawking until the moment his back was turned. "I'm not going to hurt you." He paused. "Yet."

"You're jumping to conclusions."

"Don't lie to me, Norm. Did Owen tell you to use me as the pawn? Or was that something you worked out for yourself?"

"Taylor?" Madelyn persisted in her efforts. "Please?"

"Get us some champagne, darling," Taylor repeated, his voice like acid.

Madelyn didn't know what to do. Perhaps she shouldn't do anything: fate of the gods, just deserts. She turned away, and her eyes inadvertently flicked across the room and met those of Edwina Prince. So small that it almost didn't exist, Edwina signaled for Madelyn to act and act quickly. Another three seconds of this would bring the entire room to a standstill.

Madelyn glanced back at the situation, seeing some invisible fuse burning the last inch of its length. Without thinking about it, acting on sheer instinct, she stepped forward with her prettiest, most practiced smile and held out her skirt in a deep curtsy. She could have been one of those gracious Southern women living in this very house a century before.

"Mr. Bullard." Her voice was soft and lovely with charm. Everyone on that end of the room could hear. "They're playing a waltz. I've heard that you dance it divinely."

For some moments after that, Taylor stood watching the woman he'd asked to marry him. Her performance was so completely convincing as she glided about the floor, onlookers gave him a look of dour disappointment and went boredly on their way to bigger and better things.

Edwina slipped up behind Taylor's back. "Did you see that?" he asked without turning around. "Did you see what she did?"

"She's very special, Taylor."

"Tell me about it."

"Rare porcelain must be handled carefully."

Amazed, Taylor turned to meet the smile of his stepmother. "I don't have to go through all that rigamarole of explaining, do I?"

She laughed. "Have you and I ever had to do much explaining?"

Taylor pulled her into his arms and placed a kiss upon the top of her head. "Not very much, darling. Not very much." Except for Madelyn, he loved Edwina more than anyone alive. "I'm going to marry her, Edwina. She pleases me . . ."—he shook his head—"so much."

How often had she gotten out of bed when Taylor had cried out in his sleep? Edwina wondered. How often had she studied him when he wasn't aware and had seen that sadness creep about the edges of his mouth, the frightened, almost pathological mistrust in his eyes?

She drew him out onto the dance floor. She had taught him to dance too. "I think I can remember enough steps to keep up with you."

"You old fraud," he said, laughing. "I'm the only one who knows you for what you really are."

Edwina was glad Taylor was marrying Madelyn Grey. He needed her, more than he knew probably.

"What a trauma," she mused, "being understood by another human being. I don't know if I can stand it."

Taylor hardly heard her; his eyes kept sweeping the floor for Madelyn, and when they met, he smiled sheepishly. *Truce?* he said with a cock of his head.

It'll cost you, she said and let her smile reach her eyes. *How it'll cost you.*

"Now," Taylor demanded much later after he'd manfully done his duty to Edwina and several of her friends who had been lying in wait for him the moment the dance had ended, "tell me why you look so smug, Mrs. Champion-to-be."

The music had started again, and he'd ducked behind the peonies and the bottle rack and skirted the floor to find Madelyn standing at the edge of the band platform.

Whirling around, she laughed and let him catch her tightly in his arms. "It's called 'Saving Taylor's Hide.'"

"Tough hide?"

"I rather like it."

"You'd better. You're stuck with it. Now, back to where we were before we got so rudely interrupted."

His kiss came down upon her mouth with passionate fierceness, and Madelyn closed her eyes and reveled in the bliss of it. He wanted her and nothing was as sweet as his body's familiar urgency. She let her head drop back.

"Let's get out of here," he whispered against the side of her throat as he rained kisses there. "I can't wait for you. Let's go skinny dipping in the lake. Let's make love on the grass. In the water."

He lifted his head and looked at her with deeply burning eyes, pleading eyes. "Let's fly to Mexico. Tonight."

Adoring him, Madelyn held his scarred jaw in her palm. "Edwina would kill us. I vote for the lake."

Grinning, he swung her around. The final cadence of the music was striking.

"Well, well, well," drawled a bourbon-slurred voice. "The mystery guest has finally arrived."

"This is a bloody nightmare," Taylor said.

Chapter Eleven

W allace Prince's looks weren't a threat to anyone because no one could be that beautiful. The photograph published next to Madelyn's in the *Daily Times* hadn't come close to capturing him, and she doubted that any camera could. His eyes were soft and brown and filled with a vulnerability that he tried to offset with a mocking curve of his mouth. To complicate that, his clothes were a rebellion. A sultry silk shirt opened midway to his waist and was tucked into tight Italian-cut trousers. A gold chain nestled into a mat of fine brown curls. The rings upon his fingers were only microdots shy of vulgarity.

Coming into this room dressed as he was, as drunk as he was, was a bald statement: *I don't want to be here. One or the other of us should leave.* A statement to whom? Her? His father?

It was the moment everyone had been waiting for. When the ''twins'' finally came face to face. Madelyn's brain was a computer gone crazy: searching through hazy memories, juggling known facts, juxtapositioning them with intuitions and impressions and wondering, *Should I feel something for this man?*

Wallace was doing the same thing, and his long hands restlessly turned a glass between them. His brows drew together as he pondered.

"Wallace." Taylor pressed Madelyn's fingers in a reassurance that hurt more than it helped. "What's up?"

Wallace fleetingly lowered his eyes. "I'll spare you the embarrassment, dear brother," he murmured rakishly, "of not asking you the same question."

A muscle twitched angrily in Taylor's jaw. "Be careful, Wallace."

Unfortunately, the band had chosen this particular time to take its break, and in the interim silence Owen's voice could be heard all over the room. He lifted his head and saw what everyone else saw—the bright tension between Wallace and Madelyn.

Then, in the instant telepathy between father and son, Madelyn understood Wallace Prince. A lifetime of disappointed reaching out for Owen was in his look. Wallace's appearance tonight was an outcry against circumstances he could not control. He was more afraid of life than she was.

Owen's face turned an ugly shade of red.

"Cheers, Father." Lifting his glass, Wallace mockingly threw down the last swallow and bowed to Madelyn. "I would ask you to dance, Miss Grey, but I'm a bad risk tonight. I've disappointed my father, you see." He laughed too quickly. "I don't know why he's surprised. I disappoint everyone."

"I'll kill that boy," Owen was heard to mumble as he started elbowing people aside in his plow across the room. "With my bare hands."

"But I must congratulate you, Miss Grey"—Wallace touched his temple like some Shakespearean protagonist—

"on your superb sense of style. One poor girl actually had a nose job to make herself look like me. Can you imagine it' It was a total waste, of course. The Princes do have excellent noses, but we have so many less desirable traits, a you can see." He hiccoughed softly and asked like a puzzled child, "Miss Grey hasn't had a nose job, has she Taylor?"

Taylor could have gladly taken Wallace out behind the mansion and thrashed him within an inch of his life. He gripped his arm, hard. "Not here, my man. Not tonight.'

"What's the meaning of this?" Owen overpowered them all.

With a sardonic smirk, Wallace rolled his tongue around the inside of his cheek. "I don't think Miss Grey looks like me. Do you, Father?"

"For which we are all eternally grateful, Wallace.' Taylor threw his arm around the intoxicated twin and compelled him to follow. "Come along now. Easy does it This won't hurt a bit."

Owen promised himself that this was the last time Wallace would ever behave this way. Where in hell was Edwina? He gave a bewildered father's shrug to those nearest. "Beautiful children, aren't they? Makes you wish you were young again."

"Not that young, Governor."

Laughter.

Owen lifted both his big hands for a "Proclamation.' "Ladies and gentlemen. Your attention, please. Since we're all gathered here, we might as well pass the hat." He waved away the repartee and patted one of his pockets. "Seriously now, folks, I have the speech right here. Guaranteed to set your heart afire."

"And empty our pockets too?"

"Especially your pockets." Owen's laughter boomed. "But Edwina keeps me on the straight and narrow.

Owen,' she said when I was dressing, 'not on an empty stomach.' A true daughter of the South, my Edwina. A born First Lady."

Taylor had reached the door, and Madelyn was glancing over her shoulder, meaning to join him. From across the room another woman obviously had the same idea—a striking Castilian creature with stunning black hair and eyes the color of onyx. Serina Prince, and just as Madelyn would have fallen in step with her, Edwina's hand reached out and caught her own.

Please, her look begged Madelyn. *A moment.*

"I give you Edwina!" Owen thunderingly announced.

If she were nothing else, Edwina was a trooper. Startled, realizing that Owen had just dumped everything into her lap, she masked her irritation. She signaled the head waiter with a clap of her hands.

"We're so pleased you all could be with us this evening to lend your support," she said brightly. "And now"—here she bowed demurely—"dinner is served."

The waiters exchanged a look of sheer horror, and a frenzied scurrying commenced—partitions being slid back and doors thrown wide while the caterer went into acute hysteria.

"Every time I hire out for this gig something like this happens," he wailed.

"The waiters aren't complaining," hissed his assistant as he began jerking pans of rolls out of the warmer.

"And why should they? This'll put an extra ten dollars on their checks and leave me holding the bag."

The stir of getting everyone seated gave Edwina the opportunity to loop her arm through Madelyn's and walk her to the door. When they stepped into the corridor Taylor was making the turn by the three tall windows. Serina Prince was walking after them, her long skirt billowing out behind her like a crimson sail.

"You can catch up." Edwina flicked an anxious look t
the ballroom. "You won't be missing a thing in there excep
an hour of excruciating boredom. Believe me."

Madelyn smiled. "There are worse things than bore
dom."

"Wallace despises these affairs, but Owen has th
outdated hangup about family appearances. By midnig|
maybe Howard will be raising such a ruckus no one wi|
even remember that Wallace was here and gone."

Madelyn didn't reply.

"You know"—Edwina flicked her fingers at the disap
pearing trio—"when Taylor first came to this house,
thought it was about the most awful thing that eve
happened to me. I threw a fit, I can tell you. I let everyon
know I didn't marry Owen Prince to raise a teenager alon
with Wallace. What I really wanted to do was to sho\
everyone how a plain little Tennessee girl could steal a bi
Kentucky man's heart and have all the social accouterment
to show for it—jewels, clothes, servants. And then Taylⱺ
stole my heart."

"He has a way of doing that, doesn't he?"

"You really do love him, don't you?"

Flushing, Madelyn kept focused upon the place wher
Taylor had been. "Did he tell you?"

"I know Taylor too well to have to be told. He's als
very protective of what's his. There would've been rea
trouble tonight with Norman if you hadn't done what yo\
did, Madelyn. I don't suppose you'd tell me what Norma
said."

This was Madelyn's opportunity to get in her lick, enjo
a little revenge upon Norman, a luxury she hadn't bee
afforded with Ellwyn Muse. "Would it serve any purpose
It's over and done."

"But he did offend you, didn't he?"

"Mrs. Prince—"

"I wish you'd call me Edwina. And, Madelyn"—
Edwina grew more intense—"I'm not my husband. We're
two different people. Sometimes we're . . . very different."

Above everything, Edwina was a true hostess. "All
right, dear," she said. "I won't press you. But if anything
or anyone makes you feel unwelcome in this house, please
come to me."

Agreeing that she would, Madelyn heard herself asking
the question she realized she'd wanted to ask all along.
"Mrs. Prince, do you think Virginia Prince is my mother?"

Edwina didn't appear in the least shocked. "I've wondered that a dozen times since you first came here. I
honestly don't know. But if she is . . ."

From somewhere out of sight came laughter—Taylor's
rich mirth and that of Wallace, and a woman's higher
pitched giggle. Madelyn stared at the little eighteenth-
century table where she'd laid Owen's check down before
she'd walked out.

"You know, I came here that day for my mother," she
explained. "I had no idea it would ever come to this. But
one thing I know—if Abigail were able to say how she felt,
she would say she doesn't want anything that's not given
with a free heart. But she can't say that, Mrs. Prince. So
even though I started this mess, I have to say it for her. I'm
sorry. I should never have come here."

Edwina's fragile features misted. How many times had
she seen the same killing pride in Wallace? Today, in this
age when everyone was out for whatever they could get?

She impulsively cupped her hand about Madelyn's jaw.
"Taylor is very lucky, Madelyn. If you ever need a friend,
I'm here."

The servants of the Prince household were veterans,
prepared for any emergency. Tonight when Taylor kicked

open the door that led into the breakfast room, a uniforme
man and woman hurried to meet them.

"Everything's ready, Mr. Champion," the man sai
with an anxious bow. "Arlene has eggs and biscuit:
gallons of coffee and all the trimmings."

"Coffee first, Simon." Taylor glanced around to mak
sure Madelyn was bringing up the rear. "Wallace, fc
God's sake, if you must lean, will you kindly wait until
can get you into a chair?"

"I thought I was in one." Wallace gave a wounded sigh
"Sorry."

"This, darling," Taylor called back as Madelyn walke
through the door, "is the real Prince house."

He propelled Wallace in the direction of a chair an
introduced Serina. "Arlene and Simon make sure we'r
fed." An elegant dark-skinned woman with snapping eye
bowed her head at Madelyn. "And," he continued, "the
see that all hangovers are unhung, all appointments me
and all secrets are kept. This is the last and most importar
secret, Simon. Miss Grey and I are going to be married."

"*Taylor!*" choked Wallace.

"*Taylor!*" Serina whispered.

"Taylor," Madelyn said with much less enthusiasm, an
Simon narrowed his eyes for the slightest fragment of
second and said nothing.

"See?" Taylor kissed the top of Madelyn's head. "Sh
can't wait."

The breakfast room was of carved mahogany paneling
Twin chandeliers hung from a white ceiling with their bras
so expertly shined it looked wet. Twelve open-back Chip
pendale chairs sat around the table with priceless sati
seats. Beyond the glass doors was an extravagantly land
scaped terrace whose kidney-shaped pool sparkled lik
turquoise.

Serina hugged Madelyn's arm by way of congratulation:

nd said she had to look in on Clay because he was teething.
Taylor perched on a stool near the china cupboard and
pulled Madelyn back into his arms to growlingly nibble the
back of her neck.

"You're embarrassing Simon," she protested.

Laughing, he kept her imprisoned and murmured, "A
nun would embarrass Simon."

To Simon's mind, flirtation should be conducted in
private and then only if it were absolutely unavoidable. He
unloaded his cart of food: scrambled eggs, hot, buttered
biscuits, an assortment of jellies and jams, crisp bacon and
tiny smoked sausages, and on a side dish, sliced ham with
molasses. The coffee had already been poured. Wallace got
the first cup, and he stood with it to study Madelyn from
over its rim.

Was Wallace thinking the same thing she was? Madelyn
wondered. Are you my other self? Why don't I feel
something? Why haven't you triggered some long-buried
memory that would clear all this up?

Returning with two-year-old Clay, all sleeper-clad and
drowsy, Serina announced at the door, "Look who just had
to come."

She gestured to a small white-haired black woman who
carried herself with the dignity of one who has long since
accepted life on its own terms. "Cleo," Wallace said.

No one knew exactly how old Cleo Washington was. She
had been taken into the Prince household when Zedechiah,
Owen's father, owned seven hundred acres of prime Virginia farmland, and she'd been in her teens then. She'd nursed
Owen from the day he was born, and then the twins. It had
never occurred to Cleo, at least not in the last forty years,
that she wasn't as much a member of the family as Owen
himself.

With her back as straight as a reed, Cleo walked with the
aid of a brass-handled walking stick. Arthritis had twisted

her hands dreadfully, and she wore a shawl about he
shoulders, though it was a warm night—for her old creak
ing joints, she said.

"My stars, Cleo." Taylor lifted one of her hand
"You'll never get beautiful if you keep hours like this."

"I wuzn't beautiful when I wuz twenty, Taylor Champ
on, and I'm not about t'get prettier now. An' you shou
talk, with that face."

Taylor made his own expression as fierce as possible. H
walked the old woman toward the table. "Don't you kno
I'm a tough man, Cleo? You're supposed to watch your ste
around me."

"Yeah," Wallace glumly intoned. He dragged out a cha
and straddled it. "Ask Norm. Taylor's tough."

Norm was not a subject open for discussion, and Taylo
flashed his stepbrother a quick warning.

As Serina buckled Clay into his high chair, she said
"Have another cup of coffee, Wallace."

Cleo held up her pinky finger. "You're 'bout as tough a
this. An' I could still tan your hide."

"Cleo once gave me a choice between a lickin' and
woodpile," Taylor explained, laughing. He poured tw
cups of coffee and placed one in Madelyn's hands. "She'
never gotten over the fact that I chose the lickin'."

"What I've never forgiven myself for, is not givin' yo
the lickin' anyway."

Madelyn sipped and smilingly replaced her cup to it
saucer. She held it just above her waist with an unconsciou
grace. "My goodness, Taylor. What did you do?"

After thinking a moment, Taylor chuckled. "Beats th
hell outta me."

No one could remember, and Cleo ended the matter wit
a definitive thump of her stick and never saw the fond wink
exchanged over her head. "Well, I'm sure you deserve
it."

After she had finally settled like a fussing hen upon her nest, Cleo asked Simon to bring her a sweet roll with extra icing. She sat bolt upright in her chair, not allowing her back to touch the carved wood.

"Cleo has an outrageous sweet tooth," Serina whispered to Madelyn. "She goes to great lengths to pretend she doesn't. All the servants indulge her, and no one would dare tease her about it."

The old woman's eyes came to rest upon Madelyn, and so, Madelyn thought, did everyone else's. "Come here, child," she said and waved her forward. "You're th' one, aren't you? The one who claims t'be my bebe."

The breakfast room grew so quiet that the music seeped through the walls from the ballroom. Wallace was watching the scene as if the breath had ceased to move in and out of his body.

"Not claiming, really," Madelyn guardedly replied. "Trying to remember, yes."

"Come closer."

Moving nearer Cleo's knee, Madelyn surprised herself by stooping down to peer up at the wrinkled old face.

"Pretty, pretty eyes." Cleo smoothed back an escaping tendril of Madelyn's hair with her arthritic claw. "Used to brush my bebe's hair when she was little, yes I did. Brushed it 'til it looked like that dark molasses my daddy used t'make."

Madelyn asked the question that Cleo had obviously been brought into this room to answer. "Cleo, do you remember me?"

"Lawd, girl, I missed that child so much I could close my eyes an' bring her back in my mind." The black face crinkled, and Cleo shook her head. "Wouldn't it be easy for me t'say you wuz her?"

"Cleo," Wallace said sharply. "For God's sake, is she Waverly, or isn't she?"

"Patience, boy." Cleo shook her head at Wallace "Years—they change a person, inside. They change faces."

Madelyn didn't know if she'd failed the test or passed She was weary of games. She grasped one of the gnarled hands. "Would you know Virginia Prince?"

"Miss Virginia?" Cleo's nostrils dilated with some old and secret slight. "Miss Virginia had her own girl. 'Twas the babies for me. As diff'rent as night and day, they were. Him . . ." Sniffing, she nodded at Wallace. "Following Waverly around lak she was his mama. An' Waverly actin' lak she was a little princess. Spoiled rotten, my bebes wuz. I don't 'pologize for spoilin' my bebes."

The old woman seemed to drift off into her nostalgia, while Madelyn leaned back on her heels and visually conferred with Taylor. His support was an electric thing, as it had been during the interview at the exhibit. *I'm here*, his look said. *Go with your instincts*.

Drawing in a breath as she came to her feet, she walked to the scowling young man and said: "Wallace, is there anything about me you remember?"

Wallace's fingers were kneading the back of his neck, and he jerkily came to his feet. Madelyn's smile dwindled. Why was she doing this? They were two strangers.

"There's no need to go through this," Taylor said and walked up behind Madelyn. "Either of you. Wait for the records to come. A little more patience, Wallace."

"We've been patient," Wallace lashed out. "Fingerprints, footprints. It all comes back to the same thing, Taylor. I used to lie awake at night wishing Waverly was dead. And then I was grown, I couldn't hate a baby girl anymore. I didn't think about her after that. I've never been able to imagine Waverly grown. Yes, Madelyn could be Waverly. But she could be anyone."

Madelyn stared at Taylor in dumb amazement, then at Wallace. "Hated?"

"Easy, darling," Taylor said as he circled her waist, but she pulled free.

Her eyes swept around the room in fascinated misery. "Hated?"

Serina walked up behind her husband, touched the side of his handsome head. She knew better than anyone the scars left upon her husband. "Don't do this to yourself, honey."

Since Abigail's announcement, Madelyn had looked upon Waverly Prince as some kind of character out of a fairytale—spirited away by a once-glamorous mother, a tale of ill-fated romance. Never once had she thought of how it would feel to be the other twin, the unchosen one, the one who would always ask, "Why didn't she love me enough to take me too?"

Now Madelyn and Wallace were operating on some wavelength all their own. Twin or stranger, she placed both hands upon his shoulders. "I'm so sorry, Wallace. So very, very sorry."

Wallace struggled with his composure. "Everyone's been keeping score, you know. Adding up the twins to see if they matched. You? You'd be the twin with nothing who turned into everything. I'd be the twin with everything who turned into nothing."

What pain! Madelyn took one of his hands. "They said you were a pianist."

"Pianists are sissies, don't you know? I'm a lawyer."

"I should never have come here." Dropping Wallace's hand, Madelyn began moving heavily toward the door.

"You had every right to come here," Serina protested.

"What's she like?" Wallace called after Madelyn, a terrible desolation in his voice.

Madelyn turned, amazed at his question. "You think people who are hurt in here"—she touched her heart, meaning the soul—"aren't as disappointed because they're simpler. But Abigail always knew she wasn't right. It hurt her because she couldn't keep up. But she never lashed out.

She never wounded anyone deliberately. She wanted, more than anything I think, not to be blamed.''

So wrapped up were they all in the high drama, no one had been watching Clay, who had been toddling unsteadily about the room. Now he stumbled upon Madelyn's feet with a babyish cry. Madelyn swept him up into her arms, and as if his weeping were somehow for the tragedy of Wallace and herself, she comforted him with shushing sounds.

''Mama,'' he wailed as his dark brown eyes spilled their fountain of tears. ''Mama.''

Serina began getting up from the table.

''Poor baby,'' Madelyn crooned as Serina crossed the room for him. ''Mama's coming, see? Mama's coming. You're a Little Tom Tinker, aren't you? What a mama's boy you are.''

Blinking at this strange dark-eyed creature whose voice was musical and clear, Clay stuck his finger in his mouth and sniffed.

Madelyn giggled and began to sing the old nursery rhyme as she hugged him. ''Little Tom Tinker got burned with a clinker and he began to cry, 'Mama, Mama, what a poor fellow am I?' Is that you, hmm? Little Tom Tinker?''

The next moments were one of those small tender tableaus where women fuss over babies and make maternal sounds that no one ever practices and that don't include the menfolk at all. Wallace was too absorbed in his own brooding to notice, in any case. He didn't even pay attention to Taylor, who walked thoughtfully over to Cleo.

Bright tears were glistening in the old, half-blind eyes, and Taylor felt a strange vibration in the air. He touched one white curl and softly teased: ''What's the matter, old-timer?''

She looked up at him from beneath heavily wrinkled lids. ''De Lawd sabe us all.'' When Cleo was very disturbed she fell back into the heavy dialect she was born into.

"Cleo?" The stray bewilderments of this evening collected into a knot in the pit of Taylor's stomach. He locked his teeth. "Cleo, *tell* me."

"Listen t'mah bebe, Ah use t'say," she replied in a singsong chant. "Ah'd dress 'er up, mah bebe, an' show 'er off. 'Sing fer Miss Virginny,' Ah'd say. Show yo' mammy how you kin sing."

A muscle ticked at the edge of Taylor's mouth.

The old woman's back straightened taller. Her cane came down upon the floor with a snap. "I taught that song to Waverly Prince before she was two years old," she said.

By the time Taylor got Madelyn out of the breakfast room it was well past midnight. His repertoire of meaningless exits and clichés was exhausted. No one should jump to conclusions. Wait for the evidence. Careful, careful. His shirt was sticking to his back by the time he reached the corridor. His pants felt wrinkled and clammy, and his stomach was jumping.

"I need to think," he said as they rounded the exact same corner where they had met an eternity ago.

"We don't have to say good-bye to Edwina and the governor, do we? I want to go home."

The mention of the governor started the whole thing over again in Taylor's mind. Norman's treachery. Why? Why was Owen setting in motion such a campaign against Madelyn? What was he afraid of? Madelyn had to be his daughter and Owen had to know it. It was the money. Or the talk at campaign time. Or both.

"We don't have to say good-bye to anyone," he said and grabbed her arm. "Let's go out through the garage instead."

She seemed unable to keep walking. She clutched at him. "I'm Waverly, aren't I? Owen Prince is my father. I'm Waverly Prince."

"We don't know that."

"Wallace thinks so. Did you see his face?"

"This isn't adding up."

"Cleo thinks so."

"I don't want you hurt, Madelyn."

"That miserable little creep Norman."

"Norman's history."

"I never really believed it. With all the talk, I never believed it."

They avoided the front of the mansion by way of the east tower. On the ground floor was another kitchen, much more elaborate because this side of the house was where Owen and Edwina lived. Owen conducted much of his off-duty politics from this wing. Even Wallace hesitated to invade its sanctum. Everything was dark. Only a small lamp upon a table had been turned on.

Taylor drew Madelyn quickly along, and then he suddenly came to a halt. He twisted his head around, searching. "What's that?"

"What's what?"

"That smell."

Madelyn took a deep breath and crinkled her nose. "Smoke?"

"Something's on fire!"

The looks they exchanged were horrified, and Madelyn rushed along the doors flanking the lift. "Here!" she exclaimed, waving frantically.

The door was locked, and Taylor didn't hesitate. "Give me a hairpin."

"Taylor?"

"Quickly, quickly!"

He picked the lock in less than a minute, and the door banged back on its hinges as Taylor charged into the darkness and flooded the place with light. The room was not on fire; it never had been.

It was a paneled, draped, and carpeted office surrounded

by built-in bookcases filled with leather-bound lawbooks. The furnishings were all antiques including the great Jacobean desk and executive chair. Antique mirrors were framed with heavy brass. Console tables bore priceless vases and silver appointments.

"Owen knows how to live," she murmured grudgingly.

"Owen knows how to spend money."

"There." She pointed to the wastebasket beside the desk.

Taylor peered into the now-empty metal container. The ashes were still warm. There was a tightening at the back of his neck where his hair was standing up.

"Let's go." A chill crept up the backs of her legs. "This scares me."

"We're not breaking and entering."

"We weren't invited."

If it hadn't been for Norman Bullard's charade, Taylor wouldn't have been so quick to suspect Owen of skullduggery. But something was breaking up. It involved him and most certainly involved Madelyn. He drew open the bottom drawer where Owen kept a series of personal files. Stooping to one knee and resting on the heel of his shoe, he flipped through the labled tabs. He knew these files from memory. Many of them he'd compiled himself.

Madelyn leaned over his shoulder as he pulled out the file on Virginia Prince and opened it. The contents were about the same as he had at the paper. Except that here Owen had his old marriage license, Virginia's college diploma, some health information.

"Are her fingerprints in here?" she asked.

"Fingerprints aren't on birth certificates."

"Well, let me see it anyway."

Taylor turned over several items and came to the end of the file. "It's not here."

Feeling a dark premonition, Taylor replaced the file and

pulled out the one of Waverly Prince. Owen had misplaced the records, he'd said. He'd misplaced a lot of things; the file was empty.

He took her out through the garage, and when he opened a door and drew her out onto the lawn where he'd parked, his face was hard and set. "I want you to take the Mitsubishi and go home. Here're the keys. Go to the boat and wait for me."

Madelyn shook her head. "You can't confront the governor with this, Taylor. Come with me now."

"I'll get Wallace's car and be along."

"What're you going to say?"

"I'm not sure yet."

"Even if he destroyed his files completely, they're his. It's hardly illegal."

"What Norman did was illegal."

"I have a few questions about Norman." She wrapped her arms around him. "I'm coming with you, Taylor." She smiled. "We're a team now, remember? Mr. and Mrs. Champion?"

They reentered the mansion through the front because Taylor said he wanted to find the butler. When he did, he scribbled a message on the back of a card and handed it to him. "Give this to the governor, Paul."

"Oh, you'll find him in the library, sir," Paul replied, nodded to the door down the corridor. "He's been making some telephone calls, I believe."

Taylor returned the card to his pocket. "I'll catch him there."

"Very good, sir."

The fault wasn't Paul's and it wasn't Taylor's; it wasn't even Owen's. When Taylor pushed the door it opened without a sound. He glanced at the paleness of Madelyn's face and said, "Owen?"

"Hell, I tried scaring her!" Owen blurted. "It's your ball now. You're going to have to get rid of the records.

Change them. Use some of that money of yours. I've kept up my end.''

Taylor thought of going out and coming in again. He thought he should cough to make his presence known. But he didn't do anything except look at Madelyn. The silence was so deadly that they could hear the ticking of the little French clock on the mantel. Madelyn shook her head hard and grabbed at his hand.

He held a finger to his lips.

''Well, then,'' Owen went on to say, ''if I lose the nomination over this, you'll be leaving Washington too, John. I'll tell you that.''

Alarms were going off inside Taylor's head. There was no doubt as to what records Owen was worried about, but why would someone in Washington be affected by all this? What could make ripples all the way to someone in Washington?

Catching and holding Madelyn's eyes, Taylor took a deep breath and pushed open the door with a clatter, chattering as he did. ''I could have done with the vocalist, but otherwise—''

Owen was sitting upright in his chair, his brows at high peak and a palm covering the receiver. A thin sheen of sweat glistened upon his forehead and over the folds of his neck.

''Oh,'' Taylor said with a belated smile. ''Sorry, Owen. Paul said you were here, and we . . . go on and finish. We'll wait.''

''Talk to you later,'' Owen mumbled into the receiver and hung up. He leaned back in his chair and let his hands come to rest over his belly. ''Well, Taylor, I figured you'd have gone home to have your own little party by now.''

With a scald of resentment, Madelyn pulled her hand from Taylor's and stepped behind a chair.

The governor twisted his mouth and surveyed her agitated stance. ''Have a seat, young lady.''

She shook her head, and Owen groped about on his desk for a cigar. Lighting it, he asked Taylor through the cloud of smoke, "Serina get Wallace to bed okay?"

"Wallace doesn't know how to reach you, Owen," Taylor said calmly. "He tries and tries. It's not maliciousness on his part. Just inadequacy. You were awfully hard."

"Wallace is weak. I don't like weakness, Taylor. That's why you and I have always gotten along."

There is weakness, Madelyn wanted to shout at the pompous man, and there is sensitivity! You wouldn't know sensitivity if it slapped your face!

Taylor considered his fingernails for a moment. He looked up sharply. "I won't pussyfoot around, Owen. I came to talk about Norman Bullard."

Though he wasn't showing it, Owen was feeling the sadness of one who's succeeded too well at what he has set out to do. He'd wanted Taylor to overcome his background. Well, now he had, and the ideals that Owen had paid for out of his own pocket were putting him beneath a microscope.

Swiveling in his chair, Owen reached into a small pantry and removed a bottle. He spun off the cap and sloshed gin into a glass. Rising, he walked around the desk and braced himself against the top. The toes of his shoes lined up with the toes of Taylor's.

"Go home, Taylor," he ordered emphatically. "Forget Norman and go home."

"Screw it, Owen."

The tossed liquor splattered across Taylor's face and burned his eyes so badly that for a moment he thought he'd been blinded.

"Taylor!" cried Madelyn and rushed to him, her face blazing wrath as she pulled him, stumbling, toward the divan. But fury was shooting through Taylor. He swiped at his eyes with the tops of his hands and he shoved her aside. He saw his fist burying into the soft folds of Owen's belly. He started toward the governor.

Owen dropped the glass and waved Taylor toward him. "Come on, boy!" he shouted. "Your guts are twistin' you want t'do it so bad. Come on, big shot. I'll beat you to a bloody pulp like I did once before!"

Taylor threw back his shoulders and took a hard, struggling breath. His hands were white-knuckled with fury. "You pull a stunt like Norman again, and I'll have a judicial committee breathing down your neck, so help me God. I'll crucify you in the press!"

"Remember where you came from, you two-bit street punk!"

"Don't make me choose between you and her, Owen."

"You already have!"

The door slammed hard. Pale as a sheet, trembling, Edwina leaned back against it. She could see the toil of these two men as clearly as if it were emblazoned upon their foreheads—not just a conflict between father and son, but a struggle between men for the rights of men. Madelyn was staring with open-mouthed and fascinated horror.

"I could hear you two at the front door," Edwina hissed and placed her palms together. "What's going on here?"

Only in the presence of Edwina could Owen feel truly damned. Even Taylor and his affected principles could not bare him to the bone the way she could with a look. He stormed around the desk and poured himself another drink and threw it down.

"He's going to marry that girl," he said over his shoulder. "He's going to marry her."

"Good," Edwina snapped. "Taylor's of age, Owen. He can do what he likes."

In his mind, Taylor saw his debts to Owen. There came a time when debts had to be marked paid. But what then? What would Owen do without someone to follow along behind him, making everything work?

Repairing his face and smoothing his hair, Taylor walked where Madelyn stood in shock. He placed his arm about her shoulders and kissed her forehead. "I'm not up to this," he told Edwina baldly. "I can't take any more of the head games. I can't take Norman Bullard."

When he started walking to the door Edwina saw the end of something special. She didn't have to ask what Norman had done. She knew Owen. She took a step toward her husband, flabbergasted. "You're not going to just let him go, Owen. He's your son, for heaven's sake."

Owen refused to look up. He sloshed more gin into the glass. "He is a man who once lived in this house. A disloyal traitor."

Edwina's small foot came down on the floor. "Stop this, Taylor Champion. You can't leave this way."

For a brief second Taylor wondered if something couldn't be salvaged. Edwina was his mother. She was his friend. But Madelyn was his love. "Ask him if Madelyn is his daughter, Edwina. Ask him if Madelyn is Waverly Prince."

Spinning, Owen pointed his finger as if he were taking aim with a gun. "You can't prove that."

"I will eventually get those records replaced."

A leer twisted Owen's face. "I wouldn't put any money on that."

Taylor's oath ripped through the room, and Madelyn circled his waist and pulled at him. "It's all right, Taylor. Come on. Let's go home."

Edwina was pleading. "Don't destroy something here, Owen. Taylor has stood by you, and you've stood by him."

"Is it the money, Owen?" Taylor interrupted Edwina when he reached the door. "Is it Abigail Grey lying in that hospital? Is it the money?"

As Owen slammed the glass down on the table, rage poured out of him. "Don't you look down your superior nose at me, Taylor Champion. You'd be sitting in some cell if it weren't for me, and you know it. I've given you the best, and no one would've done that. I've raised Wallace when I didn't have to, and I—"

So that was it! The charade was up. After twenty-two years it was up, and it all flashed across the panorama of Taylor's mind: Wallace and Waverly were not Owen's children. All of this mess was because Owen didn't want Wallace's paternity known.

He licked his lips, then wiped across them with a hand. "I could have understood that, Owen," he said more gently. "Madelyn could have understood that."

Owen didn't even reply. He waved Taylor out of the room. But Taylor gazed down at Madelyn and prayed that she could have compassion for a man who wanted something so badly that he acted like a fool.

Madelyn's concern was no longer for herself. "Poor Wallace."

"Yes," Edwina said. "Poor Wallace."

When Edwina went to her husband and put her arms around him, Taylor shook his head. Men: in their hour of grievous pain, who did they turn to but their women? At the door he looked back. "Who is Wallace's father, Owen?" he asked. "And Waverly's?"

Owen looked like a battered army tank at his desk. "I will never tell you, Taylor. Marry the girl. We are, for what it's worth, still a family."

And as Taylor and Madelyn walked through the door and into the hall, Edwina moved behind Owen's chair. He sat so silent and still. Had she ever loved him? she wondered as she stroked the thinning hair.

"Can you tell me, Owen?" she asked.

He sighed in defeat. "Wallace's father is very big in Washington. We were friends when Virginia got pregnant. He was married. He paid me a great deal of money to marry her, to raise the children. Then, when Virginia left and took Waverly it seemed like some kind of bizarre justice. There was the money Wallace's father gave me, and there was Virginia's."

Owen leaned back in his chair and dragged his thick

fingers through his hair. "Don't judge me, Edwina. Taylor and Wallace have been my penance. I've appeased my conscience, and by damn I've paid my dues. Virginia made my life hell on earth. I don't want to find her. I don't want to ever hear of her."

Edwina poured herself a drink after that and walked to the window and stared at the moon-chased lawn. Without looking back, she said: "This may very well cost you the nomination. You know that, don't you?"

Closing his eyes, Owen let out his breath. He knew, he knew.

Chapter Twelve

The windows at the dock reflected Taylor's headlights like so many eyes flying open to see who was creeping home at this ungodly hour. Madelyn was in great need of reassurance, and she rolled down her window to hear the familiar creak and strain of the old dock, and the steady chop, chop, chop of the waves against the hulls.

Something in Taylor's life had ended tonight, and when she turned, put her hands on his shoulders, and searched along the column of his neck, he leaned toward her in his own silent need. She fastened her mouth to his and traced the lines of their joining with her fingertips.

"I don't want you to be alone tonight," she whispered.

Nodding, he followed her inside the boat. He was already dragging at his tie when she shut the door, and she placed it on the arm of a chair and fetched them glasses of chilled wine.

Over her shoulder, she said: "Don't feel sorry about

grieving over Owen, Taylor. It takes a whole man to be hurt.''

Taylor had been undoing his cufflinks, and when she brushed his hand aside and unfastened them herself, he slumped back in the chair, accepting her need to care. He caught at her hands, pulling her eyes to his face.

"I need to hear you say it," he said on a hoarse, torn breath. "Do you love me? Would you still hide parts of me away?"

"Oh, Taylor." The one thing she could do well was love him. "I know I could live without you. People can do anything. But I wouldn't want to. Everything I do—when I work and when I look at the river—you're in my mind. Every hour carries its special thought of you. I have never loved, nor will I ever love again, the way I love you."

He set down his glass with a sigh, and Madelyn trembled with desire, not to make love for the thrill but for the closeness. She didn't know if it was the right thing for him, and she got up and put a tape in the machine. The music was soft and restrained, not adding to the mood or detracting from it. The wind from off the river billowed out the curtains—cool, promising.

She bent over his head and kissed him upside-down, and they exchanged gentle, passionless touches.

"Don't ever . . . don't ever . . ." He cupped her face. He could hardly say the words.

"I will never leave you," she whispered against his cheek. "I'm not Helen. I'm not even the woman I was. Because of you I'm not afraid of the days, Taylor. Life is something . . . to be lived. Do you still want to marry me?"

He grinned. "Do you have to ask?"

Laughing, she said, "Can my wedding present be late?''

"Not if it's what I think it is."

"Not that," she said and came to sit at his feet. She placed her chin on his knee. "I want to do the auction,

Taylor. I want to . . ." She hesitated thoughtfully. "I want to do it for you, for the paper, because it's been kind to me. For the orphans too, of course, and for myself. I want to put Ellwyn Muse behind me."

She rose up on her knees and leaned over him. He looked as if he were in pain. He brought his hand up to cover his face. Letting out his breath, he said, "Oh, girl, when you give a man a wedding present, you really give one, don't you?"

Though Taylor wasn't sexually aroused, Madelyn's yearning fingers skimmed over him as lightly and as fragilely as lace. She took off his shirt and his shoes and socks, loosened his trousers. She rubbed his toes, and took down her hair so that it spilled onto his lap. Kneeling between his legs, she reached up to kiss his mouth. His eyes were closed, and she caressed his forehead and cheeks, the scar on his jaw. As she lingered at his nipples, the first stirrings cut through his haze of pain.

"Do you want me to stop?" she whispered.

He groaned. "Only if I die."

There was no pressure for anything. What happened, happened. And she liked Taylor's slowness for desire. It gave her the chance to touch him, to hold and taste him and know that it was her kiss and her eagerness that had the power of magic. She touched him everywhere. She adored him in every way she knew.

"I do love you," he whispered and took her hands and taught her the finest sensations of himself.

Then it was as if he feared to let a moment or sensation escape him, as if she, like Owen, might dissolve without warning. He led her to bed. And still Madelyn fashioned a scenario of her own choosing. She undressed with the finesse of a woman who had loved many times and many ways, and the charming irony was that she had not; everything she knew he had taught her.

He lay on her bed and studied her unhurriedly—her

small, white breasts that betrayed her emotions as surely as a blush, the soft curls that were a mystery below her white belly. And when she gracefully settled herself across his waist he clasped the backs of her legs and pulled her higher. And higher, until his caress of her was almost a thing of reverence.

With a great sigh, Madelyn's eyes closed and her head went back. She repeated his name like an incantation when his hands moved over her belly to the anxious tenderness of her nipples. Both of them became lost for a time. Outside, the monotony of the breaking waves was like a narcotic. Everything was turning inward upon its center. Even Madelyn's moan was a kind of wonder to her own ears, and she made herself accessible in ways that she had not dreamed of.

"Don't ever let me go," she whispered when he came up into her like a sword seeking the finality of its sheath. Her arms wrapped like a vise about his neck. "Don't ever let me go."

They were married on the first day of September, a Tuesday, at dusk. Wallace was Taylor's best man, and Pearl stood beside Madelyn in her new georgette gown as matron of honor. Edwina and Owen attended, and a few other close friends.

Madelyn had never been more lovely in her long ivory gown, Taylor thought. Its elegance was its simplicity: rows of tiny pleats streaming from waist to floor and a wide-brimmed hat. She had caught her hair straight back from her forehead so that her brown eyes seemed to fill her face. She didn't take her eyes off him through the short ceremony, and when he said, "I will," he lifted her hands and kissed them.

His wedding gift to her was a braided necklace of dozens and dozens of tiny pearls. He had teased her, saying if she would forgo all the nonsense about the groom not seeing the bride on her wedding day, he would give her a bauble. She'd stood in the middle of the floor weeping after he fastened it about her throat. Then they had driven to see Abigail.

"When the doctor thinks she's recovered from this last setback," he told her, "I want to bring your mother home."

The thought was staggering to her. "How would we manage?"

"I thought we could get her a live-in nurse. They could live on the boat. It was her home for all those years. Maybe she'd get better being around the old familiar things."

Madelyn had to cry again at that, of course, and he said her tears would run into the Ohio River and then they'd have to filter it at Louisville too.

The honeymoon went on for months. Madelyn was deliriously happy. They lived around the workmen at the country house, and as it neared completion so did her work for the auction. Christine had publicized the orphanage charity out of all proportion, and Taylor gave her free reign.

On the day after Thanksgiving, when the ground was shin-deep in leaves and the whole countryside was preparing for winter, Christine arrived to crate and transfer all the paintings. She came dressed in jeans and boots and directed things like a general.

"You keep changing on me, Madelyn," Christine declared as she stood with feet astride, one fist braced at her waist, a clipboard in the other. She was studying a whole row of acrylic nature scenes that Taylor had meticulously framed for her. "You're so prolific."

"Picasso did five paintings a day. That's prolific." Madelyn was critically studying her work. She was never satisfied. "Anyway, I've been saving up."

Now Madelyn's workspace consisted of two huge rooms whose partitions Taylor had removed and replaced with white square pillars. Everything had been gutted and painted white. The rooms spanned the house from east to west, and the outer walls had been replaced completely with glass.

Christine entered the last items on her inventory: two huge surrealistic works. "Well, these are fantastic. You can see something different every time you look at them."

"You're no critic."

"I know what I like." Christine waved for the workmen to crate the paintings. "Ellwyn will be at the auction, Madelyn. I had to invite him, but I let him know that we wouldn't be disappointed if he didn't show."

"I'll manage."

"Well, tell the bastard for me what he can do to himself."

Laughing, Madelyn wondered if Taylor ever compared the two of them. She wasn't in the slightest jealous of Christine; she had turned out to be one of her best and most reliable friends.

She motioned for her to follow to the kitchen. "You're so practical, Christine."

Moaning, Christine said: "I'm a bitch. Don't pretend otherwise."

"Bitches are okay." Madelyn laughed. "Maybe I'll become one."

"Take a course. You'll love it."

"I could do a feature for a magazine. 'How I Got My Degree in Bitchiness and Couldn't Find a Job.'"

"All the good jobs are already taken," howled Christine.

Tears were running out of Madelyn's eyes. "Oh, damn. I hate those unemployment lines."

Madelyn was in her working garb: one of Taylor's old shirts and her spattered jeans. Now she wiped her eyes with the tails, while Christine plopped down on a bar stool.

"Will you stay for lunch?" she said. "Taylor's coming home. We're having sandwiches. He hates sandwiches."

Christine went into another fit of laughter. "See? Your degree wasn't for nothing."

They laughed until they couldn't anymore. Sniffing, repairing her hair, Christine said, "The guys at the paper are making father jokes. Have you and Taylor decided to have a baby?"

"He's just talking." Sobering, Madelyn opened the refrigerator. "But I did catch him looking at my calendar the other day with a strange calculating look in his eyes. How on earth did you manage to snag The Arbor House for the auction?"

The blonde was arranging cold cuts from the refrigerator. "Promised them fifteen percent."

"That would do it."

Outside the glass doors of the kitchen they could see the movers loading the carefully packed crates onto the truck. Madelyn stood holding a head of lettuce as if it were an offering. "You really think this will make money?"

"You tend to the art, Madelyn," was Christine's unflurried reply. "Let me worry about the money."

Madelyn didn't say anything to that. If this thing were a bust, Ellwyn Muse would devour her like a sack lunch.

Besides being advertised in both newspapers, four hundred private invitations to the auction went out from the *Daily Times*. It was a gala afternoon, and the orphanage did its own advertising, part of it in *The Register*. Madelyn didn't get her first attack of nerves until Taylor pulled up in the huge parking lot outside the Arbor House. Everywhere she looked were cars; cars and more cars, a veritable ocean of cars.

"Well, I'll be damned," Taylor said.

Madelyn felt her jaw sag in disbelief. "What else is happening here today?"

"Nothing."

Taylor waved to the parking valet that they would go somewhere else to park. "It's really sad when the lady of the hour can't even get a parking slot."

"Oh, God," she groaned and imagined an Ellwyn Muse getting out of every one of those cars. "Taylor, I'm going to faint."

He put on the brakes, blue eyes narrowed with a half-tease. "You're pregnant," he said and arched one brow.

"That isn't funny."

"Hmm. I thought you said Ellwyn Muse didn't bother you a thimble's worth anymore."

"I lied. I want to go home."

"Well, scratch that."

"I'll embarrass you."

He curled one side of his mouth. "It won't be the first time."

Every day Taylor fell more in love with her, with every sweet, tough, shy, moody, elated, depressed, effervescent particle of her. And now he smiled. Life was too good these days. He was happy. It was dangerous to be so happy.

The Arbor House was the only really elite auction house in town. With its conservative marble exterior and brass-trimmed lights, it could have passed for a museum. The loading dock was always busy, bringing in everything from paintings that sold in six figures to antiques that someone's grandmother had left in her will for charity. The plush auditorium held four hundred people without opening up the wings. Many famous faces had been seen there—rich socialites coming to spend their money, and collectors conducting serious buying.

"I thought you'd never get here!" Christine said as she hurried across the room and showed them where their seats were. "Absolutely everyone is here, darlings, and a few we didn't count on. It's drawn people from as far away as

Florida and one collector from Los Angeles who heard about it from a friend.''

Madelyn made a sound that could have been taken any number of ways, and Taylor grinned. "She's pregnant.''

"Madelyn!" Christine reached for her in awe.

"Don't listen to him." Madelyn waved away Taylor's joke and pecked her on the cheek. "I'm terrified. Where's the ladies' room?''

Christine bridled and looked at Taylor. "I thought she said Ellwyn Muse didn't bother her a thimble's worth anymore.''

Taylor grimaced. "Madelyn tends to dishonesty.''

"Well, forget Ellwyn. He's been on his best behavior ever since he got here. As a matter of fact, I think he's nervous. He's trying to impress people like crazy. His assistant is with him. He's after his job, Randy said.''

"Wonderful," Madelyn said with keen malice. "Does he need any help?''

The auction lasted nearly four hours. Madelyn, unable to stand the pressure, spent most of her time in the ladies' room or touring the building with one of the young woman employees, who took mercy on her and showed her the storage room goodies. When she did finally take a seat at the very rear of the auditorium, Randy Morrison strolled over and murmured to Madelyn and Taylor as he squatted behind them and leaned between their chairs.

"Have you seen him?" he asked.

Taylor leaned back to whisper. "Seen who?''

Randy gave a discreet jut of his chin. "Over there. The young guy with the bald spot and the pipe. Andy Reasen. We had lunch the other day. He's been dogging Muse's heels just waiting for the moment to make his move.''

Taylor laughed. "He doesn't look too dangerous to me. Rather reminds me of another hungry young man.''

"Well," Randy retorted grinning, "he's smarter than I

am. But Madelyn said the first time she ever saw me that my name might someday wind up on your door.''

With a pretended astonishment, Taylor reared back to scowl at his new wife. ''Did you say that?''

''What did I know?'' She craned to get a look at Andy Reasen over Taylor's shoulder and privately wished him luck.

Chuckling, Randy stood to go. ''Christine said to tell you we've got one hundred seventy-five so far.''

Unable to believe it, Madelyn gaped at the reporter. ''But that's terrible. Only a hundred and seventy-five dollars? Half the stuff is sold already.''

''Terrible?'' Randy grinned. ''A hundred and seventy-five thousand is terrible?''

Madelyn locked wide, dazed eyes with Taylor and mimed the figure.

But the sum total was over two hundred and thirty thousand dollars. Somewhere around the two hundred mark, Madelyn stopped feeling anything. The figures the auctioneer called out were gibberish. Her ears popped. How was this possible?—she, the one who'd never quite fit, the one who'd never quite caught on. She had done this with her 'strangely boring, contemptible' work. Swiveling in her chair, she looked Ellywn Muse straight in the eye.

Ellwyn would have rather done most anything than attend this auction. But to refuse, or to even send Reasen to sub for him, would be an admission that he'd been wrong. How had Madelyn Grey been capable of this? How had he made such a mistake with her? She hadn't looked like a success; she hadn't said the words or given off the air.

But she was always there, year after year, so damned quiet and so damned independent. And then those portraits she'd done for what's-his-name had started cropping up, buyers coming to him to get an opinion of how good he thought they were.

Finally this. He hated her. She made him want to throw up. He could go anywhere and in any company and take credit for a dozen brilliantly launched careers. He'd been involved with anything that had ever done well in this town. Now his editor-in-chief had given him an assistant to cover the bases he'd missed: i.e., Madelyn Grey!

By now the buyers had thinned out and the only ones remaining in the auditorium were a few press stragglers, the employees of the house, and those *Daily Times* staff members who had worked the auction. Ellwyn was preparing to go when he unavoidably walked right into Madelyn and Taylor.

"Miss Grey." Ellwyn drew a mask over his hatred and nodded across the space that separated them.

Madelyn took a second look in surprise, aware of Taylor moving protectively near her right elbow. It was the first time she and Ellwyn had spoken since the fateful interview.

"My name is Champion now, Mr. Muse," she answered with cool politeness as a thrill spread over her skin. Some things never changed, did they? A shell-shocked person jumping at a backfire.

"I thought you might still go by Grey. As a professional name, naturally. Hello, Taylor."

Taylor extended his hand with a warning lurking behind his blue eyes. "Everything going okay with you?"

"Oh, yes." Ellwyn's teeth glinted beneath his beautiful mustache. "Very well indeed. And you?"

"Fine." Taylor retracted his hand and adjusted a cuff. "Just fine."

"That's good." Ellwyn glanced about the room to see if he could find something to extricate himself from this encounter. "Well, I see some of the art students motioning to me. I suppose I must see what petty little problems they have today."

Vulture! Madelyn wanted to shout. She hugged Taylor's

arm. When they moved on to get a glass of champagne, she muttered under her breath, "He wouldn't admit he was wrong about me if someone threatened to burn him at the stake."

Taylor clicked his glass to hers. "He knows he's acted like an ass."

"If he could find just one thing he could fault today, it would be all over tomorrow's paper. 'We found Miss Grey's work to be tediously repetitious.' The man's a menace!"

"You're telling the wrong person, sweetheart."

"You think I should tell him?"

"Do you?"

"It's not my way to be a screamer, Taylor."

He grinned, hugged her. "Revenge takes longer when you don't scream, but it's always sweeter."

Madelyn lifted her brows and tilted her head in a coy prettiness. "Why, Taylor, you sly old fox."

"Which is why I've outwitted the hunters, my dear."

Madelyn felt Muse's stare drilling into her back. Two years he'd taken out of her life because of his cruelties. Why couldn't she let it go? She was coming into her own now. Without him. Let it be enough.

When all the compliments had been given, all the smiles smiled, she was glad. Taylor, sensing her drained exhaustion, said he was taking her home. Madelyn waved good-bye to Christine, and saw that Ellwyn and a number of press people were in the process of leaving too. They blocked the door. Ellwyn was laughing, protesting someone's statement about surrealistic beginnings.

"Wrong, wrong, wrong." He finger-combed his blond hair and said with his usual pompous and condescending authority, "Goya, you nimcompoop, without a doubt. Don't you do your homework?"

His tone was so unforgivably haughty, so embarrassingly supercilious, that Madelyn turned to see who had triggered such insolence. Andy Reasen, and he was flushed and chagrined. He removed his pipe and turned away.

Madelyn felt the old fury rising in her. "I'm afraid you're wrong, Mr. Muse." Her voice cut across the room like a machete.

Ellwyn turned as if he couldn't believe his ears, and so did everyone else who remained in the room. Taylor, sensing a rising strength in Madelyn—what she would not do for herself she would do for someone else—stepped back. This was something he wouldn't have missed for all the money in the world.

"I beg your pardon?" Ellwyn said and turned slightly blue around his mouth.

From across the room, Christine came to stand next to Taylor. "Stop this, Taylor. If you don't, I will."

Taylor grabbed Christine. "Leave her alone."

"He'll slaughter her."

"Wait."

At this moment, Madelyn's face was radiant, triumphant. "Freud influenced the surrealists," she said with deadly calm. "Writers like Lautreamont and Breton, even philosophers like Trotsky. But not Goya."

Good Lord! thought Taylor. Hang in there, girl.

It took a moment for Ellwyn to realize that the little brown wren Madelyn Grey was coming down upon him in the presence of his peers like a falcon.

"W-Well," he stammered. "Of course Freud. But Goya—"

"The surrealists, Mr. Muse, deliberately estranged themselves from the art of the past," Madelyn told him. "Mr. Reasen is correct."

"I would say it's obscure at best." Ellwyn was sweating. Andy Reasen was grinning.

Madelyn felt her stomach rebelling. Sweat was collecting on her back and beginning to dampen the waist of her dress. *Be careful,* she told herself. *Talk slowly and keep your head*

*up. But do it now, for Andy Reasen, for yourself and for all
the corpses Muse has strewn along the way.*

"That's because you're not an artist, Mr. Muse," she
said with sterling clarity. "You're only a critic."

Yahoo! Taylor wanted to shout. At least give him one
good kick while he's down!

Ellwyn felt like a thousand eyes were gawking at him. By
the time Louisville stopped talking about this, he would be
a laughingstock. He'd shot this girl down, for pity's sake.
Why hadn't she stayed down? He hated her. No respect. No
one had any respect anymore. And what would he do if that
weasel Reasen moved up over him? He couldn't stay at the
paper after that. He wasn't half through with his life yet. He
didn't want to start over somewhere else.

Madelyn smiled up at Taylor as if she'd just walked out
of some terrible room and was turning to shut the door.
"Let's get out of here," she said under her breath.

Taylor grabbed her hand and fell into step, but not before
he took one good look over his shoulder to see Andy Reasen
gesturing with the stem of his pipe. The people standing
around Ellwyn Muse weren't even looking at him; they
were slowly migrating toward the low-key assistant. Ellwyn
realized that he was being left alone. By the time Taylor and
Madelyn reached the front lobby, Ellwyn was standing by
himself, gnawing at his beautiful blond mustache.

"I don't believe it," Madelyn said as they reached the
car and she slid into her seat. "If you hadn't been with me, I
couldn't have done that."

Taylor's heart turned over. "Yes, you could." He leaned
over and kissed her, held her face and gazed at her for long
moments. Drawling facetiously, he said, "I declare, my
little girl is growing up."

She stretched her arms to the top of the car. "Your little
girl is developing bad habits, but vengeance is sweet,
Taylor. So very, very sweet."

Laughing, he started the car. "You call what you did vengeance? Go on, my sweet angel, I wouldn't change a hair on your head." He revved the engine. "This car is running like a bloody thrashing machine."

They drove over to the houseboat. The hospital had said that Abigail could be released the following week. Everything was stocked and ready. The sun was far past its zenith, and the afternoon was growing cold. As they swung open the car doors, Taylor's telephone signaled him.

"Oh, no. You're not going back to the paper, are you?"

He lifted the receiver. It was the Prince chauffeur. He had a parcel for him. Taylor told him where they'd be and that they'd wait for it. They pulled up their coats and walked along the deck.

"It looks so lonely without all the plants, doesn't it?" she said. "All empty. No L'il Abner."

Taylor laughed. "I'm sure the whole dock gave thanks when L'il Abner moved to the country."

She laughed. When the chauffeur arrived with the box, they walked down the gangplank. Madelyn turned on the heat and put hot water on for tea while Taylor opened the box.

"Would you look at this?" he said as he emptied out a clutter of odds and ends that covered the whole top of the table.

Madelyn placed cups and saucers on the table. "What?"

"It's from Cleo. A bunch of Virginia's things she found in the attic. She said you might want to see them."

As Madelyn dunked tea bags, she watched her husband go through some old yellowed greeting cards, a few musty letters. There was a framed picture of Virginia and Bounty Fair and the bracelets the twins had worn at the hospital. A pair of baby shoes and a perfume bottle.

Taylor accepted his tea with a thoughtful glance at her. "She's really convinced that you're Waverly."

Madelyn shook her head as she read over some letters. "These mean nothing to me. I quit thinking about it. I'm Madelyn Champion now."

In an off-hand gesture, Taylor sniffed an aging handkerchief dotted with yellowed perfume. He spread out a leather glove, fawn-colored and still soft. "She means well."

When Madelyn saw this she stood quite still, as if sleep were overtaking her. Taylor sensed her change and looked up, still holding the glove. Her eyes were fixed on it—unblinking, unaccepting. Her lips were parted, but there was no sound.

"Madelyn?" he said and offered her the glove.

She jerked her head back as if she'd been hit, then she rubbed at her cheeks. She swallowed, blinked rapidly, and then walked into the tiny feminine bedroom.

Taylor followed. Her eyes went upward to a small storage space above the closet, and he questioned her with a sound, for there were no words between them. He knew by her shaking hands that he was to open it. Inside was a suitcase, a really terrible one with a decal of Florida on its cracked side. Taylor pulled it down and flipped it open. Inside were old garments, nothing more.

"Abigail's," she said in a strained high voice. "Before she got so thin. I just put them away. I . . ."

She bent over it and rummaged through the musty folds. When she withdrew the mate to the glove, Taylor wasn't too surprised. It wasn't as soft and well preserved as Cleo's. It was stiff, as though it had gotten wet, but it was unmistakably the mate.

Neither of them spoke as they returned to the kitchenette. They sat down at the table and stared at the tea in the cups as if the tiny pieces of settled leaves in the bottom held the answer to the future.

Finally, Madelyn took a long, slow breath. She sat very straight, and Taylor knew that she had made a decision. She was herself again, and a visible strength was filling her. Coming to her feet, she cleared everything away—the teacups, rinsing them and putting them in the pantry, the suitcase which Taylor replaced, without the glove, to the shelf.

She gathered up their coats, handed him his. After she put hers on, she stood looking at the glove for a time. Then she smiled. "Are you ready to go?"

Taylor was buttoning his jacket. Not understanding her at all, he folded his arms across his chest and stood absently rubbing the scar on his jaw. "What are you going to do?"

"Nothing," she said and opened the door and stepped outside.

It was growing colder, and when she walked along the catwalk to the rear of the boat, stood gazing out at the river where it picked up the deepening red of the sun. Taylor came to stand beside her, wanting to help but not knowing what it would be except to be with her.

"You could get a lot of money with that glove, you know," he said.

"I don't want money."

"But Abigail might. I mean, Virginia." It would take some doing to think about Abigail as Virginia Prince, no matter how much he'd prepared himself for it.

Madelyn faced him, leaning her hips back against the redwood railing. "What good would money do her? She can come here and live in her boat like she's always wanted to do. What if she is Virginia? Owen Prince would insist on putting her in some fancy hospital. Unless he wanted to buy me off and not tell anyone. No, my mother has more future as Abigail Grey than she has as Virginia."

"But she's not Abigail, Madelyn. And you're not Madelyn Grey. You're Wallace's twin sister. And"—he grimaced, then shrugged—"my sister on paper."

She slipped her arms around him. "I'm not in the slightest your sister." She pressed her cheek and felt his buttons scoring her cheek. "Wallace thinks Owen is his father, Taylor. You know better than anyone how much he needs that."

With a kiss upon her hair, Taylor wondered at her unselfishness. Not once had she thought of what being Waverly Prince could mean to her. When she detached herself and stood staring down at the glove, he stared at it too. She stepped to the railing and tossed it overboard.

"Madelyn!"

The piece of pale, fawn-colored leather floated for several seconds, turning a darker color; then, as it was caught in the moving current, it was sucked down and out into the Ohio River. Taylor almost wanted to throw himself in after it and bring it up. Did she realize what doors this was closing?

"It's evidence," he said in a shocked gasp. "You can't destroy evidence."

Madelyn looked up into his puzzled and troubled blue eyes. She could remember him that day, standing like a monument against the sun. She could remember Owen's look when he'd written that check and how Taylor had come after her, had protected her.

"Even if Wallace and I were Owen's real children, I wouldn't tell him," she said. "Fatherhood is earned, Taylor. Just like daughterhood or anything else. Owen doesn't want a daughter. If he did, he wouldn't have let anything stand in the way of claiming me. He would have acted on the feelings of his heart. He was good to you in this way. He'll probably be good to Wallace now. I don't need someone's grudging courtesy. I have everything. The love of a lifetime, and it fills all the empty places in my life. You're all I need or want."

Taylor didn't kiss her. He held her very close as the cold

wind blew in off the river. Her heartbeat was strong and steady against his chest.

"Come on," she said, detaching herself and taking him by the hand. The sides of her mouth tipped up in an impish little smile. "Let's go. I know what's wrong with your car."

Letting that sink in, Taylor smothered a grin and gave her a nudge to precede him. He wanted to go home too but not for the same reason. He wanted to make love to this wonderful woman he'd married. He wanted to have a child with her. He wanted more than he ever wanted.

"You think so, huh?" he mumbled.

She marched ahead of him with determination. "I read the Mitsubishi manual after I rode in yours that day. It's the EGR, Taylor. You see, the exhaust gases are introduced into the intake manifold by way of this valve, the Exhaust Gas Recirculation valve. It operates from a signal in the carburetor. At idle speeds, the vacuum to the EGR valve is cut off. This causes the EGR to close and keeps the exhaust gas from going to the intake manifold."

Taylor promised himself he would not laugh. "Really?"

"I need to clean the valve base and remove the exhaust deposits from the mounting surface, that's all. It isn't receiving its vacuum signal when it should and the valve diaphragm isn't cutting off. You know that rough sputtering you're complaining about?"

She was so beautifully grave with that brain of hers clicking along a hundred miles an hour that Taylor had to clear his throat. Vigorously. "You . . . uh, you can do all this, huh?"

She looked over her shoulder, her expression a mixture of coyness and patient chiding. "Taylor, you just have to wash the valve assembly in a solvent. A wire brush or wire wheel will do it. Or tapping with a soft-faced hammer. What idiot couldn't do that?"

Leaning over, Taylor pecked her upon the lips and gave her behind a fond swat. Oh, boy, it was going to be this for the rest of his life. Well, it would never be boring, would it?

"No idiot, my darling bride," he said and laughed because she was so perfect. "No idiot at all."

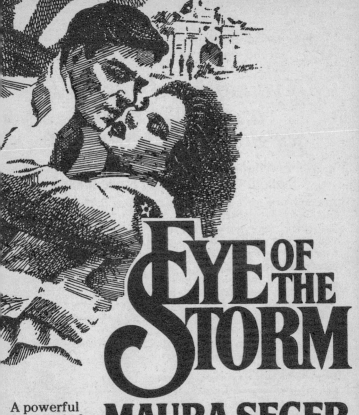

EYE OF THE STORM

MAURA SEGER

A powerful
portrayal of
the events of
World War II in the
Pacific, *Eye of the Storm* is a riveting story of how love
triumphs over hatred. In this, the first of a three book
chronicle, Army nurse Maggie Lawrence meets Marine
Sgt. Anthony Gargano. Despite military regulations
against fraternization, they resolve to face together
whatever lies ahead.... Also known by her fans as
Laurel Winslow, Sara Jennings, Anne MacNeil and
Jenny Bates, Maura Seger, author of this searing novel,
was named by ROMANTIC TIMES as 1984's Most
Versatile Romance Author.

At your favorite bookstore in March.   EYE-B-1

READERS' COMMENTS ON SILHOUETTE SPECIAL EDITIONS:

"I just finished reading the first six Silhouette Special Edition Books and I had to take the opportunity to write you and tell you how much I enjoyed them. I enjoyed all the authors in this series. Best wishes on your Silhouette Special Editions line and many thanks."

—B.H.*, Jackson, OH

"The Special Editions are really special and I enjoyed them very much! I am looking forward to next month's books."

—R.M.W.*, Melbourne, FL

"I've just finished reading four of your first six Special Editions and I enjoyed them very much. I like the more sensual detail and longer stories. I will look forward each month to your new Special Editions."

—L.S.*, Visalia, CA

"Silhouette Special Editions are — 1.) Superb! 2.) Great! 3.) Delicious! 4.) Fantastic! . . . Did I leave anything out? These are books that an adult woman can read . . . I love them!"

—H.C.*, Monterey Park, CA

*names available on request